Chaperones

MEGAN KARASCH

ISBN: 1-4840-9445-X
ISBN-13: 978-1-4840-9445-7

Acknowledgements

I could write, "see first novel – 'Tales from my Hard Drive'" – here, but the people mentioned below deserve some effort.

As I've said before, and will say for eternity: first and always foremost, my mother, father and sister. They are still, as they have always been, my heroes – the kind that step into a phone booth and change into super humans every time they speak to me. I don't remember a time any one of them disappointed me or weren't ferociously loyal, loving, caring or entertaining. I couldn't write, fabricate, or wish for a better family. Thank you again and I love you more than even Shakespeare could have expressed.

My beloved Tim Davis: I can't think of a world worth living in that doesn't include you. You supply me with laughs, creativity, kindness, support and wisdom in astounding amounts. I thank you again and I love you.

The following dear friends (in alphabetical order) and all-around amazing individuals who have championed this second writing effort by reading, proofing, critiquing, criticizing and praising it: Allison Cohen, Erin Gebo, Alicia Harris, Jennifer Hoffman, Lisa Richards Keston, Danny Llewelyn, Barry McCrossan, Dana Cohler Moncrief, and Jaime Richardson. I love you all and I thank you for your limitless patience, friendship, love and support.

To my precious friends and family that I don't have the time, space or, let's face it, patience to mention by name: You are also loved and integral parts of my life and endeavors. I remain confident that these extraordinary people know who they are and how special they are to me (of course, I will take questions to address uncertainty). I thank you all as well.

To my copy editor, Daniel Levin Becker who again had to read a story unlike anything he'd ever choose to pick up and revise it into a clean, smooth piece of literature – which he again expertly completed: Thank you very much.

To my cover artist, Erik Chrestensen: I thank you for your patience and your talent and for masterfully bringing my mother's and my artistic vision to life.

To the team at JKS Communications: I have only just begun working with you but you have already made my life infinitely easier. I thank you for your enthusiasm and support and look forward to continuing to work with you.

The "Sawrey Boys" at Grizedale College, Lancaster University 1996-1997 (most of whom will never even see this book) and Lancaster University: Believe it or not, you were, in large part, inspiration for this novel. That said, please don't read yourself into it, it's fiction. I thank you for the bar crawls, the entertainment, the company and for opening my eyes to a new world.

And finally, to England: I will always love England for its magnificent landscape, its charming pubs, its quaint towns, its witty citizens and its clever television.

Author's Note

Notwithstanding any of the acknowledgements, this book is a work of <u>fiction</u>. The characters, incidents, pubs and dialogues are products of my imagination and are not to be construed as real. Any resemblance to real life people or places is entirely coincidental. Oh, except my cat, Squeaker — she's real (and a total badass).

Chapter One

"Honey, I have huge news. Amazing news. Life-altering news that I just cannot wait to share with you!" I had planned to say to my boyfriend, Brandon, while driving the twenty-five minutes it takes to go five miles in Los Angeles. My intestines were in knots and I managed to chew each of my nails so far down that I struck blood. I knew he'd eventually be happy for me, because he would agree that opportunities like the one I was moments from sharing with him come once in a lifetime, but the road to that emotion would certainly be paved with tears and heartache.

I pulled up to Brandon's house, took a deep breath, and then several more, and walked in. That's when something, call it Murphy, Mother Nature, The Force, or a different being with a screwed-up sense of humor, threw a wrench into the middle of my plan, shattering it to smithereens.

The house was empty. Throwing my keys on the counter to make myself comfortable, I noticed a picnic basket wrapped in an absurdly large, candy-apple red bow — the kind of bow most often seen wrapped around cars in commercials that "hint" to women that their husbands are lazy deadbeats if they don't drive a luxury SUV into the living room and waste a hundred feet of ribbon tying it around the thing. A paper sign rested atop the basket: *Don't even think about opening me. I mean it. Pick me up and take me across the street to the park. Don't worry, I'm watching you, it's safe. I love you. —* *Brandon* xoxo

Never having enjoyed surprises, I opened the left side of the lid slightly and found another note: *Seriously?* Laughing, I opened the right side: *Satisfied?*

You've got another note. Stop your snooping and take me to the park. Enter where we always do. I acquiesced to the demands in the notes, picked up the basket and walked out.

Upon entering the park, I immediately happened upon a trail of rose petals that led me into a pocket of trees I had always avoided because it seemed an ideal hiding place for knife-wielding lunatics. Today, however, petals paved the way and I knew this madness was Brandon's doing, not the elaborate plan of a psychopath. I picked up the rose petals as I walked, eager to keep mementos from what I felt was going to be an extraordinary day. I put a few of them up to my nose and breathed in that intoxicating aroma unique to a rose. In my world roses always announced something wonderful. I received them on my first date with Brandon and on our six-month and one-year anniversaries. He also sent them to me a few times when I was working on photo shoots, "just because."

As I walked further through trees, I began to hear the vibrant strings of the Spring movement of Vivaldi's *Four Seasons*. My smile grew painfully wide while I listened. As the music grew louder, I walked faster, excited about what I would find beyond the trees and also itching to get out from the dark, insect-ridden thicket. *What the hell was crawling all over my legs?* The sunshine greeted me again as I stepped out into a wide-open field smelling of fresh-cut grass. Dogs chased Frisbees, children swung high on the swing set and played messily in the sandbox, and picnic blankets lay in luminescent, kaleidoscopic designs around the lawn. The sounds of laughter created a staccato pattern around Vivaldi's violins. Though there was dynamic activity on all sides and I was concerned that the kids on the swings were going so high they might fly right off, I eventually focused in on the giant heart outlined in rose petals a few feet ahead.

Brandon stood in the center of the shape, tall and proud, his upper body covered in a tee with a printed tuxedo shirt and jacket, his hands in the pockets of khaki shorts. I chuckled at his shirt, as it so perfectly demonstrated his playful nature. Sunglasses concealed his warm, chocolate-brown eyes and the sun glinted off his sandy blond hair, creating a reddish tint. My eyes began to fill with water and I ran the last few steps toward my darling Brandon, dropping the basket and the rose petals I had accumulated en route. I threw my arms around him and attempted a graceful, dramatic embrace, as though I had just come off an airplane to find my beloved who had been at war for twenty years, but my momentum was too great and it carried me onto his toes, practically knocking him into the bottle of champagne lying beside him inside the heart.

The ends of Brandon's hair around his neckline sat in a pool of sweat and his back was damp. We unlocked our embrace and he smoothed my hair back from my face. He gave me a long, tender kiss hello, followed by multiple quick lip-to-lip pecks. As he held my face in his hands and our lips continuously met, I knew he was seconds from asking the question virtually every girl looks forward to from the moment she sees Prince Charming slide the glass slipper onto Cinderella for the first time.

After a few minutes of passionate lip locking, Brandon removed his sunglasses and held my hands in his.

"Andrea," he said. "Standing in the spot where I met you at a party I didn't really want to go to, I know you are the woman who makes me glad I'm alive."

He knelt down and reached his hand into his pocket. A second later his hand emerged, shaking slightly, closed around that classic black velvet box I had dreamed of since before I even fully understood its significance.

Brandon stared deep into my eyes, his eyes shimmering as they began to accumulate tears, and continued. "The last year of my life has been damn near nirvana and I would be a total fool not to tell you now and every day following that I love you. My darling Andrea Joanna Lieberman, will you marry me?"

I looked down at Brandon's handsome face, tears sliding down my cheeks like a light rain in early June. I tried to stare into his eyes, but the sun bounced off the diamond, creating a prism of color and rays of light. The world was silent, save for the sound of my galloping heartbeat.

"I have to tell you something," I said. *Now? I'm choosing to tell him now?* I should have had my head examined, but there wasn't time. I had no choice. I had to tell him. *But look at that diamond! No, it's not fair to him. The 1.5 carat princess-cut in a platinum antique setting with — holy shit, is that ten baguettes? Dammit, focus, Andrea!* Sure, the diamond would have been the envy of everyone I knew, but it would have to wait. Brandon deserved the whole truth. *Seriously, though: did he pick that out by himself?*

"Huh? Is it something other than 'yes'?" he asked, with squinted eyes and a furrowed brow.

"Sort of."

"What?" Brandon began to rise from the posture he had taken before I destroyed a moment so perfect that *perfection* seemed a demeaning term.

"Well, no, wait. Kneel back down."

"Hon, I think the moment has passed." He closed the box, which made a deafening *POP*. I jumped.

"No, it hasn't," I said, placing my hands on his shoulders and pushing him down.

He again bent down onto one knee and opened the box.

"Okay, perfect. Try again."

"Fine. Willyoumarryme?" he said, his voice slurred and lackadaisical this time, his eyes looking up and away in the distance.

"Bran, I love you so much. And because I think you may be *the one*, I have to say, I can't marry you right now."

So that was me ruining — twice — what should have been the most beautiful, romantic moment of my life.

"Is that a no?" he asked with genuine confusion and a quickly expanding dollop of anger. "You forced me to ask twice so you could say no?"

He rose again, shoving the ring into his pocket as I bit my lip, smiled, and shrugged like a toddler caught stealing candy from a jar.

"It's not really a no," I said, attempting to hollow out the deep hole in which I stood.

"But it's not really a yes," he clarified.

"Right, it's not really a yes."

Brandon ran his hands through his hair and tilted his head back before looking at me with alternating expressions of bewilderment, resentment and pain. "Damn, Andrea. I don't know what to say to that."

And neither did I. His reaction had left me speechless. And ill. That I had caused such pain to someone so unbelievably dear to me, and for reasons not at all his doing, made me more nauseas than the fast food bacon chili cheese fries that sent me to the emergency room for a stomach pump.

"Well, when do you think you'll know?" he asked after moments of searching for what to say next.

"About six months."

"There's a specific timeline?"

"'Fraid so."

"I know this proposal was unexpected. But I thought we were on the same page."

"Well, we aren't *that* far apart," I muffled, staring down and chewing on my thumb where the nail used to be.

Brandon took a seat on the grass, his knees bent up to his chest and his arms draped over them. I sat likewise. A genuinely kind and understanding man, he tried to grasp why I would utter such an ugly response to his beautiful question.

"Okay, Andrea. What's the issue? You think you don't know me well enough?"

"No. I don't think I know me well enough." *Who was I, Jerry Seinfeld? Surely I could have done better than: It's not you, it's me.* But the truth was... well, that was the truth.

The tears that had originally formed and fell from the sublimity of the scene now fell from sadness, heavier and more imposing — like an East Coast rainstorm in January. I had little doubt that I was sitting beside an incredible man; someone whom, if I whittled wood, I could see myself whittling with when we were too old to care how utterly lame it is to whittle wood. He'd be there for me through the years to share the most joyful of times; he'd be next to me, holding my hand, through those dark times when you can't find words strong enough to express sorrow. But I wasn't ready. I was old enough to be ready. I should have been ready. But I wasn't.

Being the only child of a teacher and a pediatrician meant I would forever be suffocated with attention. My mother witnessed and attempted to moderate a colorful variety of mischievous behavior all day, all year, and my father was privy to every type of illness that could befall a child. I had been doomed from the words "push, Mrs. Lieberman, push!" As I grew up, my parents uttered a broken-record like *no* to virtually every request I made to venture beyond a quarter-mile radius from my home, continually reminding me of all that could go wrong in any given situation. I was, therefore, taught to fear everything that could be considered risky even by *Sesame Street* standards. And I learned it well. Consequently, I had missed a lot of life.

In elementary school I was not permitted to ride the bus because "they'll just hire anyone to drive those things," as my father would say, to which my mother would add, "I know, and they're almost always alcoholics." I wasn't permitted to play outside when it was too dark, too hot, too cold, too windy, or "just didn't feel right." In my teens, I was not permitted to go to concerts because of the "undesirable" people that attend them. "I don't trust men with spiky hair, long hair, or dyed hair, they all pierce their privates" I can still hear echoing in my mother's high-pitched hysterics. I couldn't go camping with friends in college because of "lions and tigers and bears," and "don't get me started on those wildfires." A group of my friends went backpacking across Europe after college; I was at home reading their postcards: *Off to tour the Sistine Chapel and tomorrow, a gondola across the canal. You would be in heaven here!* Or *At the Parthenon, Andy, the view is outstanding!* My life filled up with post-event gossip from people who went to interesting places and did interesting things. By the time I had discerned that most people didn't fear the things I did, that it was abnormal behavior to be afraid of virtually every living thing, fears were embedded so deep in my psyche I wasn't sure if they could ever be removed. And once I figured that out and connected that anxiety to how my parents had raised me, despite how much I loved and cared for them, I maintained some amount of enmity towards them.

By my mid-twenties, I had had enough. I wanted to be less afraid; I wanted to live rather than fear dying. I had accumulated more than my share of instances that lent themselves to the conclusion *regret's a bitch*. I had heard "you should have been there" so many times it was sure to be my epitaph. I no longer wanted my fears, quirks, and idiosyncrasies to ruin my relationships. Since I was about fifteen I had had numerous "relationships" with men, all of which lasted less time than a Los Angeles rainy season. I had always believed I needed a man's protection, an uncommon state of being for a woman born in the eighties. However, because I had never learned to be on my own, I had never learned to deal with anything on my own, and my fear of living and my dependency on others both grew faster than any sort of independence or resourcefulness. More often than not, my curfews, my ever-growing list of places not to visit, and my resulting quirks landed me on the receiving end of *the talk*, which usually began with some form of "look, you're an interesting girl, but…"

And then, when I was twenty-four, Brandon walked into my life: the man whose first hello came at a time when I had resigned myself to being alone, when I wanted a man as much as I wanted to be tied to a bowling ball and thrown into ten pins. But our love had grown at too fast a pace for me to keep up. I truly, deeply loved Brandon and I feared losing him the way I had lost the others; however, I also found it hard to achieve the personal growth I desired and knew was necessary while in a relationship. That was, until Tom Henson entered the picture and handed me the ultimate in bravery-building activities.

"Tom Henson is sending me to England for six months to shoot castles and cathedrals for *Adventure Magazine*," I said, uncomfortably shifting my weight to avoid the pins and needles I stood on waiting for Brandon's response.

"Holy shit, baby!"

"Yes, holy shit, indeed. This isn't exactly how I envisioned telling you, though. I'm really excited about it. Scared shitless, obviously. But excited. I hope you'll be happy for me."

"Wow, talk about sink or swim," he said. Not the ideal phrasing, but not a wrong one, either.

"Thank you."

"And you're not trying to break up with me?" he asked. "Because there are easier — closer and safer — ways."

"No, Brandon, I'm not. I'm just not ready to commit my life to you. I don't know what I'll find out during my trip, but barring a lobotomy or a proposal from Prince Harry, I believe I'll come back sick of my own thoughts and words and ready to start a life with you, forever."

"Then why aren't you saying yes?"

The true answer was that I was frightened of the possibility Brandon would no longer love whatever version of me returned from abroad. In addition, if there were even the slightest chance of my coming back from England and discovering I wasn't finished with "me time," I didn't want to be attached to the extent of an engagement. I wanted to come back self-reliant. When I said yes to Brandon, I wanted to be certain it was because I *wanted* to be with him, not because I *needed* to be with him. And I had to be free from him to make that transition.

It also felt wrong, and perhaps disrespectful, to get engaged and a few weeks later leave my fiancé for six months. From the time I had put pillowcases on my head and ripped flowers from my parents' yard to play bride, the magical moment of the imaginary proposal was always followed by the excitement of faux wedding planning. My visions never included the phrase "of course I will marry you; let me just take this half-year trip to England first, which I'm taking partly to get away from you," which is about as romantic as a drunken wedding in Vegas surrounded by a room full of hookers and Elvis impersonators. However, trying to remain sure of my conviction while watching Brandon's expression transform from sublime to sorrowful squeezed my heart into a pulp. But I was doing what I knew had to be done.

"Because the timing just isn't right. I hope you understand and that you'll be supportive, Brandon," I said.

"Of course," he replied. "This does seem like a wonderful opportunity… "

"Thank—"

"—for someone else."

"What?" His lack of confidence in me, my work, and my abilities annoyed me, but certainly helped remove lingering doubts about my decision to go abroad.

I immediately thought about what my best friend, Ashley, had said when I sought her advice the day before. I could always count on her to be forthright and honest — even when the advice stung like a razor nick doused in lemon juice.

"To hell with Brandon if he's not happy for you!"

"Okay. Thanks, Ashley, but it's not quite that easy."

"Well if he truly wants what's best for you, he'll be happy for you."

"Yes, but being happy for me and not breaking up with me are two very different things."

"He's not gonna break up with you. Just be honest. Tell him how great this is for your career. He'll understand *that*."

"I know, but he'll be so scared for me. Even more so than I am."

"Is that possible?" she asked.

"I guess we'll find out."

"I'm so excited! I can't wait for you to go."

"That's really very sweet of you. I'll miss you too."

"Of course I'll miss you, Andrea, but this is going to be so good for you."

"Yes, if I make it through. Hell, if my parents make it through."

"You will all be fine and you will all be better off," she said, with almost too much logic for my comfort. "Brandon needs this too; he could back off you a bit. Let them all see what your friends know you can accomplish. Let *yourself* see what we believe you can accomplish." I should have married Ashley, but nature had decided I liked boys. "Focus on your camera," she said. "It'll make you feel better. Think of the amazing pictures you'll take."

It was only a thin layer of protective coating, if any, but my camera was something of a security blanket. It hid my face and my emotions and somehow made the world safer. Were it not for my camera, this trip might never have been possible.

"Andy, this is a tremendous career move," she added, enthusiastically. And she was right. Apart from personal growth, the assignment offered substantial professional advancement. For the first time, I would have photographs published in a reputable magazine, moving me closer to my occupational bulls-eye: shooting fashion spreads in Italy for *Italian Vogue*.

"Yeah, okay. My career. I'll think of my career," I told her and myself simultaneously.

"And Brandon should too," she asserted.

"That's true, of course he should," I confirmed.

"Excuse me? For who?" I asked, giving Brandon an opportunity for redemption.

"I'm sorry. For you, Andy," he said. "I just know how terrified you get."

I looked down and away and said nothing, hurt by this statement of fact.

"And being away from home by yourself is only going to amplify your fears."

"I know," I said under my breath. I didn't know what to say to contradict him; he wasn't wrong. But that was why I was going. So I could journey away from fear, arrive back in the US and say, with confidence, "I'm not that girl anymore" (or at least be further down that path).

"And the timing's a bit strange."

"I didn't know you were going to propose." It was, in fact, a complete surprise. We had agreed several times that we would not get married until after we lived together, which in my head was still years off. I had lived alone for just two years and was still grappling with the challenges of being on my own — all of which I welcomed.

"If you had known, do you think you might have accepted the trip anyway?"

"Yeah, maybe... Yes, Brandon. Definitely. I need this, I really do. But, I need to know that you'll be here for me."

Brandon turned to me and looked deep into my eyes. "I'll be here." And then, "My God, what did your parents say?"

Although Tom Henson had been my father's best friend for longer than I had been alive, the moment I revealed to my mother and father that he had offered me a job in England, and that I had accepted it, was quite possibly the most frightening moment of my existence — on par with the combination of riding in a helicopter and swimming in the ocean, both of which I was sure yielded nothing but an early death. I blurted it out quickly over dinner the night after I had finalized the details with Tom, using Band-Aid logic: the faster you do it, the less it will hurt.

"Guess what? Tom Henson gave me this tremendous opportunity for a photography assignment in England! More potatoes please," I said, all in the same tone I would use to announce I had won the lottery.

My parents stared at me for a second as though my head were spinning around like a dreidel. Then they both ran to the phone, grabbed it at the same time, and played tug-of-war in an effort to be the first to call Tom. My father let go of the handset, sending my petite mother flying into the wall, and then used the speed dial on his cell phone. I didn't hear so much as a "hello" before the castigation began.

Listening only to my father's end of the conversation, this is how it went:

"We've been friends thirty years, Tom, and you effing ruin my life?!"

"Oh, the best interests of your magazine come before those of my daughter?"

"Well it's not gonna be a great experience for her if she doesn't come back alive!"

"Don't tell me whether I should or should not be happy for my daughter!" And then he spat out many adaptations of the F-word I wasn't even aware he knew and slammed down the phone as he does to telemarketers who call during dinnertime.

After a few deep inhalations, my father regrouped, looked at me and calmly said, "Sweetie, Tom seems adamant about you going to England. Therefore, I have just one question for you, 'what have your mother and I done to deserve this?'"

My mother also called Tom and pleaded with him to take back his offer, but when that proved futile she pointed a silent rage in my direction. When I visited the two of them she would lock herself in her room like a three-year-old scolded for eating Twinkies for dinner, but she left self-help books strategically placed around the house: *How Do I Make it Right?: A Guide to Dealing with Problem Children* and *Why Do My Children Hate Me When All I Gave Them Was Love?*

Several days after the big reveal, I stopped by the house at dinnertime, certain my parents would be at the table. They had a strict routine that included dinner from 6 to 7 p.m. Always. I gave them tremendous credit for never faltering and for scheduling every day of their lives around a 6 p.m. dinner (in addition to the myriad other rules that structured their days). If I timed it properly, I knew I could stop my mother from retreating to her bedroom. Sure enough, like clockwork, the two were sitting at the kitchen table when I walked through the door.

My mother looked up at me and dropped her fork. She placed her hands and elbows on the table, fingers tapping. I hadn't seen such a look of disappointment since the time I tested out new scissors on her purse straps and proclaimed "it wasn't me!" while holding the purse with segregated straps in my left hand and the instrument of the crime in my right.

"I lost my appetite. I'm going to my room. I'll eat dinner tomorrow," she said.

"Mom, come on. Isn't this silly?"

"How did you know I was at the table? Were you watching us from outside?"

"No, mom. I've developed psychic abilities."

"Andy, don't patronize your mother."

"Sorry. You've been eating at the same time, in the same place, for at least twenty-five years. So I guess I just got lucky. Please talk to me. I don't want to leave with us not speaking."

"Then don't go."

"Mom, I have to go."

"If I die while you're gone, you're gonna be sorry."

"I'll fly home for the funeral," I said.

"That's not funny."

"Tell me about it. Look, it's six months. That's all. Six months. One semi-annual sale at Nordstrom and I'll be back."

"Your father and I have never left the country, and we're perfectly content."

"Dad has left the country."

"Right, but that was a very long time ago."

"Well, I'm not you," I declared.

We held a staring contest for minutes, my pained expression contorting more by the second. With squinted eyes and pursed lips, I implored her; finally, I broke her. Her face dropped and her body released, giving in to the idea of discussion. She allowed me to explain that the trip had absolutely nothing to do with them, at least not in a vengeful way, and that my agenda was to improve my craft and myself, not to destroy them. "This is about me, not you," I told her.

"I don't understand what you can't get from being here," she said. "We let you go to the Valley, Santa Monica, wherever you want."

It was nearly impossible to explain my rationale to someone who thought a nearby beach town would provide sufficient substance and culture to make a well-rounded individual.

"Mom, really? Santa Monica? That's not even ten miles away. And I don't think there's so much as a museum on route. I want to see other parts of the world."

"Then buy a pic—"

"And not through someone else's pictures. I'm a photographer. I want to *create* the pictures."

She didn't respond.

"You've done a mighty fine job trying to keep me from growing up. But I'm twenty-six. It's time."

"We didn't mean to keep you from growing," she said. "We just want you to be safe."

"Well, whatever the reason, it's resulted in me feeling young and fearful. And inexperienced. And irresponsible. And I want to fix that."

"We can fix it together. You can get a dog."

"No, that's not… well, maybe when I come back. But that's not the fix. At least not now. Mom, at this point, it's either this trip or therapy. And the trip's cheaper. But I do love you and I need to know you'll be here for me when I go."

During our conversation I realized just how little my parents understood the way their overbearing parenting had stunted my growth. (It was good to know, though, that they thought my level of responsibility and independence was such that I could raise it by taking care of a dog.) They seemed genuinely hurt and confused, but then, so was I. Where was my "congratulations, Andrea!"? And what about "we're so proud of you, sweetie"? I was saddened that I would leave the country without receiving such sentiments. Instead, we talked consistently about the opportunity for the next week until they finally spoke to me like the same daughter they had smothered with affection for twenty-six years.

"They're coming around," I said.

I leaned into Brandon and placed my head on his shoulder. "I'm really sorry I ruined the amazing day you planned."

He tilted his head, resting it sweetly on top of mine, though sarcasm continued to seep through. "No problem. I'm sure we'll have other once-in-a-lifetime days to eclipse this one."

I understood Brandon's bitterness and I understood his sorrow. I cupped my hands over my face and the tears continued to fall. Hampered by a cornucopia of emotions, I laid down in his lap. He had planned an evening of romantic festivities at a nearby hotel to celebrate our engagement — silly man, so certain I would say "yes, of course I will marry you" rather than "not right now, I'm leaving for six months" — but we opted out. Conversation was awkward and a halo of sadness hovered overhead.

Chapter Two

During the four weeks prior to my trip, I spent a lot of time with Brandon, seeking constant reassurance that we were on solid ground despite my rejection (sort of) of his marriage proposal. He assured me that we were, but it took longer than I had hoped for him to look at me in the same amorous way he had before the words *not right now* spewed from my lips. I also spent a lot of time with my friends, all of whom were shocked that I would agree to such an enormous endeavor without a gun pressed to my temple or the receipt of an actual pot of gold upon completion. I said goodbye to them at a fantastic soiree replete with "inspiring" phrases such as: "Wow, Andy, that's really brave; I never thought you'd go through with it," and "Your parents know you're going to England, right? The one that's across the Atlantic… that England?" While talking to them about what a good idea it was for me to go, the remarkable photographs I would take, and how much I'd learn about me, various cultures, and the world, I realized I was still convincing myself. I uttered a continuous loop of "I'm so excited, I just can't wait; really, I can't wait. What an opportunity this is!" too many times for it to be authentic. Despite the quips, the smart-ass remarks, and the betting pool revealing the odds-on favorite that I wouldn't make it the entire six months, the consensus among my friends was that England was a step in the right direction.

"Now remember, I don't want to hear from you while you're gone," Ashley said.

"Your sensitivity is overwhelming. What if I'm dying?"

"You sound like your mother. However, now that you've gone and used the D-word, if you're dying you can call me. Nothing less, though," she laughed. "Obviously we'll email, but you really need to be away from here for a while. From your mother. From Brandon. And even me. And did I mention your mother? We'll all be in the same places when you return."

"What if Brandon won't wait for me?"

"Then he's an asshole."

"Comforting. Can you do better than that?"

"No, I can't. I can't promise you he'll wait, but I really, really think he will."

I looked at Ashley and shook my head. She wanted to be helpful, but not so much that she would lie. I loved her for that. "Better. But not quite there," I said.

"Andy, there're no guarantees. But you'll talk often, you'll see him soon, and it will be fine. You have to believe in him, like he should in you."

"You're right."

"Now, go kick some British ass," Ashley said, as I took a deep breath and hugged her goodbye, relying on her sage advice more than ever before. "Oh, and if you really cared about me, you'd bring me back someone British. Accent of Prince William, face like Ryan Gosling, body of Jon Hamm."

"Nothing unrealistic about that. You got it."

Chapter Three

On the day my journey would begin, I stood with my parents at the departures curb at Los Angeles International Airport and wrapped my arms around them for the last time for six months. My mom's ability to shed tears was astounding — I didn't think our little ducts could manufacture such a copious amount of fluid. My father, true to form, was holding back his tears, almost successfully. His lips quiver when he tries not to cry; as we stood outside the airport doors, they were on overdrive.

"Goodbye, mom. Goodbye, dad. I'll email you."

"Every day?" my mother asked, black mascara streaks now running down her face.

"I can't promise that. But I will keep in touch. I love you both."

"Now, I want you to get a fire extinguisher as soon as possible after you land," my mother said.

"I really don't think that's necessary."

"Didn't London just have a massive fire?" she asked.

"Yes, in the 1600s, but I imagine they've put it out by now," I said, making a mental note in spite of my sarcasm to ensure that my apartment building had at least one fire extinguisher per floor.

"We love you," my mother said before leading my father away. Once she thought she was out of earshot, I heard her add, "I'll never forgive Tom for taking away my little girl!"

When my parents walked away, they left me standing next to Brandon, the one person I was sure to think about every day I was gone. In a bit of a panic, on the way to the airport, I had asked him to marry me five times; each time he had responded with "not right now." I suppose a proposal in a Jeep Cherokee on the highway with a sobbing bride-to-be and her parents in the back seat wasn't what he envisioned as the ideal way to become affianced.

"I love you, baby. See you in three months," he said, wiping the tears from my eyes.

I nodded my head. "Me too, Brandon. Three months." I would see my beloved again halfway through the trip, a much less daunting amount of time to think about than the entire six months. I had already begun the countdown.

We gave each other a monstrous hug, squeezing almost unbearably tightly.

"Text me when you land," he said.

"I will."

"Or call if you want, but please let me know when you land."

"I know, honey, I will. I love—"

"It doesn't matter what time it is."

"I know, Brandon. I love you. Goodbye."

I walked into the airport and, as the doors closed behind me and the sight of Brandon vanished into the air, I experienced a feeling of dread greater than my fear of spiders, snakes, earthquakes, and thieves combined: what would become of us?

Chapter Four

Istepped into the maze of ropes enclosing the security line and the reality of the distance soon to be between me and my loved ones — and the duration! — struck me like a cartoon frying pan to the face. *What the hell was I thinking?* I couldn't shake the feeling that I was going to vomit. I called my mother, expecting her to share in my panic and help me get out of this ridiculous mess, but the person who answered the phone and claimed to be my mother didn't at all resemble the lady that had raised me.

"Hello honey, you okay?" she said in a calm voice, as though I had just gone across the street to the market.

"What? Do you have amnesia? I'm leaving for six months!"

"I know, dear. It's exciting, isn't it? Now, I'm reading *People.* You must have to board the plane soon."

"I can't do it. I can't go."

"It's irresponsible to back out now. Mr. Henson is counting on you. We don't shirk our responsibilities."

"Well, maybe *you* don't, but I do. I'm coming home. And getting a dog."

"It'll be good for you, dear. Go out, see the world. We think you should be on your own for a bit." I would sooner have expected her to tell me they planned on cryogenically freezing themselves for the six months I was gone. What was wrong with her?

"Be alone? *You* think it's a good idea for me to be alone?" Something was amiss. I had entered an alternate universe where logic reigned supreme.

"Your father and I talked about it, and we agree you should put some distance between you and Brandon."

"Wait. What!?" Never mind; logic was farther off than the United Kingdom.

"Yeah, the proposal seemed a little rushed. Take some time. Think about it."

It was the first they'd ever mentioned of me rushing into a life with Brandon. They had always spoken fondly of him. It didn't make sense.

"You don't like Brandon?"

"No, he's fine, I guess. We just think you're too young to get married. And you've only been with him a year. What do you even know about him?"

Too young to be married? I was twenty-six. My mother had been twenty-two when she got married, and by that time my grandmother had already labeled her an old hag in danger of dying alone. And what did I know about him? One year wasn't exactly three dates.

"You know, when I get back, I'll probably accept his proposal."

"We'll see, dear," my mother said dismissively as I heard her flipping the pages of her magazine.

"So you're not scared anymore that I will be all alone more than 5,000 miles away?"

"Oh, is it that far? I didn't realize. Don't worry, we'll find ways to cope," she said, closing out the strongest case of denial I had ever heard.

There was too much to process between my mom's silly blather about my relationship and the fact that I was leaving home to be on my own for half a year. Thankful that I had finally received any blessing for the trip, I let the conversation lie, took several deep breaths, and stopped trying to back out.

I was concerned at her comment, though: how *would* they cope? They had little in their lives besides work. Since the day I moved out, I had visited them at least once per weekend and sometimes during the week. Whether I showed up announced or not, I would find them sitting in the same two chairs, bouncing between my mother's and my father's favorite television shows. I tried to encourage them to leave the house, take up hobbies. I brought them brochures from UCLA for extension courses I thought they might find interesting. They told me I was being intrusive and to leave them alone. Me, intrusive? Where would I have picked up such a trait?

When I at last made it to security, to the surprise of no one who had ever met me, I held up the line. As it turned out, mace and pepper spray were not fit to be carry-on items.

"Are you out of your freaking mind, lady? You can't bring these on board," the TSA agent declared obnoxiously, as though any idiot would have known that.

How were you supposed to ward off the terrorists, I wondered?

The lethal sprays were gifts from my father, coming with the warning that if I didn't contact him when I ran out so he could send more I could no longer call myself his daughter. That was fine; I was terrified enough of the world to spray the hell out of an errant hair that hit my shoulder. Even with the extras in my luggage, I knew I would run out. Of course, it didn't matter much, because I also believed there was a good chance the phantom puppeteer holding up the airplane would take a lunch break and let go of the strings.

Before he let me go, the nasty agent also took my Breathalyzer. "But I was gonna ask the pilot to blow in that," I said.

"I'm pretty sure that wasn't gonna happen. Now move on."

When I finally made it to the gate, I stared at the tiny speck of a cockpit in one of the 80-ton metal coffins I was only moments from boarding, and wondered how effective it could possibly be given how small it was in relation to the rest of the plane. Being a first-time air traveler, and having taken as few science classes as my education would permit, I couldn't help but be baffled by what kept those things suspended in mid-air. While pondering the mysteries of air travel, regretful that I had never taken an online course in aerodynamics, I also wished that my parents had gotten me used to flying when I was young, so that by the time I was an adult I could accept with confidence that something so heavy could travel through the sky as if on invisible wires. Unfortunately, my mother had held steadfast to a lifelong refusal to travel by plane, and my father hadn't been on one since he married my mother, so there had never been any chance for me. With limited time before boarding, I accepted that, at least for the time being, air travel would remain as big an enigma to me as Regis Philbin's success on television.

At the first minute wine became available on the flight, I shot a glass of red. I was moments from popping in a sleeping aid, putting Eric Carmen's "All by Myself" on a loop on my iPod, and drifting off, when something caught my ear.

"Mummy, what if I have to go to the loo? I might have to poo, you know."

"Well, you're just going to have to wait, luv, aren't you?"

It wasn't the content of the conversation that caught my attention, but the accents. To risk a rash generalization, Americans love the British — my family included. My father's adoration manifested itself in numerous *Fawlty Towers* marathons that were not only a hilarious way to spend a day but also wonderful bonding time for the two of us. John Cleese had fostered numerous inside jokes that we would share throughout our lifetimes. Brandon watched several British science fiction shows that I could never connect with, but he talked about them often and, as they played in the background, I found the dialogue witty and interesting. My mother shared my love of *Downton Abbey*; Ashley shared my love of British leading men — Hugh Grant, Gerard Butler, Colin Firth, Robert Pattinson, David Beckham, and, well, I could go on for days. I was enamored of the adorable way the Brits added a question mark to ordinary statements, turning them into rhetorical questions. With each new accented conversation and the anticipation that all my conversations for the next six months would involve a beautiful dialect, my hands unclenched and my shoulders fell about a foot. My eagerness to begin my real-life introduction to British culture prompted me to do something I never, ever, ever did.

"Hello," I said to the middle-aged man sitting in the aisle seat next to me.

"Well, howdee, there, ma'am, what's yer name?" *Dammit, I should have known by the bolo tie.* A cowboy fresh off the dude ranch. Having no interest in a discussion with an American stranger, I had to put a quick stop to my invitation for conversation.

"It's Andrea. Hey, can you excuse me for a minute? I want to get something out of my carry-on." Of course, I had my sweater, my pillow and enough magazines at my seat to occupy me for several flights around the world — unnecessary, as I also had my iPod and enough meds to sleep for a week. What else could I possibly have retrieved? I rummaged through my bag for a moment and gave up.

"Oh, silly me. My sweater's already on my seat. My apologies."

"No problem there, little filly." *Christ.*

I retreated to my original plan: I tossed back a sleeping pill with a fresh glass of red and slept for the next nine hours, waking just in time to feel the plane losing altitude and plummeting toward the ground. I started breathing heavily.

"Holy shit! What's happening?"

"Calm down there, little lady," said Cowboy Bob, resting a hand on my shoulder.

"Calm down? Calm down? We're crashing!"

My ears popped as I felt the air pressure dropping with the plane. Vision still cloudy from the remnants of my Lunesta-induced sleep, I looked around for the oxygen mask.

"Where's that mask?" I asked, frantically pushing every button I could find above my seat, including a few above the neighboring ones. Everyone around me began to stir as well, wondering what I could be so panicked about.

"My mask doesn't work. Why won't my mask work? They promised us masks!" At the beginning of the flight, while I was taking half of my carry-on out and putting it on my seat, I listened intently to the what-to-do-in-an-emergency instructions and I distinctly remembered the mention of oxygen masks. But I couldn't locate one. I felt the plane fall a few more feet and heard a screech.

"What was that? Were we hit?"

Flight attendants rushed over to my seat, trying to temper my panic attack. As they ran down the aisles from both directions, I heard various voices shouting: "What the hell's going on over there?" and "What's that commotion?"

"Stay calm now, lady, ya hear?" Cowboy Bob said, a ray of light from the window bouncing off of his iPad-sized, shiny belt buckle. I closed my eyes, put my head between my knees and gripped the arms of the seat as if doing so would save me from a thousand-foot drop. The plane began to right itself.

When the plane came to a stop, I picked my head up and looked around. All passengers were alive; none injured, even (though many stared at me like they wished I were). That plummeting I felt, the plane moving toward the ground… that was the plane landing. We had touched down safely at Heathrow Airport in London, ten minutes before the scheduled arrival time.

"Never can be too careful," I said, smiling widely at the flight attendants who stood in front of me with arms crossed, lips pursed, and eyes narrowed. I wondered whether I could hide under the seat in front of me until everyone else disembarked. I couldn't. Security officers and the pilot compelled the other passengers to remain on the plane an extra half hour while they questioned me.

I ran down what surely sounded to ordinary humans like a horribly fabricated list of excuses but to me were the absolute truth: "I was disoriented from a bad dream and sleep aids... I'm new to flying... I didn't know that that's how it feels to land."

"Christ lady, you can't be serious," said the pilot. "Didn't you notice that no one else was concerned?" *No, sir, I was too busy panicking.* Story of my life. It didn't matter.

"I'm really sorry, sirs. It's a misunderstanding, really."

"Bloody 'ell, Miss."

They searched through my bags and asked me what I was doing in England and how long I would stay. Their faces dropped and their heads shook when they heard I would be on English soil for six months. It was a crushing start to my journey.

As the passengers were finally permitted to leave the plane, I heard rumblings from people on all sides.

The Brits: "Mummy, what was wrong with that lady?" "Well, she has some mental problems, doesn't she?"

And the Americans: "She made us late, that psychotic bitch."

I put on my sunglasses, lowered my head, and walked on. Heathrow was gigantic and I had little idea where to go. I heard directions over the loudspeaker, but they were in at least five languages, none of which sounded like my own. I followed the herd to a huge line at customs. I made it through with little trouble besides the officer's annoyance at my plea to keep my sunglasses on and whisper my name, employer, and address in England. When I finally made it to baggage claim, I opened my phone to text Brandon.

Hi babe, in London. Had a safe flight, apparently. Can you let my father know? It's hectic here. Talk soon, love you xo

It was a case of what-they-didn't-know-wouldn't-hurt-them. Now that my on-board debacle had finished, I could say I had made it through with only some pride shattered and a few death threats from overly dramatic passengers. Brandon and my parents would worry needlessly were I to tell them about the scene I had caused. All they needed to know was that I had arrived safely.

I grabbed my luggage from among the bags that had been unceremoniously chucked down the carousel like yesterday's garbage, and walked over to where I saw taxis. But these were not the hybrid sedans to which I had become accustomed. These taxis were old black town cars like in the movies, with front doors opening back-to-front and back doors opening the other way. And the passenger side, well, that was backwards too. It was as though I had been transported in time and I was excited — so much so that I walked right up to a car and began to crawl inside. But as I did, I heard yelling.

"Oi! Oi! Stop! What are you doing? There's a Q!" I slinked backwards out of the cab. *What the hell's a Q?*

I turned back to find a line of people pointing up at a sign I had somehow missed: TAXI QUEUE.

Oh, a queue, not a Q. "Okay, okay. So sorry. I didn't see it. My apologies."

Chastened and standing in the queue, I surveyed the scenery. It was all concrete and bland, industrial. I was disappointed. London looked nothing like the Oliver Twist town I had expected. Expectations are a funny thing: colossal ones can ruin what might otherwise be a pleasant moment; bad ones can make an unpleasant scenario seem enjoyable. Having learned of England from art history and Hugh Grant films, I had galactic expectations: cobblestone streets, magnificent architecture, beautiful men wearing newsboy caps and buttoned-down collared shirts that creep out at the neckline of their V-neck sweaters, with accents that make the crudest phrases flow like eloquent prose.

However, only moments after the person manning the taxi line motioned to me and said (phonetically) "'ello, luv" the disappointment began to fade. The ride toward the center of London revealed suburban towns — albeit blurrily, thanks to the speed of the cab driver, which suggested he was going for a personal record — where many small brick homes were packed amidst the greenest of foliage. And when we finally came to a stop behind a line of cars in Trafalgar Square, I realized that my expectations had not been nearly high enough. It was indeed the splendor I had dreamed of. I stuck my head out the window and stretched my neck to look up at a statue of Lord Nelson, surrounded by four massive bronze lions guarding his honor. I saw exquisite buildings with elaborate facades and columns in every direction. No strip malls in sight. No hideous beige stucco in a single-file line of chain stores. No 99-Cent anything or shop names ending with *King*. Compared to home, it felt old and important — and this was from the limited view of a taxi. My hopes rose even further as to what I would find when I would be able to walk around and devour the scene.

Adventure Magazine had arranged for me to stay in corporate housing that would serve as home base while I traveled around on assignment. My new six-month residence was located on Marsham Street, in the City of Westminster, just minutes from St. James Park, Victoria Train Station, Westminster Abbey — the heart of London. When I thought about how my lodging would look before I reached my destination, I had envisioned an old brownstone cottage atop a stony path, packed tightly among a group of identical cottages in a neighborhood surrounded by nothing but green-ery, heat rising from smokestacks, me jumping from rooftop to rooftop, singing "Chim chimney, chim chimney, chim chim charoo." Of course, that vision was a picture of London in the early 1900s — from *Mary Poppins*. London is a modern metropolis now. And this was real life. So the apart-ment was actually in a five-story red brick building with white trim around its edges and windows. Similar apartment buildings and townhouses lined the street, trees interspersed between them. I walked up the stairs to the second level and opened the door to my contemporary, fully furnished one-bedroom place. The light-colored wood floors creaked slightly as I walked around my stylish kitchen, which had black granite countertops and wood cabinetry matching the color of the floor. It had a modest living room, bathroom, and bedroom, all with blinding white walls. Slightly sterile — and no chimney sweeps to speak of — but lovely.

I had booked my flight so I would have a two-day cushion between my arrival and my first day of work, in case my plane was delayed or we were diverted to a desert island and I had to swim to shore. It's exceedingly dif-ficult to plan for every possible catastrophe, but allowing no time for any seemed illogical. Certain I would need that extra time to make up for some sort of calamity, I was completely thrown when we landed in London on schedule. I was grateful for the extra days, however, with the effects of the red wine and sleep medication fast eclipsing the rush of adrenaline from the cab ride. I pulled what I hoped were clean sheets from the closet and put them on the bed. I fell onto the mattress and it curled around me, holding me captive, but I enjoyed its welcoming embrace. I flipped through some shows on the "telly" (as I had heard someone at the airport call it) but mostly slipped in and out of consciousness, my eyes too heavy to open, my body feeling tied to an anchor.

The following afternoon, fully rested, I was spry and ready to take on England — in the touristy sense, not that of a psycho rebel-patriot. It was when I began my primping routine that I discovered the silly little shower. The showerhead was loose, one of those handheld things attached to a large silver coil that can be pulled off the wall. But that's not how I was accustomed to showering: I typically rinsed under a nice, stable nozzle. But in England I stood, 5'9", staring at a showerhead that rose to about 5'4", leaving me no choice but to remove the hose if I wanted the top half of my body to be clean. I showered in a tub a foot off the ground, with a curtain that for some specious reason extended only halfway across, in a room full of cold air with water spraying everywhere because, though it was an inanimate object, the hose twisted and curled and seemed to prefer to squirt in one direction — toward the wall. I missed home.

Having finally finished my routine, I thought about touring alone and realized how much I wished Brandon was by my side. And if not him, anyone. I was lonely already. What was I going to do for the next six months? I breathed deeply, thought about the stunning scenery, the pictures I would take, and the stories I would tell when this trip ended, and I understood anew that this was the time — my time — for adventure. Bolstered by this realization, I was energized and prepared to see some sights.

Having read in numerous travel guides that London was a haven for pickpockets, I fastened a money belt tight under my clothes. I put my camera in a bag strapped diagonally across my chest for less access to passersby. I pulled a purse over my other shoulder so it lay diagonally in the opposite direction of my camera bag. And I placed a can of pepper spray in my pocket, thumb on the trigger, and headed out the door.

Chapter Five

Using the hand that wasn't wrapped around the pepper spray, I pulled out the sightseeing spreadsheet I created, which had been organized by area, price, and importance. Number one on my list under the heading "Must See!" was a landmark of great historical significance: Harrods Department Store — a place I had learned of while sobbing over the heart-wrenching round-the-clock footage of Princess Diana's death. I had a fleeting thought that landing in London and heading first to a store was a silly waste of time in such a grand city, but the thought passed so quickly I gave it no attention. I was twenty-four hours from spending six months shoulder-deep in culture; pampering for one day in five acres of unnecessary, overpriced luxury items was acceptable — and necessary given the previous day's harrowing flight experience. Harrods also housed a memorial to the late Princess so I was confident that all of my bases were adequately covered. I took out my trusty travel guide, piled on my map with a pop-up Harrods protruding toward the sky, and held it out while walking down the road. Only the Hawaiian shirt and the straw hat were missing from the image. The guide recommended taking the underground subway (the "tube" to locals); since I was in London, I'd do as the Londoners did. I walked to the nearest tube stop and looked inside — which was when rational me and everyone-is-out-to-get-me me collided. "We" debated whether the tube was really such a good idea. Men wearing trench coats, as though they were planning to flash their junk to unwitting spectators. *Of course, it was quite cold.* Kids wearing matching tracksuits and hooded sweatshirts, traveling in packs, as though they were searching for a bystander to "jump" on gang initiation day. *Although, that's what kids wear and why should they travel alone?* It was dirty and damp. *Though fairly well lit.* What if I fell off the platform? What if a Brit who still blamed us for electing George Bush pushed me off? The Andrea with delusions of destruction won the debate when I allowed her to waste too much time wondering how my parents would find out that I had been killed on the tube. I would go only to places I could walk. Unfortunately, Harrods was a forty-five minute walk — an Ironman Triathlon to those of us who hail from Los Angeles; it would have to wait.

My not-so-savvy refusal to use the United Kingdom's most efficient and popular mode of transport whittled my touring options down by more than two thirds, unless I wanted to spend my life savings on taxis. My first stop would be Westminster Abbey — five minutes on foot, door to door.

I picked up my pace to pass the tube station, then worried about looking the wrong way while walking across the street and getting flattened by a car. Many of the streets had *look left* or *look right* painted in large letters next to the curb, but what if I approached a corner where a multitude of cars or pedestrians blocked the prompters? Although the option to go back to bed briefly ran across my mind as the safest way to spend the day, it was also the dumbest. I slowed down, vowed to look in every direction possible as I crossed the road, and walked on.

I quickly uncovered another issue to solve: hunger. My stomach was groaning, seemingly louder than the street traffic, and I felt faint. I pulled a granola bar from my bag and wolfed it down in seconds, wasting no time on chewing. But it wasn't enough. Fortunately, the tube stop was just a few feet from a small café where people appeared to be snacking on pastries and filling up cups with coffee, that luscious pick-me-up I had come to rely on. I studied the long line of people and the bins of items labeled as bagels and noticed that the latter items bore no resemblance to the bagels I knew and loved. They were small, thin, and pale, like the dough had not yet risen. I gave it a pass, saddened at how Britain had mangled such an otherwise perfect breakfast treat and I grew concerned: if the British could mangle the bagel this badly, what chance did *I* have?

I opened my map to a pop-up of the Abbey and noticed that its pointy protrusion upward really was quite phallic, a fact which did not go unnoticed by my fellow pedestrians.

"Miss, I don't know what you're searching for with that thing, but this isn't America. Put it away."

I flipped through a couple of the other cut-outs in the book and, particularly upon viewing Big Ben, realized that the map book was a gag gift that should have stayed at home with the others I received at my going-away party (a baseball cap with an "X" through the Union Jack and the phrase THE YANKEES ARE COMING, THE YANKEES ARE COMING; a straw hat with the Queen's arm protruding out the side, which waved at the press of a button; a T-shirt that read ASK ME ABOUT MY DENTIST). And with that, I decided that purchasing a new map was in order.

I continued down the road, looking up, down, side to side, and possibly diagonally at every crosswalk. I ignored the people who attempted to push me into the street when I took a tad too long determining when it was safe to walk.

"Um, you can walk across now, unless you're waiting for it to become morning in America." How do they know I'm American?

I knew Westminster Abbey was an important landmark in Britain where monarchs are crowned, royalty say their vows, and science heavyweights Darwin and Newton and scriveners like Dickens and Chaucer were laid to rest. In just a few minutes, I looked up to find myself in front of the impressive structure, shocked that I had arrived so quickly and that a building of this repute was not hidden behind gigantic walls and a hundred-foot-wide moat. It appeared too important to stand out in the open for any patron, worthy or not, to walk inside. From the tourist entrance, the massive building looked like two adjacent towers, the grey of a dolphin's belly, embellished with intricate carvings and statues embedded in the facade. Each tower stood over two hundred feet high, one with a bold brass clock near the top and all corners topped by pointed spires. Connecting the towers was a smaller structure about two-thirds as high, rising to a point in the center at its highest peak. I was instantly awestruck.

Outside the entrance sat a middle-aged vendor behind a glass partition, a full head of grey hair and kind eyes partially hidden by a thick set of bifocals. I smiled as I began to fumble with the currency I hadn't yet tried to figure out.

"Hiya. Sixteen quid, please."

And a quid would be what, exactly? "Quids? I have only pounds, sir," I said.

His cheeks began to quiver as he bit back his laughter. "That'll do as well, Miss," he said. *Okay, so quids equal pounds. Got it.*

I picked through the money in my hands as though looking for something in particular, perhaps a beacon of light to point to the correct configuration of currency.

"Can I help?" he asked, tapping his finger, annoyed now at how much time I was taking at his window.

"Oh, no, I've got it," I lied.

As the line grew longer and tempers shorter, I stuck out my hand holding the equivalent of about two hundred US dollars.

"I'm sure what you need is here."

"Yes, you could get in every day for three months, Miss. Carry on."

Hoping he took only enough for the one visit, I thanked him and walked inside.

I tiptoed through the opening to the Abbey, where rows of chairs for religious services lined the floor and a colossally high vaulted ceiling loomed overhead. I stepped a few feet past the entrance and marveled at the wooden pews that marked the sides of the Abbey, each row lined with small gold lamps covered by red lampshades, and the gold ornamentation on the wall behind the top row. Elevated at the top of the back wall was a large, circular stained-glass window with rows of hexagonal windows directly beneath, all of them too high and far away for me to make out the exact images. I was exhilarated by the psychedelic array of colors the sun created as it shone through the glass.

Feelings of wonder aside, I couldn't linger long. It wasn't that I didn't find churches beautiful — I did, but with an abundant helping of spookiness. After all, churches are places to pray for the dead, for people to grieve, and the windows tell stories of those who have died. I had steered clear of all houses of worship for those reasons. I had never attended a funeral, my mother having shielded me from those of the two people I knew who had died, and I had never prayed in a religious structure. It was eerily quiet inside; no sign of life except the haunting whispers of the praying visitors. The light was dim. Candles flickered.

I instantly recalled my first and only venture inside a church: I was six years old. I had been walking my dog in a circle in my front yard, not being permitted to go beyond the two-foot high gate by myself. The walk was proceeding without incident until a squirrel decided to taunt my precious canine from a nearby tree. My dog took off and I took off after her, the chase leading us into a nearby church. It was pitch black inside, minus the small stream of light creeping in the open front door. I followed the sound of my dog snarling in search of the squirrel, and I heard rustling. And I soon heard the sound of people yelling, at me, to leave. However, due to the darkness, I didn't see anyone's faces. I bumped into chairs, statues, and an organ before hands grabbed me. Startled by what I was sure would be the clutch of a kidnapper, I screamed just as the lights popped on and I found myself in the middle of the beautiful funeral service that my dog and I had destroyed. Apparently the participants had been standing still, waiting for someone to fix a blown fuse. Once the lights came on and I saw their angry faces, I grabbed my dog's leash and ran. Therefore, my last memory of a church was being chased out of it by an angry mob. I recalled my mother's expression when I returned home; I also remember that as punishment I was locked inside the house for at least a week, an eternity in my mind at the time. As my memory receded, I assume my imagination filled in some of the details. Being the fearful sort, though, my memories of the event haunted me for years. As those memories flooded back, I felt more nervousness than solace and I bee-lined for the door.

I walked out of the Abbey hoping the knots in my stomach would untangle, but they didn't. They persisted for a reason other than fear — it was shame. One of the world's most striking, historically important buildings was just feet in front of me, and I couldn't go through it.

While snapping some shots of the exterior and trying to talk myself out of what I knew was an illogical panic, I suddenly found myself in the middle of the infamous English downpour. Had someone taken a picture of the scene, they might describe it as *bleak* or *gloomy*. To me, though, there was nothing bleak about walking through London in the rain. In Los Angeles, the rain halts all activity, as though the water were a force field locking people indoors or, when they do "brave" the elements, from driving faster than 20 miles per hour. In London, life goes on as planned under the weight of the rainfall. I was a figure in an Impressionist painting, walking in the midst of distinguished-looking silhouettes of people dressed in long fitted coats, no visible detail on any faces, holding umbrellas that wove together in an intricate Escheresque pattern. I stood on a corner under an overhang and placed my umbrella at my feet to savor the rain and take photos of the stone from the buttresses that flew across the buildings, the columns that delineated the entrances, and the pointed rooftops as they glistened through the droplets. I tilted my head back and closed my eyes to inhale the scent. When I was done, I bent down to grab my umbrella but came up empty; it was gone. I rotated my head like an owl and saw someone running in zigzags down the sidewalk, carrying my umbrella. I started to dart after the thief, but once he became a mere speck I gave up. Surprised that I would close my eyes in public, I marched on thinking about how to keep blinking to a minimum. I was relieved in a sense, however, that the robber took only my umbrella and left my personhood in tact. I soon felt water soaking my hair and seeping through my shoes and conceded that rain is beautiful only when you're not sopping in it.

Lacking a guidebook with a crude picture of a convenience store, I walked down the road like a lost puppy until I happened upon a Boots Pharmacy, where I was greeted at the entrance by the second Brit who could have benefited from a good punching (the first being the crook keeping dry under my umbrella).

"Oh, dear, we're all wet, aren't we?" she said, in a tone that seeped pity and condescension so thick you could spread it on a scone.

"Well, *I am*, yes. You seem to be perfectly dry," I said, with only a fraction of the lady's sass.

"Oh, we must carry an umbrella, mustn't we?"

"Oh yes, ma'am, I guess we must. Wait, I did, until a little mugger took the one I brought with me," I said.

"Were you hurt?"

"Well, not physically."

"That's not really a mugging, now is it? It's really more of a pickpocket situation."

Do my pockets look like they could fit an umbrella? I failed to come up with a response that did not include sarcasm equal to her condescension, so I remained silent, gave a polite smile, and turned to search the store for an umbrella to save my drowning ass. As I turned away, however, my foot slipped in the puddle of water that had accumulated while I was chatting with the "insightful" chipper lady. Sliding, I stuck a hand out to find balance, then my other hand, which landed on a display of candy that I held on to as I walked in place, slipping with each step as though on a treadmill. I gripped the candy display, hoping to pull myself to an upright position and regain traction. No such luck. Within seconds, my feet slipped out from under me and I felt the candy display teetering back and forth before it came crashing to the floor along with me.

So there I sat, near the entrance to Boots, in a pile of candy and a puddle of water with my pop-up map by my side, open to Big Ben. The weight of the humiliation crushed me further when I heard "store cleaners to the entrance" over the loudspeaker. What's more, the person speaking forgot to turn off the loudspeaker while he talked to a coworker — leaving me to hear more: "oh, wait, what happened? Are you serious? Bloody Americans." Disgraced in surround-sound, I watched as customers entering the store leapt over me, none slipping on the candy or the water, none offering to help me up but one who said, "Americans should really have chaperones, shouldn't they?"

A man I erroneously thought was a friendly cashier finally walked over to assist me. As he pulled me from the mess I had created, he said, "You shouldn't tour England without an umbrella, you know. I'm sure your map thingy says that somewhere, doesn't it?"

Yes, and it also says No Taxation Without Representation. "No, no. I've actually not heard that before. It's lucky I met you."

I managed to sort myself out and buy an umbrella, as well as a new map, just in time for the clouds to clear and the sun to come out from hiding, mocking the wet dog I had become.

With the newly clear day and the new positive attitude I was trying by the minute to embrace, I walked to Buckingham Palace to determine whether it lived up to the hype. Once out front, I was caught in a pool of paparazzi, throngs of people holding their cameras overhead and swarming the gold-tipped black wrought-iron fence enclosing the palace, a massive white rectangular building with two horizontal lines of square windows. Maybe due to its simple shape and functional appearance, it was an appealing building that, if its walls could talk might say (in a prim and proper tone): Excuse me, Miss, but rather important business takes place here. The crowd of people, myself included, looked upon it in wonder — after all, the Royals lived just inside the walls. The tourists contemplated all sorts of silly queries: "Do you think the Queen will come out and wave?" "Why does the Queen need such a large house if her kids moved away?" "What does the Queen do besides drink tea?" As senseless as the questions were, they came from the right place: the feeling that we were lucky to be there.

I took a picture and texted it to Brandon: *Just meeting the queen for tea. It looks like she won't show, but I still have this great view of the palace! Love you. xo*

The crowd grew swiftly, leaving me feeling suffocated and trapped, and indicating that it was time to leave. I pushed through, gripping my belongings tightly, and walked across the street to St. James Park where I meandered through the pathway down the middle. Mammoth trees lined both sides of the trail, overlapping overhead to create a large canopy. The park was serene, and although I longed to sit on a bench and watch the ducks swim around the ponds, I felt the chilly air and noticed that the world wasn't as bright as it had been before. It was getting late in the day and I was concerned about being out past daylight, especially in a park. Parks are prime spots for ne'er-do-wells, the brush providing perfect cover, and a hoodlum with a brilliant accent is still a hoodlum. I walked briskly, one finger back on the pepper spray.

About a block from my place, I came upon what the Brits call a "chip shop," a fast-food fish and chips joint serving food greasy enough to be wrung out but delicious enough to keep me from caring. I placed some money on the counter, took my newspaper-wrapped fish and chips to my room, and fell onto my couch. As soon as the satisfaction of sitting hit me, I became immobile. I could feel a throbbing bruise blossoming on my left thigh, my ankles swelling, and my arms becoming too heavy to lift. I peeled the oil-soaked paper from my fish and inhaled my dinner. I considered taking a bath, if only because I felt like I was cloaked in Crisco, but fell asleep before I could work out the logistics. My first day of work would begin at sunrise.

Chapter Six

While I was spending the day walking industriously around a foreign country, my father was walking aimlessly around his own house. The background of my ambling had been street traffic and the jubilant sounds of a bustling city; my father's score had been my mother's operatic wail.

"We've lost our baby girl!" she bellowed numerous times.

"No we haven't."

"She'll never come back."

"Honey, we've made sure that's not going to happen."

"What if she meets that Matthew Crawley character from *Downton Abbey?*"

"Okay, then she'll never come back."

My mother's wailing grew an octave higher and ten decibels louder.

"Honey, stop. She's not going to meet him. Now, remind me, did you say the toilet in the guest bathroom needed fixing?"

"You never know; she's an attractive girl," she said. "What? No, the toilet's fine."

"Oh, right. What about the desk in the office, didn't you say a leg was broken?"

"I'm going to put some pictures together in case something happens to her and the police need a reference. No, the desk is fine."

My father walked into the yard and began pulling weeds, or what he thought were weeds. My mother stared out the window, her eyes puffy and red from her two-day cry-a-thon.

"Honey, why don't you let our gardener do that? You're pulling out my begonias."

"It's fine, dear."

After yanking out random stalks and leaves from the backyard, my father looked around and nodded proudly, though the yard looked exactly the same as it had before his bout of "gardening," minus a few begonias.

"I think I'll add some more flowers next weekend," he said. "The side yard looks a little bare."

"Okay, George. We can pick them out, but let's have the gardeners plant them. You've never planted flowers before."

"Maybe it's time I learned."

My parents continued with their routine. They watched movies they had already seen multiple times on television and conversed with each other only minimally.

"Normally Andrea would be here today."

"I know, Annie. But it's going to be a long six months if you say that every time she would normally stop by."

"I can't help it."

"Please try."

"Okay, you're right. We should have dinner soon. It's almost six o'clock."

"Yeah. You know, we're going to be fine, Annie."

"I know we are," my mother replied as she started chopping vegetables from a pre-made salad in a bag. "We just have to find ways to stay busy."

Chapter Seven

At 7 a.m. I opened my closet, perused the clothes I had brought from home, and rejected each item. I had traded my chic Los Angeles attire for what I believed was a sensible UK one, but now I was disappointed and further resented my tube-aversion for causing me to skip Harrods. In England, I would dress like a J. Crew display mannequin in winter — a bland ensemble of jeans, a tee under a solid-colored sweater, and black boots. *Comfort sure can be boring.* My hair was a perfectly symmetrical ball of blonde frizz. Inside or out, the air was damp — a staunch enemy of curly tresses. I'd pick up a flat iron as soon as I could find a pharmacy other than the Boots that had assaulted me the day before. Once again I packed myself in like a paranoid Girl Scout with pepper-spray ammo, my money belt strapped tightly around my waist under my clothes, and my camera bags and purse strapped in crisscross fashion over my clothes. I walked outside to brisk air and clouds hanging overhead.

I decided to sample one of the "bagels" at the shop near my apartment. I also bought a cheese Danish, in case the bagel was as tasteless as it appeared, and a monstrous cup of coffee. With the long line of people waiting to be served, I again placed some money on the counter and allowed the brusque, frazzled cashier to take what he desired. I walked out the door, took a bite of the doughy, more-dry-than-matzo, item, and let the realization sink in that it would be six months before I would have a real bagel.

In just a few blocks I saw the tube again, and this time I was determined not to let it get the best of me. I would defeat my white whale du jour. I stepped into the waiting area and looked inside. People pushed past me as though I were but a circling fly and walked right in. It was easy for them, swarms of them. But it was dirty and loud. I heard the crackling of the wheels against the railings — metal on metal — and the announcer's warning to *mind the gap* as the subway car screeched to a halt. I thought again about the people who have died on those tracks. Those who had failed to mind the gap and fell between the car and the platform — or, worse, who were pushed by a crazy person. What about those cornered on the inside of a car by a ruffian who shoved a gun in their face? There would be nowhere to run. Or those who got trapped when the engine stalled, then died of starvation? I sat down and put my head between my knees. Eight minutes later I looked inside and steadied my resolve. *Shit*. I couldn't do it. I started to walk away, but when I made it to the other side of the entrance I turned back as if someone had tapped me on the shoulder. I looked around at the people effortlessly boarding the trains, their ages ranging basically from 0 to 100. *How bad could it be?*

I took a breath, deeply inhaling toxic fumes, and approached the ticket machine to figure out how to buy a subway card. It asked me first to pick a zone. I looked around at the maps on the walls and felt them coming to life. Faces emerged from the middle of the colored lines and I heard hearty, ominous laughs. A line began to form behind me; the whispers quickly grew in volume. Despite my obvious confusion, no one offered a helping hand. I felt like the people surrounding me were pointing and cackling, the walls closing in. I turned to the waiting patrons. "Oh, nuts, I left something at home," I said, and ran away, allowing the public transportation system to win another round of "how to scare Andrea out of doing the things normal people do."

My feet ached tremendously and I felt the blisters that had formed the day before rubbing against my soles and oozing a sticky fluid. I cursed myself every painful step to the office — and there were many. I made several wrong turns and asked for directions twice from two of the most harmless-looking old people I could find, both of whom said something like "the tube's much quicker, innit?"

"Was that word 'in-nit'?" I asked one of them.

"Sorry... is it not?"

To conceal the fact that the tube scared me like the clown in *Poltergeist*, I responded that I didn't at all mind the "bloody freezing" weather and rather enjoyed walking — with a limp.

When I had finally reached my limit of traveling in haphazard circles, I asked a third "sweet" elderly person to direct me. He laughed and pointed me toward the door to my left; I had arrived. It was a wonder I had missed it, given the group of women with their hands and noses pressed to the glass door, as though their fingertips had plastic suckers, eager to witness the arrival of the American. I paused for a moment to let the three ladies detach themselves from the door and scurry to their desks before I went inside.

"Hiya!" they yelled in high-pitched synchrony.

"Hi there," I said, scanning my new six-month stronghold. *Adventure*'s satellite office was a large white square, stark as a psych ward, with the exception of a poorly framed and crooked rectangular picture of the London skyline on one wall and a discolored cover of *Adventure*, depicting Stonehenge, blown up and framed on the other.

"You can see why we're recreating a UK issue, can't you?" said one of the ladies, who I later learned went by the name Gemma, pointing at the *Adventure* cover, which was nearly as old as Stonehenge itself. Gemma was a tall, very thin, pretty girl in her early thirties with light brown, stick-straight hair just past her shoulders, porcelain skin, and light brown freckles visible only in certain lighting. The size of her jeans suggested that she approved of her slender figure and longed to show it off, as did her low-cut top and exposed décolletage.

"It does look like it can use updating. And the poses are just all wrong for their structure," I responded, hoping to prompt laughter but obtaining only befuddled expressions and the lonely sound of crickets.

I bowed my head a little and walked further inside. The floors matched the walls — bare — no boxes, few cabinets. It was as though they had just moved in but the moving van hadn't yet arrived. Ikea's finest reception desk stood in front of two rows of three cubicles each, separated by a pathway topped by vomit-brown carpeting.

I started to place my things beside an empty desk when one of the other ladies broke the silence. "Well, then, what are the walls like in America?"

"What? Huh?" I looked toward the other girls for assistance with comprehending the question. To no avail, though; they looked around the room, also avoiding it. They might as well have been whistling.

"Come on then, tell us," she probed again.

"Oh, I'm sorry, that was a real question?" I replied, to which I received a few laughs. *Phew.* "I'm sorry, you are?"

"Millie."

"Well, Millie, the walls in America do pretty much what they do here. You know, hold up the ceiling."

"Oh," she said with a blank expression that, I would learn, was not one she wore some of the time but simply her face all of the time. Millie was a short, stout girl with dark, frizzy hair, vampire-pale skin, and eyes as vacant as her expression. Her bright red cheeks looked as though they were victims of an explosion from a container of blush, which I initially thought was caused by embarrassment. The redness never faded, though, and I wasn't sure she knew she should be embarrassed. Her innocence and ignorance revealed her to be at most twenty-one, as did her full, pleated skirt and mismatched blouse. On first impression, she was several wicks short of a candelabrum — but I didn't want to be judged solely on my Stonehenge comment, so I tried not to let the wall question define her character.

"Hiya, I'm Claire," said the third lady, extending a hand. Claire, similar in age to Gemma, was a nondescript character. She was sweet looking but soft-spoken and petite, with brown hair and eyes, wearing clothes as plain as her appearance; you could pass her by without noticing. But to me she was kind and helpful. She gave me an *Adventure* email address and we discussed office procedures.

"Would you like some tea?" she asked, handing me a laptop.

"Oh, um, sure. Thanks." I hated tea. Always had. But, without knowing whether refusing tea in England was a treasonous crime redressed by beheading, I gave a gracious nod.

A dual effort by the staff in the London and Los Angeles offices of *Adventure* had yielded a loose itinerary for my trip. I glanced at the three-page document, wondering why they had allotted six months to complete the tasks and assemble the issue. Had I merely gone from castle to cathedral to castle, it seemed several weeks would have provided ample time. Upon further discussion, I learned that the trip would be more complex than mere glamour shots of monuments, with some shoots including elaborate scenes with props and models. The publisher had requested that we take a library of pictures at various times of the day, which required me to shoot each landmark at dawn, midday, and evening if possible, using my professional judgment as to whether a new time of day added something special to the shot. The itinerary also provided buffer time for travel, inclement weather, and re-shoots. Claire told me that Millie had spearheaded the London team that prepared the itinerary; therefore, extra time was likely built in for human error too.

I spent the day researching and taking notes on the places I'd go and what I hoped to accomplish for the magazine. The office was largely silent, apart from Gemma's commentary on men she was perusing on a dating website and Millie's questions as to how the men actually got into the computer — other than which she said very little, which I had already learned was a gift. Claire occasionally chimed in with, "You alright?" and several "Need more tea?" comments. The tea was mere hot water with leaves that smelled of lavender and tasted of vegetation; learning to politely refuse tea catapulted to the top of my to-do list.

The first day of work was one during which I put my head down at 8 a.m. and picked it up at 3 p.m., wondering what the hell had happened. At that point, Gemma stood up from her desk, eager to complete the workday. "I'm knackered. Let's all get to know each other, yeah?"

The rest of us looked up at Gemma and then at each other, confused at such an abrupt and early end to the day.

"We've worked hard, I need a drink. Grab your coats," she added.

Gemma hadn't worked hard, but she was excited about the happy hour she had arranged at a nearby pub, and, as my first-day nerves hadn't fully settled, I conceded that a drink would help to relax them. "Sure, sounds good to me," I answered.

"Smashing," she said. "No better way for you to meet the two blokes you'll be traveling with and for me to decide if I want to shag one of them."

"One of them?" asked Claire.

"Yes... at a time."

"Ah, right then."

"I'm sorry?" I asked.

"Oh, what about?" asked Gemma.

"No, I mean I don't know what you're talking about. You must be mistaken. I'm traveling alone."

"Oh, I don't think that's correct, is it, Claire?"

"Didn't you know, Andrea?"

"No, no, I didn't know." I started to panic. I had few thoughts other than how powerless I would be if these people tried to take advantage of me. I thought of dreadful scenarios, the type you'd see in graphic reenactments on *Dateline. Tonight at 11: What happened to Andrea Lieberman? The journey and disappearance of the castles-and-cathedrals photographer.* How would I protect myself? Assuming "blokes" meant men, I had additional concerns, maybe even more alarming: how unattractive I can be in the morning, and whether I had brought the right accessories. Women never want to feel undesirable to men, whether or not sex is on the table. It adds stress; the mere presence of two men would increase my morning preparation ritual by at least twenty-five minutes.

They must have been misinformed, I thought. I called Mr. Henson to clear up the confusion.

"Hi, Andrea. How's your first day going?"

"Um, it's great, Mr. Henson. Look, the girls just told me that two people are traveling with me. Is that right?"

"Yes, that's right. No one told you?"

"No, it only just came up."

"Oh. Well, we found these really great guys to help out with the shoot."

"Okay, that's great. But you know, I can do this on my own."

"No, Andrea, you can't. As I hope Claire told you, this trip is a lot more than a snapshot of a window and a column. Besides, the lawyers have advised against sending you alone; too much liability. And our insurance company won't let us. It's out of my hands."

My heart sank a little at the news. I was disappointed to be deprived of a soul-searching adventure where I could learn about myself and my ability to survive. But simultaneously I breathed an enormous sigh of relief and felt the queasiness that had been mounting since I took the position begin to dissipate. Due to my general unease with living, how I would have made it through the six-month trip alone was as big a mystery to me as air travel was. But Mr. Henson had handed me something new to fear: two strange men that the magazine had hired to accompany me, who would be virtually my only company for half a year.

"Well, do you know them?" I asked, indiscriminately gnawing at my fingernails that had only started to recover from the previous chew-fest.

"No, but I've spoken to them several times and checked out their references. They're impressive, a lot of publishing experience."

I started asking Tom a thesis-length list of questions. How well had they been vetted? Did we have their police records? Had they ever appeared on *America's Most Wanted?* What about England's version of the show?

"Andrea, if you don't want to go, tell me now. I can still replace you."

"Oh, I was just kidding, Mr. Henson. I couldn't be more pleased. Just one more question, though. We're not sharing rooms, are we?"

I held my breath waiting for him to answer.

"No Andrea, you're all sleeping on your own."

"Wonderful." That was a relief; at least I had a place to hide in an emergency. "Thanks again for the opportunity, Mr. Henson."

And that was it. If I wanted to go on this journey, I would have to do so with two foreign men — well, foreign to me, anyway.

"You alright?" asked Claire as I sat in a daze, allowing the new information to simmer.

"Yeah, I think so. I'm just wondering how I'm gonna tell my parents."

Chapter Eight

Gemma had swapped her low-cut blouse for an even lower-cut spaghetti-strap tank top that happened to be in her purse — I imagined her grabbing it every morning along with her cell, keys, and a pair of matching undies — and took her coat. I walked out behind her, followed by Claire and Millie.

"I love happy hour," said Millie as the door shut behind us. "Maybe because I'm always happy anyway."

As we walked up the road, I was proud of the way I stealthily regarded the street signage — *look left* and *look right* — while crossing each intersection.

"Andy, no need to examine the curb. Just follow us, we won't let you get hit, yeah?" said Gemma with a nod and a knowing smile. Okay, maybe not so stealthily.

A few blocks later we arrived at The Humping Camel, a place I labeled as a traditional British pub: dark oak walls and even darker wood floors; all rustic, no gloss. A rotund and toothless old man with a thick accent and suspenders stretched to their limit stood behind the bar — a man I imagined spit-cleaned the glassware. Electronic trivia games sat atop the corners of the bar and a large jukebox adorned the back wall, playing Adele as we entered. Gemma sat at the edge of a large table facing the door and immediately winked at a man she thought was attractive, declaring, "he'd get it." When a less desirable man entered, she would turn to us and say, "oh, he'd never get it."

Before I could ask, "he'd get what?" Claire leaned in to me. "She's always on the pull, get used to it." I had never used, much less heard, the expression *on the pull* before, but it became crystal-clear very rapidly what it meant. I then began my own game: guessing which men Gemma would give "it" to. I was often wrong; her standards were such that about eight out of ten men would get it.

"Oi, lads, over here," Claire said waving two gentlemen — my travel companions — over to our table. I sat up ramrod-straight and tried to steady my trembling legs, preparing to meet them. The first one, Gemma stated, would "never get it." Claire told us it was Robert, the copywriter. Robert was the British stereotype: 5'11", lanky, pasty-white skin, prominent freckles and reddish-brown hair — not bad-looking, but he wouldn't stand out in a circle of other men.

"Hiya. You alright? I'm called Rob," he said, and shook all of our hands.

The man behind Robert received Gemma's most emphatic reaction of the night, "ooh, he'd get it... again and again." Contrary to the English stereotype, he was tan, at least 6'2", with dark hair, green eyes, and a muscular build.

Before the second man reached our table, Claire leaned in and whispered, "That's Harry. Half-Italian, half-English, Oxford graduate. He's a photographer and an art director."

Harry was so good-looking you couldn't help but blush when he looked at you. It didn't seem fair to the remainder of the male species — or the female species, really, as I suspected there was only one of him. *Aren't we working on cloning, though? We should start with Harry.*

"You alright? I'm Harry, lovely to meet you," he said, taking a hand from each of us and giving them all a kiss. I wanted to curtsy in response. After the formal introductions, Harry clapped his hands together. "Right, we need drinks. I'll go to the bar. You lot get cozy. So tell us what you fancy," he said, directed at me.

It took my entire arsenal of willpower not to respond with "you," but I made an even bigger fool of myself. "I'm sorry, I thought you said just you were going up to the bar."

"That's right, just me. So tell us what you'd like."

"You keep using the word *us*, but you mean just you."

"Oh, Americans are the best." Then in a slow, Southern drawl he said, "sorry, ma'am. Please tell me what drink you'd like to have; I, by myself, am going to the bar." He tipped an imaginary hat, and when he did I got a whiff of his cologne: an intoxicating mixture of vanilla and mint leaves. Though I have no confirmation, I'm sure my cheeks turned a shade of Millie-red.

Though Harry was easily the best looking man I had ever seen without a movie ticket, his inviting smile and easygoing demeanor made me comfortable. "Easy there, buddy. I'm not from the South. Anyway, I'll take a Sam Adams."

"Oh, come on, then. Try a British lager," he said.

"Why not a Cains," said Gemma, chuckling.

"Well, I don't think we need to kill 'er just yet," said Harry.

"Yeah, a Sam Adams will work fine," I chimed in.

"How about a Carling, that's pretty weak," Rob added.

It was a word I recognized. "Yeah, let's do the weak one."

"Yep, good thought, Rob. A pint of Carling, then. Yeah?"

"No, no, Harry, that's way too much."

"Okay, a half pint, then."

"Is that a lot?"

I had no idea how large a pint was, so I attempted an ounce-to-pint calculation in my head while fumbling with the money I still hadn't quite figured out. Roaring laughter erupted. I had become the table's jester.

"That's alright, luv, I'll get it. I think we all want a drink before the bar closes," he said. "You can get us a round in a few days, when you have that all sorted."

Harry returned to the table with drinks and crisps (potato chips to us Americans) for everyone and I learned that a pint was merely a full-size glass of beer, not some zany English measurement. Earlier that day, a famous British newscaster had died — he would definitely have "gotten it" from Gemma — kicking off gossip and discussions about all things British. I felt alienated and alone — but then, I was. I understood each separate spoken word (well, most of them), but when they were strung together the conversation was unintelligible to me. My eyes wandered around the bar: groups of people conversed, some pounding the tables in fits of laughter; a table of young men and women in professional attire played drinking games, affably taunting the gent forced to chug a whole pint after a wrong answer; friends caught each other up on subjects from office gossip to the dating scene. I observed their mannerisms and took in the array of accents. It was not at all distinct from a night at a bar in my hometown — the people interacted the same, which, for a reason unbeknownst to me, was surprising. It didn't look foreign, but it certainly felt that way. I wanted to chime in to my table's discussions with factoids or witticisms, but I could never find the right moment. I wanted to know everything about them; I had thought the feeling would be mutual. But there would be plenty of time for that. Regardless, I was entertained by the way Gemma turned even the most benign of Harry's statements into dirty comments.

"Remember that interview he did of the Prime Minister last year during the labor strike? He really had the man by the balls!" Harry said.

"Ooh, I'd like to have them both by the balls," Gemma responded in the tone of a C-list porn star.

"What? That's ridiculous. He never held someone's balls," said Millie, giggling with embarrassment at having said *balls* — for which I couldn't really ridicule her.

Claire sat as silent as I did, which I feared was more uncomfortable for her — she was most likely familiar with the discussion topics. We occasionally exchanged awkward smiles as we caught each other observing the parties happening around us.

After about an hour and four glorious pints of Carling, we began musing about the assignment.

"You excited about our trip, then?" asked Harry.

"Huh?" I said, caught off-guard.

"Huh?" repeated Robert in a mocking tone. "This is England. We say, 'Excuse me, can you please repeat yourself.'"

"Oh, I'm sorry," I said, almost inaudibly.

"Just taking the piss."

"What? I mean, excuse me, can you repeat yourself?"

"Joking, I was joking with you." All of this banter was confusing enough without the entire table chuckling at my expense.

"I didn't know until today that you two were coming with me," I said.

"Didn't you?" asked Harry.

"No. I thought I was going alone."

"Well that would be boring, wouldn't it?"

"Yeah, I guess. I had originally wanted to go by myself but I'm not sure I'd feel safe."

"Well, this should be great news, then. You aren't going alone," said Harry, smiling with teeth so straight and sparkly you'd swear he'd just jumped out of a Crest ad.

"Yes, I'm quite relieved." I said. "Neither of you've ever been convicted of a felony, right?" I added, my beer partially covering my lips.

"I heard that, Andrea," Harry replied.

I put my glass down on the table. "Well, then, maybe you want to answer it?" I said, laughing but not joking.

"Of course not, you half-wit," he said playfully. "They don't hire criminals to work for *Adventure*. But I don't think Rob heard you. Care to repeat your question?"

Yes. "No, I do not, thanks."

"Are you a good traveler?" Rob asked.

"What do you mean by 'good'?"

"Are you easygoing? You know, a take-it-in-stride kind of bird. Sorry, I mean girl."

Not unless take-it-in-stride means paranoid, skittish, and panicky. "Well, I haven't traveled much, so I don't really know."

Rob and Harry turned towards each other, sharing an *oh shit* facial expression. "Well, this should be quite an experience, then, shouldn't it? Shall we call it a night?"

"What else would we call it?" asked Millie.

"Millie, you aren't going to join us on our little voyage through the UK, are you?" Rob asked.

"No, I'm quite scared of foreigners."

"Foreigners? We're not—"

Rob placed an arm on Harry's shoulder. "Leave it," he said. "We understand, Millie. We'll take on those British foreigners for you."

"Oh, thank you," she replied nodding her head and smiling, teeing up a line of eye rolls for the table.

"What a shame, though," I said, which was only partially true. While the confirmation that Millie would remain in the office while we were hundreds of miles away offered great solace, it also removed many opportunities for comedy.

We all said our goodnights and Gemma told Harry that if he didn't want to say goodbye to her then, he could do it in the morning. A man likely accustomed to being hit on, he smirked, winked, and neglected to respond.

I asked everyone to pose for a quick picture to text to my friends back home, with two motives: to say hello and to prove that Harry was real.

Hey Ash: The Adventure *staff above. Check out my travel partners, Harry and Rob. Too bad your single ass isn't here! Say hi to the girls for me.*

I received a text back from Ashley in seconds. *Travel partners? What's that about? And, uh, Harry… wow! Ask him if he wants a US green card.*

During the cab ride back to my apartment, Ashley and I exchanged several texts so I could catch her up on the news. In response to my concern that I would be alone with two adult males, she implored me to trust in Tom Henson and *Adventure* and try to enjoy the voyage. I had mace, pepper spray, and my own room: I would be fine. Not surprisingly, the Harry picture circulated quickly amongst my girlfriends, after which I received an influx of texts consisting of hyperbole, sex jokes, and, for the first time, offers to carry my camera gear around England.

I nearly went to bed before remembering I hadn't called my parents since I arrived. Rather than have the UK embassy knock down my door, I decided to ring them and put their minds at ease. A hundred-foot wave of stress pummeled me as I picked up my phone: how would I tell them about my male cohorts? There was no chance I could make it through the entire six months keeping it a secret; besides, I wanted to share all of the details of my trip with my loved ones. I took a deep breath and put the news to them with a positive spin.

"Cheerio, my lovely parents!"

"Oh, thank God you called. We were going to call the embassy," my mother said.

"I know you were. Hey, I've got great news. I'm not traveling alone anymore. Two guys are coming with me. Aren't you thrilled?"

"*Two* men, huh? Hmm…. okay. What are their names?"

"Harry and Rob."

"Well, it's better than you traveling by yourself, I guess. How are you? Are you cold? Do you have a sweater? Has there been a fire?"

"They're called 'jumpers,' mom, not 'sweaters.' I'm not cold, I've witnessed no fires, and I'm doing great."

"Have you used the subway? I hear it's dangerous."

More confirmation of the lineage of my madness. But I wouldn't validate them. "No, not yet. Haven't needed to. Will do soon, though."

"Okay. Not alone, though, I hope."

Of course not. I don't have a death wish. "We'll see."

"How's the staff?"

"They seem alright. One is a bit of a slut, one appears quite stupid, and the other virtually a mute. I haven't figured out the two guys yet, but they seem nice."

My dad took the phone. "Is either of the men joining you handsome?"

"What? Dad, I have a boyfriend. Fiancé. Boyfriend. I don't know. I didn't notice. Put mom back on." He did. "Mom, one of them is *really* cute."

"That's great dear. Which one?" she asked.

"Harry."

"Oh, I'm glad Harry is good-looking. That should make the trip more fun."

"Thanks for that. Anyway, how are you two? Keeping busy?"

"Yeah, we both have lots of work to do," she responded.

"I mean other than work. How was the weekend?"

"It was fine. Your father did some gardening."

"Dad doesn't know how to garden."

"Well, he's, uh, learning. He's fine. We're fine."

"Okay. Remember, I left you those brochures."

"Andy, stop," my mother said. "We have our own lives."

"Do you, though?"

"Andy—"

"Okay, okay. I better get going," I said. "I'm leaving for Canterbury in the morning."

"Okay, sweetie. We love you. Bring your mace. And get a fire extinguisher."

"Seriously, mom, you need to look into that issue. Love you both."

I hung up the phone too drained to have another conversation rationalizing the existence of two mysterious male travel partners. I sent Brandon a text: *You alright? (That's British for 'how are you?'). An uneventful first day. Had a few pints (a pint's just a glass of beer, who knew?) at happy hour. Off to my first cathedral tomorrow! Will call you after. I love you. xo*

Chapter Nine

Bang! Bang! Bang!
I bolted up from my pillow with a start, unsure what I had heard. The room was black as an abandoned highway in the desert.

Bang! Bang!

What the? I knew I was hearing a banging sound, but my brain had not yet awakened enough to comprehend the noise. Instinctively, I rolled from the top of my bed to underneath it.

Bang! Bang!

I trembled and looked around, but saw only darkness. Was someone trying to break the door down? I was beginning to orient myself to a waking state as I vividly recalled my dream of a gang of Englishmen who began a trend of beheading American women. The banging got louder. Maybe I wasn't dreaming. *BANG BANG THUD!* I thought about calling 911, but when I reached for my phone on the end table I remembered I didn't know whether there was such thing as a 911 in England. What about the operator? Was that "0" or something else? I froze, shocked that I hadn't learned the basics of how to save myself in an emergency. What if there was a fire? Damn, I had turned into my mother.

"Andy, are you up yet?" *Bang! Bang!* I wiped my eyes and looked at the clock: 5:30 a.m. Finally adjusted to the morning, I realized I was supposed to be ready to leave. I crawled out from under my bed, flipped on the light, ran to the door, looked through the peephole, and saw the handsomely dressed, completely put together Rob and Harry laughing and slamming their fists against my door.

"Shit!"

"I take it you're not quite ready, then?" Harry shouted.

"Um, not exactly, just give me a few…"

I looked in the mirror and added the word *hours*. My hair sprung out of my head like a fern tree and mascara circled my eye like a Target logo. The beer pints were pounding against my brain, reminding me that I had drunk too many too quickly, Rob and Harry looked as though they had stepped out of a Hugo Boss catalog, and we had a train to catch in half an hour.

"Maybe the 7 o'clock train would be better?" Rob shouted as I ran around my apartment thrusting on jeans and a sweater — oops, a jumper — with a toothbrush dangling out the side of my mouth.

"Don't worry luv, you aren't *in* any of the photos," Harry added. And it was a damn good thing.

I finally pulled myself together, at least decently enough to be seen, thanked whatever higher power is responsible for deodorant and hair bands, and raced out the door. We rushed to the nearest tube station, Charing Cross.

Still not quite comfortable with the idea of the tube, however, I put forth an alternative. "Why don't we walk?"

"To Canterbury?" asked Rob. "Are you a nutter?"

"I, um, don't know."

"Sorry, Rob asked if you're crazy. You don't really mean to walk almost 60 miles?"

"Right, that would be stupid," I said. "Taxi?"

"I don't know how much they're paying you, luv, but a one-way cab fare to Canterbury would pretty much top out my month's wages," said Harry.

"Something wrong with the tube, Andy?" asked Rob.

What isn't wrong with the tube, Rob? "No, it's fine," I said, as I tried to muster up courage and not spill my entire bag of crazy on two strangers. "It's just musty, that's all."

"I'm guessing you don't have an Oyster card, then?" Harry said.

"I certainly do not have one, nor do I know what it is."

"Oh good heavens, Andrea. It's called research. You should give it a go sometime," Rob said.

The ticketing machine I had stared at with confusion the day before was in reality quite simple. Rob and Harry already had "Oyster" cards, refillable smartcards used for public transportation in London, that they added money to with the swipe of a credit card.

"Watch me, luv. You get one demonstration," Harry said. And it was all I needed. It took him literally seconds to throw cash in the machine and pull out an Oyster card for me.

"You can manage that, can't you, Andrea?"

"I believe I can, Rob. Thanks."

As I shadowed my local guides through the terminal, I attempted an air of confidence. I watched toddlers stepping easily into the rail cars with the excitement they would show at an amusement park and began to regret my past two days of fear. So many men in trench coats, though. How was I to know it was safe?

"So, if you haven't been on the tube, how did you get around the past couple days?" Harry asked.

"On foot. Was a little scared to ride the tube."

"That must be why you're limping."

"Afraid? Of what?" Rob asked.

Terrorists. Bombs. Flashers. Pickpockets. Unruly infants. "Oh, I don't know. I just thought I would wait until someone could teach me."

"But you thought you were traveling alone."

"Yes, that's true. Um, okay, I guess I just had to get used to England first."

"We aren't so scary," said Harry. "You'll see."

I held my breath for a large portion of the ride, and we stepped off the tube just as my skin took on a bluish appearance and I was about ready to pass out. From there, we transferred to another mode of transport that propelled forward without a human manning the wheel: the train that would ultimately take us to my first non-London UK excursion, Canterbury Cathedral.

During the hour-and-a-half ride, I longed to allow my eyes more rest, and I would have had Harry not metamorphosed into a human cuckoo clock.

"Wakey, wakey! You have to get orientated to London time, Andy."

"Orientated? Don't you mean oriented?"

"No, I don't think so. Shall we get you some tea?"

"No thanks, no tea," I groaned.

"Come, look out the window. It's lovely, isn't it?"

"Nothing's lovely before several cups of coffee." But as he nudged me, pushing my face into the crevices of the window and the piles of dried-up gunk still waiting to be cleaned from the first time a two-year-old spit up on it, I opened my eyes. Lovely was an understatement. It was a virtual color palate containing a vast array of greens, from deep, rich tones to light, almost yellow shades — all of them new to me. After that, it was impossible to close my eyes for fear that I would miss a new shade or image of this luscious landscape. After only a half hour of the British countryside, I was starting to have a new definition of beauty.

"So this is your first time in England, I gather. Ever been outside of America?" asked Harry.

"No. Actually, I've only been outside of California a handful of times," I said, my eyes still fixed on the scenery outside.

"You're joking? Bloody Americans. You think you have it all on your one little continent," Rob said.

"I don't know about 'little.' You know, England can fit in America's coat closet. Anyway, I've always wanted to travel; I'm just a little... well, I haven't really found the time. What about you two?"

"Let's think. I've been to about thirty countries," said Harry.

"Yeah, I'm about the same, give or take."

I turned my gaze away from the world outside and pointed it across the aisle at Rob and Harry with amazement. I felt young and immature; inferior, even. What must they have thought of me?

"Well, let's start with your favorite," I said.

"Country or town?" asked Rob.

"Either."

"San Sebastian, Spain," they said in unison.

"Oh, it is fabulous, isn't it?" said Rob.

With emphatic voices and eyes wide with excitement, they compared stories about their respective trips through Spain. Although I tried to follow, I couldn't keep up. It is more convenient for those who live across the Atlantic to traverse Europe and beyond, being so close to so many countries, many of which barely rival the size of California. However, I felt like a child staring up at grown-ups while they told me a bedtime story of mystical far-off lands.

As they bonded over a "holiday" (vacation) they had each taken back-packing through Catalonia in Spain, I was the voyeur, green with envy and foaming at the mouth considering whether I would get to see the same worldly wonders one day. They paused several times to explain bits and pieces to me while they spoke, but their exhilaration at remembering their trips took over and they mostly conversed with each other. The level of en-thusiasm they shared was infectious; I couldn't wait until one day I would talk in a similar manner about my six-month UK adventure.

I was reminded of the conversations my friends had had with each other when they returned from their trips to Europe, and the jealousy I felt. Rather than continue to be the missing part of their voyages, I began to insert whatever questions I could conjure whenever there was a lull. "If you could go to one place, anywhere, tomorrow, where would it be?"

"Greece," they responded, again simultaneously. Greece was a coun-try about which we could all three fantasize, whether exploring the ruins in Athens or wading through the shimmering, crystal-clear waters of the Greek Isles. Somewhere in the middle of a debate about whether the back-drop of Greece was the only redeeming quality about the film *Mamma Mia!* (with Rob sticking up for the soundtrack), the train whistled to a stop and we arrived at the birthplace of Christopher Marlowe, the scribe whose prose is said to be rivaled only by that of William Shakespeare, and the subject of Mr. Chaucer's tales: Canterbury, Kent County, England.

A short walk from the train station brought us to High Street, where we walked down rows of charming shops, attached to one another, with low-sloping chocolate brown wood-shingled rooftops. And a few streets later we came upon the glorious cathedral: a radiant structure, composed of varying shades of stone from mustard-yellow to pale grey, standing taller than the surrounding buildings and looking much statelier with its re-peated ornamental carvings. It was a long building, flanked by rows of tall rectangular windows rounded at the top and marked by several towers with pointed spires. We had arrived too late in the morning to capture the sunrise shots we'd hoped to get. Of course, "sunrise" is more of a time than an event in England, as you can seldom tell the sun exists. It was cold. And it had been dark for large portions of my days there so far. Still, there remained a substantial difference between the overnight hours and the day-time, so I was sure the sun was up there somewhere. It was kind of shitty of it not to disseminate warmth, though. At any rate, the assignment was to take shots at several times of day, and since we had missed the dawn we would have to spend the night. Looking around at the quaint English town we'd have additional time to explore, none of us complained.

We walked around the outside of the cathedral. I snapped long shots of the building and zoomed in on the layers of detailed crevices and facades, feeling sure-footed behind the lens. I had never cared much for the study of history growing up, especially European. I'm not particularly proud of that fact, but it felt useless to spend time on eras so long past. I'm not racist, I don't want anyone else's land, and I believe in equal rights; there are no lessons I am doomed to repeat by not having a complete understanding of how we got to where we are. Convinced that my brain had a limited capacity for remembering things, I had always preferred to fill it with knowledge about the recent past and present. But now it dawned on me: whoever built this structure did so in approximately 600 A.D. — I didn't have the ability to count how long ago that was, but I felt in my bones that it was impressive. There were no buildings in California that I knew of that had the prestige to even be mentioned in the same sentence as what stood before me. It felt like an honor to be allowed, requested even, to take pictures of this cathedral, and I therefore took great care in deciding what to shoot and how to shoot it, with the hope that I would do it justice.

The west side of the cathedral sat on the Stour River, a waterway lined on one side with closely packed, red brick homes and on the other with the cathedral and an expansive lawn that served as a public park.

After I had snapped the scenery surrounding the cathedral, it was time to head inside and explore, which is when my enthusiasm, and confidence, waned. I hesitated. Until now, Rob and Harry's presence had forced me to suppress some of my usual hysteria to avoid total embarrassment. But one can only hold one's breath for so long. It was time to exhale.

"Why don't you two go in without me?"

"What? Why?" Harry asked.

"What are you on about? This place is incredible. Don't you want to see the inside?"

"It feels like death in there."

"You haven't been in there so you couldn't know that, could you?"

"And if you haven't in fact died, how could you know what death actually feels like?" Rob added.

"I just know. I'm sure of it. Churches always feel like death. And they're haunted."

"You've frequented many churches, then?"

"Well, not really; not many."

"How many?" Rob asked, already annoyed with the response he anticipated.

"Well, one. But before you ridicule me, you should know that it was a very traumatic experience."

"I bet it's stunning," Rob said.

"Oh, ease up on the poor girl," said Harry, confirming his role in the good cop-bad cop duo.

I told the story of my dog-squirrel-church fiasco. Rob and Harry took delight in the tale, and as I heard myself tell it I too realized the lunacy of the whole thing. That I could still feel terror at what was in essence a scene from a sitcom did seem ludicrous — but I felt there was little I could do about it. As the trite saying goes, it was what it was.

"While I am quite amused by your story, I'm not at all amused by your behavior," said Rob. "If I remember correctly, you did agree to a *castle and cathedral* tour, which inevitably includes the interiors of castles and cathedrals."

"Yeah, I see your point. I thought I could do it, but I can't."

"Okay, I'm not entirely sure what it is you can't do, but let us explain what you'll find in there—"

"I know what I'll find. Darkness. Ghosts. Possibly goblins. Jesus hanging on the cross."

"Well, images, maybe. I don't think Jesus himself will be hanging in there. And there are no reenactments here that I'm aware of. Now, stop your whingeing and let's go in."

I took a breath and started to walk forward, but paused.

"Andy, we can have you replaced. For fuck's sake, this is your job," said Rob, sternly.

His words pelted me in the gut. I let out a huge puff of air and conceded. It *was* my job.

Harry rubbed my back, lending credence to my panic attack. He then took my hand and slowly led me to the threshold of the entrance. I looked in and stared up at the ceilings, which seemed a thousand feet high, and looked ahead at the multicolored glass windows.

"Come on, luv. You can do this."

Rob took my quivering hand from Harry's and pulled as though he cared nothing for its attachment to the rest of my body, yanking me across the threshold into the cathedral. It was dark, dank, and dour. I couldn't smell mold but I felt it must be present, eating up the walls and spreading mycotoxins. I walked slowly across the stone floor and looked around at the wooden pews. The craftsmanship was divine, perhaps literally. I felt myself taking short, hard breaths, but I had trouble obtaining a sufficient amount of air. I was getting light-headed. As some daylight peeked in through the windows, I snapped a few shots. We headed towards the back, where light was sparse and shadows created by the flickering candles roamed the walls. The floorboards creaked under my feet. Doors opened with a groan. And that was all I could stand.

I whispered to Harry, "You can shoot, right?"

"A little bit, but—"

"Great, snap away," I said, and handed him the camera. I ran outside and sat on a bench. Staring back at the cathedral, I derided my own ridiculousness. I stood up a few times to walk back inside, but I talked myself out of it each time. I was unable to stop my brain from recalling my mother's stories about her mother visiting from beyond the grave or from imagining the faces of the angry mob that had chased me out of the church all those years before.

Fifteen minutes later Harry came running out with Rob. They were both screaming. "AAHH! He's after us. Jesus is after us! Go now! Save yourself!" Harry ran into me, wrapping his arms tight around my waist. Rob stood by us, panting, feigning hysterics.

"Oh, thank God you're alright. It was horrible, just horrible," said Harry, as he gripped me tighter.

"Well aren't you the Abbott and Costello of *Adventure Mag*. Look, I know; I've a fear or two. But I'll get over 'em." *Well, some of them. Someday. I hope.*

"Well, let's hope it's sooner rather than later, because, my dear ego-driven Yankee, the point of the trip is to take fantastic photos for the magazine, not to fix your mental problems, isn't it?" Rob asked — a question that wasn't really a question. I sank in my own skin.

"Did you at least get me some good shots while you were planning your big finish?"

"Yes, we did your job for you quite well," said Rob.

I sank further. His words were hammers that battered home the nails of my disappointment. It was a song with a familiar tune: letting my unfounded qualms keep me from yet another opportunity. I had missed several whale-watching adventures growing up because I was afraid a whale would attempt a breach under the boat and send us soaring into the sky, only to crash land somewhere in the middle of the ocean and drown. Or, as my mother would warn, "What if there's a shark infestation in the water?" I missed a graduation cruise to Mexico because I had just seen *Titanic* and thought we might hit an iceberg — in the Mexican Riviera. "And Andy, what if those Somali pirates seize the ship? They are wreaking havoc these days." On the Carnival Jubilee? How did I not know better? That therapist my friends recommended daily really would have come in handy. I had to stop permitting irrational fears to prevent me from living.

"Harry, let me see your work." I took back my camera and thumbed through the pictures he took. They were decent, but not good enough.

"I'm going back in," I declared.

"Hey! They're not that bad," Harry moaned.

"She should go back in regardless," Rob added.

I turned toward the cathedral and was startled by a glimpse of the forlorn facial expressions on the figures etched in the windows, who seemed to be coming to life under the sun's rays, and remembered that Rome wasn't built in a day.

"Never mind. You'll have to go. I'll direct you."

"You can't be serious, Cyrano?"

"I am. I just want a few more. Let's look at your shots: we need to be closer to the windows in this one; the altar in this one is too dark, let's shoot it from the other side; and I'd also like a long shot of this hall. Please, Harry."

"Alright, luv, this one time—"

"But to be clear, it's for the good of the magazine," Rob interjected.

"Of course," I confirmed.

Harry went back into the cathedral and I stood near the doorway providing him with direction. When he emerged again, I flipped through the pictures; an improvement, but I knew I could do better.

"These are okay, for now. Thank you, Harry." As we walked away, regretful for having shunned my responsibilities, I reconfirmed Harry's sentiment to myself: *never again, Andrea.*

Later that day, we sat down to a supper where I would consume my first ever lamb kebab with another traditional English alcoholic beverage, cider and black (cider mixed with black currant juice).

"So, you have a deep-seated fear of stained glass. Any other inanimate objects we should keep you away from? Perhaps a certain type of door you think might take you down?" Harry said, with a smile and a disarming wink.

"I've a list of fears that's long and distinguished and I'm not drunk enough to divulge it." Harry and Rob were eager to discover the additional nonsensical items in my catalog of demons, so we spent the next couple of hours getting to know each other by the British Book — *i.e.*, playing drinking games.

"Okay, Harry and I will tell stories and you take a drink every time we mention something that scares you."

"Well, then. I should be passed out in no time."

"To be fair, we'll take a drink with you," Harry conceded.

"Take it away, Harry," I said preparing for a mortifying night of drunkenness.

"Okay, one evening in Rome—" [*Drink*] "Wait, really? I haven't said anything yet."

"It's evening."

"You're scared of the evening?"

"Well, in Rome. I don't know anyone in Rome."

"Fine, okay. I'm walking alone [*drink*] and I come upon a church [*drink*] with an abandoned car [*drink*] by the entrance."

Rob took over the story. "An old man [*drink*]. An old man, are you serious?"

"Old men can be creepy. And what is he doing around a church at night?" I was getting drunk.

Rob continued. "An old man comes up to me [*drink*] and asks for the nearest loo [*drink*]. Wait, this is just silly. You're afraid of the bathroom?"

"Sometimes. And I assumed you'd point him to the one in the church."

"Okay, this game isn't going to work. You'll be dead before I make it to the part where the stranger in a cloak with a hook for a hand and glass eyeballs asks me about the ghost of my dead grandmother." [*GULP*]

Another round of laughter on me.

Harry took my hand. "What happened to you, luv?"

"Nothing. That's the problem. I suffer from over-coddling."

"Sounds serious. Parents?"

"Yes. What about you two? You close with your parents?"

"'Fraid I lost both of mine," said Rob. "Car accident."

It was sobering. "Oh my, I'm so sorry." The sadness of the moment muffled the surrounding noise. What if my parents hadn't been around to warn me that there might be a fire, storm, or earthquake every time I left the house?

"Wouldn't you know, the driver of the other car lived. Drunk bastard," he added, throwing his head back to finish his pint.

"I hear ya, mate. Lost mine too. Bottoms up," Harry said, also throwing down a nearly full glass.

"How did you lose yours, Harry? Can I ask?"

"You can, but I don't know. I literally lost them. I have no idea where they are."

"You what?" Rob asked, incredulous.

"We were all walking together at a county show one day. I stopped for an ice cream cone, turned around and they were gone. That was twenty years ago. If they're alive, they're total wankers and if not it's quite tragic."

We didn't know whether to chuckle or cry at Harry's explanation, but to me it was unthinkable that anyone could be forced, at such an early age, to live with fear number one on my all-time top ten. If I never learned anything else about Harry or Rob, I'd still admire them for their perseverance and courage. Though I felt colossal annoyance at my overbearing parents, at least I had that luxury. I couldn't relate to Harry's and Rob's pain, not even a fraction, and again I felt infantile. I complained of too much parental love when they didn't have any.

"I'm such an asshole. I'm so sorry for both of you." I too inhaled my remaining drink.

It was silent for a beat as we simmered in the serenity of the moment and gave some time to the memory of Rob's and Harry's respective parents. I didn't have faces or personas to add to the vision, so I just took the time to make a wish that Rob and Harry would be able to live a contented existence with only the recollection of a mother and father.

"It's okay, luv, you learn to make do," said Harry.

Harry put his arm around me and looked me dead in the eye. With his touch, each of my tiny arm hairs stood at attention between the rapidly forming goose bumps. "At least I know where to go when I'm lonely and need an experienced coddler."

"I'm here for you, Harry," I said, as I reciprocated the arm gesture and flashed what I hoped was a warm, welcoming smile rather than a half-assed *I pity you* smirk. The second or two of nose-to-nose contact with Harry was enough for me to wonder what type of skin cream he used. His face looked soft and blemish free. Despite my evening of imbibing, I knew better than to rub my hands over Harry's cheeks. But the temptation was painful.

Although photography generally works best when sober, we stumbled back to the cathedral to capture its image under the stars — well, what should have been stars. I assumed the stars did preside over the English territories sometimes, but I had yet to see them; each day I had been there so far, cloud cover had eclipsed their twinkle. But the Cathedral was spectacular under a purplish-grey hue, covered by shadows. Lots of shadows. Shadows that danced across the building. Shadows that ensured my stay would be short and sweet.

"Um, this is a bit frightening. We really should get going."

"Ah, right, your powerful fear of evening must be in full force," said Rob.

"Not evening in general. But evening in a strange place, with few people, dim lighting, and wandering shadows."

I managed to snap a couple of pictures from a distance but I quickly got caught in a familiar struggle: the desire to accomplish my task versus the fright that accompanied it — and the latter won. Nothing like a consummate professional, I cut the shoot short and hailed a cab.

Upon retreating to my hotel bed, I was haunted by Harry and Rob's reality — growing up without the two people we are taught from day one to lean on and adore — but thrilled that I was too drunk to process it completely. It did stop me from sleeping, however, so I picked up the phone.

"Hi, Brando mando, it's me, Princess Andrea!"

"Are you drunk?"

"Um, yeah. Probably. But not the usual drunk, I'm drunk in Canterbury!"

"I'm surprised you're drunk already."

"It's okay, Brandon. You do know it's evening here?"

"Yes, babe, I meant so early on in your trip."

"I've found that the alcoholic beverages really calm the nerves."

"Okay, that's good, I guess. So, how's it going?"

"Fabulous. I saw the cathedral today, it's spectacular. It's so ornate and—"

"What about the candlelight and crucifixion stuff? You doing okay with that?"

"Sort of. I had to leave the cathedral after a few minutes and let Harry take over."

"Harry? Who's Harry?"

"Oh right, I didn't reach you yesterday. Harry and Rob are the boys traveling with me. Harry's a photographer, art director dude, and Rob's a copywriter."

"You need *two* men with you?"

"Don't you feel better that I'm not alone?"

"Yes, but what, there are no women in England?"

"So, I'm having a good time and am thrilled you're happy for me."

"I'm sorry, baby. Of course I am. Are you all sleeping in the same room?"

"Nope, we've our own rooms."

"Oh, good. Is Harry good-looking?"

Too good-looking. "I don't know, Brandon."

"How old are they?"

"Well, I didn't check their IDs, but I assume early thirties."

"So, you feel okay with traveling with two grown men?"

"I'm torn, but what choice did I have? I wanted the job and Mr. Henson was clear: I was to go with Rob and Harry or go back to the US. Anyway, they're really fun to have around and I'm learning a lot about this culture. Did you know that 'fanny' here is what we call a 'vagina'?"

"That's a wonderful education you're getting, sweetie."

Brandon and I chatted about his life in LA for a few minutes before my eyes closed, demanding slumber.

I awoke the next morning completely befuddled at how the English maintained their drinking routine. My head was pounding, my face an unflattering shade of olive, and my stomach nauseous. Standing was a chore. The only comfort I found was in the fetal position, and as much as I enjoyed creative photography I couldn't think of a way to make that work. Rob and Harry, apparently impervious to consecutive nights of heavy drinking, grabbed the reins once again and went to the cathedral to take the early-morning shots before meeting me at the train station, where I sat with coffee, Tylenol, and a barf bag.

"Oi, there Andy," said Rob. "We took the final photos. One of these days I look forward to seeing your work as a photographer."

"Ah, leave her," Harry interjected. "She'll get there. She just needs to build up immunity."

To alcohol or to life? Though I had thought it impossible, I felt even more nauseated. I chastised myself as I believed Mr. Henson, Ashley, and my mother and father would have for a job poorly done. Although the words *fearful* and *paranoid* were accurate Andrea descriptors, *lazy* and *irresponsible* hadn't been. I made myself a promise that by the time we hit our next destination I would cast aside the drunken, fear-driven, juvenile behavior and reinstate the professional I knew was within me.

Chapter Ten

Once we arrived at the train station, set to go directly to the next castle on the itinerary, my newly established routine of disorganization and mediocrity thwarted my plan to restore my professionalism. Because we had left London in such a hurry, my camera charger, extra flash cards and other accessories, which I had purposely placed neatly next to my front door to take with me, still sat where I left them, forcing us to reroute back to London.

We swung by my apartment to grab my bag and took the tube back to the office. Rob "popped 'round the corner to take a phone call," and Harry and I walked in the door to find the staff watching soap operas. Claire, my favorite among the motley crew, was the first to welcome us back. "You alright? Anyone for tea?"

"No, thanks, all good." I sincerely hoped she would catch on to my consistent tea refusal and stop asking. Otherwise, I feared I would have to come clean about my aversion to tea and accept whatever ostracism accompanied it.

Millie chimed in with her unending wit and charm: "How was Canterbury? Did you hear a tale?" We smiled but ignored her, and heard from the sexually charged member of the office. "More importantly, did you get some tail?" Gemma asked, once again showing her uncanny ability to turn even the most conservative of comments into a filthy joke.

"No, Millie. No tales to speak of, but the cathedral was lovely."

"How would you know?" Harry asked with a nudge and a wink. Harry's winks sent some sort of electric shock wave through the atmosphere, causing my knees to become a fraction weaker with each one; were he to continue this maneuver, they were sure to give out. For my safety, I thought, it would be great if he never winked again — but, for my ego, I wanted him to continue winking hourly forevermore.

"I think Gemma and Millie meant to ask, how was the shoot?" Claire said. She was a woman of few words, but they were most consistently the right ones (apart from offering me tea every six minutes).

"And what are you doing here?" added Gemma. "Aren't you meant to be on your way to the next cathedral?"

"The shoot was fine but I left one of my camera bags at my place — it has my battery charger, lenses and cartridges, blah blah blah. We decided to grab it and take a few shots around London. We'll go off to the next place in a day or so."

"Okay, then. Have you chucked Rob?"

"He took a phone call. Said he was going to the corner market, back in a few."

****

"So, Rob, who's this Harry character?"

"Nice to hear from you too, mate."

"Sorry. How are you? Who's Harry? Why is he there?"

"I don't know, really. I thought it was just going to be Andrea and me but Harry showed up on the first day and hasn't left our sides since. And he is quite a looker."

"Wait, a what? A looker? I assume you mean handsome?"

"Ah, yes."

"Handsome for a Brit? Or handsome handsome? She didn't say he was good-looking."

"Well, maybe she thought you'd freak out. But never mind, that's clearly off base. Anyway, it's probably fine. He's only hit on her a little bit."

"A little bit?"

"Just joking. Although he is a tad flirtatious. But I wouldn't worry too much about it. He seems to be just a friendly guy."

"You're *definitely* gay, right? I can't have you both hitting on her."

"Gayer than a three-dollar bill. You know what? Never mind. I don't know what that means. Yes, lads are my bag. Don't worry, though, not you. You seem right uptight, even for me."

"Do they know you're gay?"

"Nope, but I'll add it to my nametag right quick."

"You know, with some men it's quite obvious."

"Well, I've left my feather boa at home, so you needn't worry."

"Maybe keep it to yourself, then."

"What? What are you on about?"

"I may need you to hit on Andrea to keep her away from Harry."

"Um, how do I put this? I realize you haven't seen me or Harry, but we're not exactly in the same league."

"Oh, don't be down on yourself, I'm sure you're dashing."

"Dashing? Anyway, this isn't self-deprecation. It's fact. My mum would find him more attractive."

"Well then, you'll have to use your charms."

"I don't feel comfortable with this."

"I can't lose her."

"If you lose her then it wasn't meant to be, man."

"I can't take that chance. I'll pay you extra. Keep him from her. Please."

"You're a real piece of work, aren't you?"

"Any chance Harry's gay? Maybe you can't tell."

"Oh, that's original, mate. 'He's not gay, he's just British. Ha. Ha.' Anyway, you'll pay me a little extra for that, too."

"I'm sorry, I didn't mean to offend. I'm sure you're all quite manly. I'm just uneasy about this Harry guy."

"Oh, I'm not offended. It's a tired joke. You Americans are just not a funny people. And, no, I don't think he's gay."

"Bummer."

"No, I just told you I *don't* think he's gay. And you and I are definitely not close enough for you to use that term."

"Huh? I don't understand."

"Here, bummer is not a nice way to call someone a gay man."

"Oh, bumm — I mean, my apologies. Yeah, we just use it to mean 'that sucks.' So, how's Andrea doing?"

"I thought you'd never ask. Doing okay, mate. She is, well, a tad scared of certain things. Many things, actually."

"I know. Why do you think I hired you?"

"Yes, it's perfectly clear."

"Okay, then. I think we're done, Rob. Keep me posted."

"Yep, will do. Cheers, Brandon."

****

Rob appeared at the office from his run to the market. "Come on, Andy, we should get going."

"Okay, I'm ready, but what's the rush?"

"We want to get to the Tower before it gets too dark and the ghosts start lurking." Rob and Harry shared a look.

"What? Wait. What? What the—" I was seconds from opening my palms and allowing my bags to hit the floor, forcing Rob and Harry to do my job for me — again — when Harry pulled my arm. "I'll save you, luv. It's just Anne Boleyn, and she doesn't even have a head."

"What are you guys talking about?"

"Yes, but she can use the head as a bowling ball." Rob laughed and took my other arm, pulling me away from Harry. "Just kidding, that's silly. She has to hold on to it. Otherwise she might lose it."

Rob used his free hand to gesture tossing a ball down the lane. "It's a strike! They all fall dead!" The ladies, clearly amused by the taunting, laughed in the background.

They pulled me to the door and as it scraped to a close behind us, Gemma yelled, "have sex with a beefeater! He'll protect you."

I was sure she wasn't joking — about the sex part, anyway. We caught the District Line on the tube and rode it to the Tower of London. On the ride over, against the backdrop of a roaring subway car lit by fluorescent bulbs, Rob and Harry gave me the *Cliffs Notes* version of the history of the Tower and the beheadings that took place there, perhaps the most famous being that of Anne Boleyn, one of Henry VIII's wives.

"Henry accused Anne of treason and adultery," said Rob. "She was convicted and then 'off with her head!'"

"Jeez, what a dick," I said.

Rob continued. "It's said that she still roams the halls holding her head under her arm."

Ghosts were, of course, on my list of fears, but I granted myself this one as leaning toward the rational side; after all, ghosts are the walking dead. Who's not afraid of the walking dead? Logically I understood it was unlikely I would see a ghost, ever, but I didn't believe in my non-belief strongly enough to not be afraid. The Tower of London also housed the crown jewels, and if I had to jump the hurdle of Anne Boleyn's noggin as it bounced toward my feet in order to get a peek, my only question was how high.

The Tower of London was a superb but haunting structure sitting on the north bank of the Thames River. Composed of brown stones piled on top of each other like bricks, varying in shade from the cream of an ivory tusk to the dull brown of a field mouse, it looked like a typical castle from a period film. The four corners of the building stood taller than the rest, topped with small grey domes and weathervanes. I walked around the outside, snapping shots from different angles trying to catch the Tower in its most flattering light. I took some pictures of the beefeaters, the guards of the castle — basically human mannequins wearing security garb from the Tudor era: red coats with bright gold buttons; black pants; tall, rectangular, foolish-looking furry hats the shape and size of Marge Simpson's hairdo. I couldn't resist participating in the classic behavior of a tourist — namely, mocking the guards as they stood stoic, attempting to force them to break character. They didn't. Poke, prod, lick, make fun: it makes no difference. As our Hail Mary maneuver, Rob leaned in as though he were going to kiss one of them. We got no response other than the guard's ever so slight lean backwards. Who could withstand such pressure? I had never seen or heard of them cracking so much as a smirk — it's as bizarre as Lady Gaga's costume closet. We joined a guided tour of the castle, meandering through the walkways, looking at and taking pictures of different views of the moss-covered stone until we came upon Traitor's Gate, a.k.a. the dungeon. Light was sparse and the rancid stench of mold plugged our nostrils. I gripped onto Harry, who was shaking.

"Are you trembling?"

"What? No, no. It's a little cold in here and I'm hungry. Just a bit of the shakes," he said, looking around and listening as the tour guide told dramatic stories of people captured, thrown in the dungeon, and killed in the Tower. I looked over at Rob, who was cowering a little bit behind us. We reached the darkest part of the hall as the guide explained what I hoped was a myth about Anne Boleyn. The guide took a long pause and the group was silent.

We heard the lone sound of water leaking from a rusty pipe. *Drip. Drip. Drip.*

Until a low-toned, but absurdly loud, "aaaaaahhhhh!!"

The three of us jumped and squealed louder, and at a higher pitch, than twelve-year-old girls at a Justin Bieber concert.

A deep-throated, hearty laugh emerged from a macho asshole who had jumped out from behind the wall. "That. Was. Awesome. I got all y'all. And good." Apparently he had thought it would be comical to further terrify his already quivering wife, consequently providing compelling support for the widely held belief that Americans are loud, obnoxious, and classless. Rob, Harry, and I looked at each other and turned our eyes with disdain to the disrespectful meathead. "Yeah, that was a good one, sir," Harry said. "You should be proud."

I couldn't help but giggle, though, at the sounds that had emerged from Harry and Rob's respective larynxes during the scare.

"You okay, guys?"

"What? What are you on about? Of course we are," Rob said.

"Yeah, what do you mean?" They looked at each other, slightly embarrassed.

"Those were some powerful yelps."

"What? No. The screaming was all part of the plan to assist that delightful man in scaring you and his unfortunate wife," Harry said.

I was dubious at the explanation, but somewhat relieved to discover that ghosts were a universal evil that terrified even the most confident of men. Through the remainder of the tour, we all stepped cautiously down the halls and I made jokes about hearing Boleyn's head roll around and spotting phantom feet.

We immediately forgot about Boleyn's missing cranium when we walked along the hall of the tower lined with the velvet ropes that enclosed the cases of coronation regalia from a long line of English monarchy: the crown jewels. Shimmering rays of light produced by gemstones under strategically placed spotlights bounced off the walls and lit up the room, while video of the Queen's coronation played in the background. Jeweled scepters, sparkling crowns, and dazzling swords — I had never seen such blatant, gaudy displays of opulence, which I immediately recognized as a missing piece in my life. I ate it up like a fat kid in an ice cream shop. I wandered through the exhibit with such intensity that my nose, finger, and possibly tongue prints were certain to remain on the display cases for days. I left the Tower planning to go apeshit on my clothing with rhinestones and a BeDazzler.

I was still working out the specifics for my forthcoming jeweled wardrobe when we entered The Spotted Cock pub to meet the rest of the office crowd for dinner.

Despite its name, The Spotted Cock was not a low-grade strip joint but an upscale, touristy bar near the Tower — nothing like the one where we had met a few days prior. The locals dismissed it as inauthentic, but it didn't matter; it existed for tourists not quite prepared for a gritty pub atmosphere. Thin dark green carpet lined the floor, and the walls displayed tacky prints alternating between hunts with foxes and those with roosters. *Oh, that cock.* The wooden bar was a glossy light oak color that matched the tables and chairs. Similar to the last pub, trivia games had been placed throughout the bar; unlike the last one, however, the bartenders and barmaids here wore matching clothing and appeared to be familiar with hygiene.

Before we could settle into our chairs or order a pint, Gemma slammed her palms down on the table. "Right. You shag a beefeater?"

"No, afraid there wasn't time," I responded.

"There's always time for shagging."

"Words to live by. Anyway, I'm engaged... ish."

"Ish? Is there a step between engaged and not engaged that I'm unaware of?"

"Is it an American thing?" Millie asked.

At once I became the center of attention. With all eyes on me, five eager individuals leaned in, rubbing their hands together like a *Daily Mirror* reporter eager to hear the dish about a teen pop sensation who had screwed her married Pilates instructor.

"Yes. About four weeks before my trip, my boyfriend proposed. Wait, I'm gonna need a drink if I'm gonna tell this story." As if from under the table, a pint of cider appeared in front of me. I took a trucker-sized gulp, stalling to decide whether I felt comfortable spilling the details of my love life to near-strangers. I took another monster sip and forced myself to open up as part of my journey.

I rehashed the events of the day Brandon proposed at the park. "And there he was… in the center of a heart outlined with petals. We hugged and he went down on one knee… "

Millie, her cheeks in her hands, let out an acute "aw!" Claire interrupted before my big reveal, "well, then it sounds like you are engaged. Congratulations!" She raised a glass.

"Yes, but what do you Americans say? If you sleep with someone in another zip code, it doesn't count?" Gemma added.

"Yeah, Gemma, I don't think that's distinctly Yankee. Anyway, I didn't say yes. I told him that I couldn't marry him now."

"Well, that's romantic," said Claire, putting down her glass.

"I wanted to say yes, but—"

"—you wanted to have sex while you were abroad. I get it."

"What? No, Gemma. No. You know, you have some type of sex ailment or something," I said. Gemma nodded and lifted her glass with pride.

"Um, another drink, please." A pint appeared again, before the request had had a chance to breathe, and I continued. "Look, Brandon's really wonderful and I feel unbelievably lucky that he wants to marry me. But I'm the least independent, most fearful person I know. And I've blown many relationships as a result. I wanted to leave Los Angeles, be on my own, grow up. And I wanted to do it without the weight of an engagement on my head."

"You aren't sure about him, are you?" asked Harry.

"Well, no. Yes. No. I don't know. I think so. I absolutely love him. I… I just didn't want to think about a wedding or any of that nonsense while I was here."

"Well, I think it's a great idea," Harry continued, only to be abruptly cut off by Rob. "Why? When someone you love loves you, what space do you need?"

"Look, she just called the engagement a 'weight' and the wedding 'nonsense.' She's clearly unsure. I think it's a great idea for her to get away and clear her head without him being there, looking over her shoulder. Otherwise she's stringing him along."

"Yes, but…" I tried to interject. No chance. The two men had hijacked the conversation, Rob on the pro-Brandon side and Harry the anti-, while the rest of us looked from right to left as though McEnroe and Agassi were on the court.

Rob continued. "Bollocks. If they have an issue, she should stay by him in their home town and work it out."

"No, I don't agree. She should work out whatever it is that she wants to fix within herself and then determine whether she can make it work with Brandon."

"But it sounds like there's an issue that's unique to the relationship she has in America, not within herself."

"She just said it's within herself, you twat."

"Maybe she's internalizing something that shouldn't be internalized."

Harry pounded his fists lightly on the table. "She should figure that out, then. Maybe it will take some alone time. Maybe it will take meeting other men."

"Finally, something interesting," said Gemma, throwing in her sex-inspired two cents.

At this point Rob and Harry became animated, gesticulating ardently, their tempers gradually flaring.

"Other men won't clarify how she feels about Brandon. She should be with him, in California," Rob said.

"Maybe she'll be more comfortable if she figures it out without him and then can return to him fully sorted."

"No, bollocks to you. If she loves him, she should stick by him in Los Angeles," Rob said, taking large sips of his drink in between sentences. His facial expression was a textbook display of frustration.

"Maybe she doesn't love him—"

And that was it — match point. Once those horrific words left Harry's lips, I heard nothing but silence, as though everyone in the pub had stopped talking and the music had screeched to a halt with a needle scratch. My patience for watching Harry and Rob bat my relationship around had reached its snapping point. I tried to process their "advice" until I thought: *what for?* They knew nothing of Brandon and very little of me. With tears clouding my vision, it was time to stop the madness.

"Helloooooo!" I said in a high-octave, mock-Queen Elizabeth voice, waving my hand.

The pitch of my reaction struck everyone in the bar by surprise and silenced all conversations. Too distraught to feel embarrassment, I waved off the disturbance and the patrons resumed talking, realizing there was nothing to see but another American with no volume control.

"Hi. Yeah. So, this is my relationship you're smacking around. And you don't know either one of us. We, Brandon and I, deserve more respect than this. So, I'll go ahead and take it from here. But thanks a ton for the words of wisdom. I'm gonna go. I'll see you boys in the morning."

I started to walk out of the bar alone, but the two quickly ran up behind me. I turned back. "Really guys, I have this, but thanks." Then again, I didn't *have* anything. Though English men appeared proper and respectful, all ethnicities have their miscreants. At any time a British misfit could jump out from behind one of those stunning architectural feats and abduct me. Therefore, despite my award-winning prideful storm-off, I jumped into the nearest cab and took it across town to my apartment, where I topped insult with injury by paying a £20 fare, went upstairs, and fell into bed and cried.

The words *maybe she doesn't love him* ricocheted between the walls of my brain as though I had yelled them from the top of a mountain in Switzerland, surrounded by sheep. I wanted to call Brandon but I didn't know what to say. I thought about calling Ashley and dialed half of her number several times before deciding I wanted to get through this on my own. I knew what she'd say, anyway: "Why do you need to prove you love Brandon to strangers?" And I had no answer.

Was saying "not now" to a marriage proposal indicative of something larger than I had thought? No, it wouldn't have been fair of me to say yes and then skip town for six months. And it wasn't fair to say yes while I still believed I had personal growing to do — growing that, if successful, would leave the status of our relationship undetermined but hopefully make it stronger. I had made the decision out of deference to Brandon. I wanted to focus on one thing at a time. Was that really the horror Rob labeled it?

I tossed and turned, annoyed at my brain for prohibiting my sleep. During restless nights at home, I often looked over to Brandon and gained comfort from his tranquility. I longed to turn over and see his face, peaceful in slumber, but an empty, lonely white sheet lay beside me — my sole sleeping companion for nearly six months. I had half a year to locate within myself the peace I found within those I loved, without their warm embrace and constant wisdom. And if I had to use a shovel, a tool belt, and a stupid-looking flashlight hat, I'd find it.

Chapter Eleven

I walked to the train station the next morning with my chest puffed out and my nose held high, as if to say "I'm still angry and I don't need your help." That is, until Harry approached me in a green jumper that accentuated his scintillating emerald eyes, coffee in hand. "Sorry about last night, Andy. I brought you some wretched coffee from that awful American chain store you like." I let the air out of my lungs. There was no way to stay angry with someone so beautiful carrying something so wonderful. Rob reacted to Harry's display with an eye roll and a grunt. He stated his half-assed apologies as well, and we boarded the train to Leicestershire (phonetically, Lester-shire). The British dictionary would be half as large if they deleted all the letters they can't be bothered to pronounce — *queue*, pronounced Q; Leicester, pronounced Lester; Worcestershire, pronounced Worster-shire; even *shite*, which doesn't need the E to be the same word as ours. Touristy Americans provided hours of entertainment as we listened to them decode British elocution. As heard on the train:

"Where are we going now, mom?"

"Ly-ces-ter-shire, dear."

"Oh, Marge, you're such a tourist," the father figure chimed in. "It's Ly-chester-shure."

"Oh, that's just silly, honey."

Yes, it was. And the Deep South accent put a very interesting twist on the vernacular. But I fear I would have sounded the same (sans Southern twang) had I not waited for my Anglo-Saxon friends to pronounce the words before I gave them a shot — out loud, anyway. But then, some of the most cherished and memorable, not to mention hilarious, parts of my trip came from the playful banter I shared with Rob and Harry regarding the eccentricities of our contrasting cultures.

"What is it with you people and your extra letters, anyway?" I would ask.

"Oh, so I guess Worcester, Massachusetts is not in America, then?"

Crap, Harry had me there… but I wouldn't give up. "That's in New *England*, smarty."

And there's the word *aluminum*, which the Brits butcher into unrecognizable pieces. The first time I heard Rob say it I was drinking a can of room-temperature Coke I had bought from a machine. I didn't have a clue what he meant until he held the can up, stroked it and said, "this is what I'm referring to, Andy. This is al-you-min-ium."

"No it's not; it's a-loom-in-um," I said. Of course, the Brits were here first, universally, so I was never the victor in any of our pronunciation debates.

Our first task of the day was a trip to Rockingham Castle, a castle that continued to serve as someone's home and, from what I understood, had been continuously occupied for over 1,000 years.

"How do you pronounce this one, rock-em castle?" I asked, half-seriously.

"No. It's Rocking-ham," Rob said, in a tone suggesting that I was foolish for suggesting otherwise.

"Oh, it's said like it's spelled. What a refreshing change."

As we walked up to the sprawling estate, I wondered whether I could slap it on my wedding registry and just how many people (or cities) it would take to split the cost. Once I acknowledged the insanity of the notion of purchasing a castle, my thoughts turned to something only a teensy bit more realistic: having my wedding there.

Originally made of sandstone, the castle was a multicolored array of the same color shades you'd find in a handful of sand from the beaches in the Western US. Other than the two cylindrical towers at the castle entrance topped with the typical corrugated trim, the remainder of the structure had the low-sloping shingled roof of a "regular" home; that said, the size and grandeur of this manor showed that there was nothing regular about it, unless you happened to be a monarch.

The threshold led us into a stadium-sized foyer. An oak-colored wood floor lay underneath our feet and a colorful painted ceiling was above. I took pictures of the images overhead of cherubs floating through puffy, comfy-looking clouds spread over a blue sky. Decorative gold picture frames enclosing watercolor paintings of war generals and bloody battle scenes lined the walls. The rooms contained a multitude of large, garish brass ornamental lamps and elaborate objets d'art that made Donald Trump's home décor look like tchotchkes purchased at a garage sale. We shot the Great Hall, a room focused around a long, thin wooden table with seating for twenty, dark wood paneling on the wall, and pictures of monarchs adorning all sides. Wooden chairs were neatly placed around the table, looking as uncomfortable as they did ornate. We shot several pictures of the kitchen, which had unfortunately been updated to modern craftsmanship but still remained inviting for tourists.

A back double-door exit led us to the main attraction: the grounds, the first sight of which was a vast blanket of grass that appeared to go on forever, like the ocean from a shoreline. The color was the green of a Granny Smith apple and manicured as though a gardener with OCD had measured each blade before trimming. We meandered along, the scent of newly cut grass etched into our nasal cavities, and entered upon the famous rose garden — seven distinct sections of fully bloomed, deep red bushels separated by white gravel paths. The shape was such that from an aerial view you would see a red and white pinwheel.

We walked along the water fountains that sat in the middle of Olympic-sized pools and snapped photo after photo. I got lost in my thoughts of eating just one meal at a table too long to see the guests on the other side (the extra-long picnic table at my local park aside) or throwing a garden party for my entire city. Touring the homes of royalty brought to life the question of just how surreal it must have been to live as a king, and how much easier it would have been with an intercom. I came out of my daze and picked up the pace when I overheard Rob and Harry agree that they were ready to leave and mosey on from the palace of kings to a festival of locals.

Each year the town of Leicester held a beer festival to attract tourists and promote its local breweries. It was an "important" cause to support, and a blissfully short walk down the road from Rockingham Castle. The theme of the festival was Ancient Greece, and although we lacked the proper toga attire we were festive in our own ways: we planned to imbibe like Greeks at an orgy, and we had brought Harry — an Adonis.

We entered a rather unsightly red brick building that served as the auditorium to a local school. The inside was dismal — cheap, thin, white-washed wooden tables with metal legs covering the floor, beige walls you imagined were once white, fliers haphazardly taped around the perimeter announcing school events. It was reminiscent of my elementary school's cafeteria, with the exception of the right-hand wall, which was stacked inch by inch with kegs of Leicester's finest — at my school, only the prin-cipal's office contained beer (as rumor had it). Hundreds of people aged 18 to 99, dressed in some type of makeshift toga, walked around sampling beers whose names I didn't even bother to learn before drinking them. We hopped from table to table, "philanthropically" tasting the beer and feel-ing terrific about our sizeable contribution to the town of Leicester. After a short while, however, the tables ranneth over with empty glasses, the ratio of cups to people reaching ten to one, and the noise level in the room, which had intensified in direct proportion to the sampling, had reached an intolerable level.

Once we were so buzzed that lifting a cup to our lips was as labori-ous as highway ditch-digging and the smell of the room was that of a frat house the morning after a kegger, we wandered several feet to a hideous pub, the Whispering Billy Goat, which I thought would be more aptly named The Flagellating Skunk. It was grimy, dilapidated, and malodorous. No trivia games, dart boards, or music; just an old, cracked wooden floor that hadn't been swept since the dawn of the Windsor dynasty, and beer advertisements hanging crooked on walls that looked as though just one violent sneeze would topple them. During the walk to the pub I somehow found the strength to consume yet another beer alongside food wading in large pools of grease — which I would never have allowed in my sight, let alone my esophagus, had my judgment not been skewed by my sampling of every type of beer made in the Mother Land. All my tact and clarity left at Rockingham Castle, and my sobriety with them, I decided to even the playing field with my new friends.

"So boys, you both know about my relationship, let's talk about what you two have going on. Harry?"

"Nothing interesting, I'm afraid. Single as they come."

"Well, I'm sure the female species appreciates it. What about you, Robbie Rob?"

"Same boat as Harry, but in my case I doubt the female species cares."

"Oh, don't put yourself down, Robbie Rob. You're adorable."

"It's Rob."

"Not while I'm drunk, Robbie Rob."

"You haven't called him Harry Harold."

"Nope. But you can see why, can't you? Well then, how do we make this interesting? Robbie, let's talk about the last girl you dated."

"I really don't think that's a good idea," he said. "Let's talk about something else."

"Come on, Robbie, it's time for you to come out—"

"What? Come out? What are you on about? Come out of what?"

"—of your shell. Open up," I said.

Harry joined me on my side of the table and sat close. Despite the hours of walking shoulder-to-shoulder with strangers in an unventilated room through a thick plume of sweat, smoke, and alcohol, he smelled like he had just rolled around in a Jasmine garden. I wondered whether he heard the whirr from my nose as it continually tried to capture his aroma. "Yes, tell us then, Rob. Your best-sex-ever story."

"Wait a minute, sex really ups the ante, doesn't it?"

Harry put his hand on my thigh and gave it a squeeze. *The thigh? It had to be the thigh? The part of my body more marshmallow-like than day-old marshmallows?* "Yes it does," Harry said. "But we're friends now, aren't we? Come on then. Out with it."

Rob took a shot of rum, the sight of which made me queasy, and stumbled into a story. "So I was with this girl. You know, two boobs, fanny, long hair, the works."

"Yes, yes. All seems normal so far," said Harry.

Not really.

Rob, still stammering, continued. "And we were at... we are at a party."

"Just couldn't wait, huh?" said Harry trying to brew excitement from Rob.

"No, couldn't wait, so horny we were." Rob swallowed hard and took a gulp from the beer he was using to chase his liquor. "Anyway, she took a seat on the toilet — closed lid of course — and I climbed on top of her, facing backward. No, wait, she got on top of me, that's right."

"Do you mean facing forward?" I asked.

"No," he said, laughing nervously and gesturing with his hands to work out where all the parts fit. "I mean, yes, of course. That's how that would work."

"Sounds kinky, man," said Harry.

Still puzzled but having no desire to make Rob feel more awkward than he appeared, I attempted to stand up and save him from trying to finish his fabricated sex story. But the entire room moved with me and I quickly fell back down.

"Maybe slower this time. I'll assist." Harry put his hands around my waist and helped me stand. "Well, aren't you a tight little bird," he said.

"Excuse me?"

"Your stomach. Nice and flat."

"That's true. It is, I noticed too," said Rob.

"Oh, well I, uh, thanks," I said, giggling and looking at Harry, my cheeks warm from the redness I knew was overtaking them, and my heart racing.

"Okay, I have to leave," I said.

"Wait a moment. I told my story. One of you has to give it a go," Rob begged.

"I'm not so sure we got the whole story. But I won't make it through another one today. Tomorrow. Night, boys. I'm gonna call Brandon."

"Oh, great," said Rob. "I'm sure he'll be thrilled to hear from you. We'll join you for the walk back when you're done."

"Unless you want to call your parents too. Let us know," I heard Harry say as I walked out the door. I was definitely too drunk to call my folks, but I did find it odd they hadn't been trying to call me every half hour.

I stepped outside. Despite the thin layer of warmth created by my thick buzz, the cold of the night bit into me like a rabid dog.

"Hiiiiiiii Bran man, how're youuuuuuuuu?"

"Oh my god. Is there anything to do besides drink in that country? It's like you're on a shots and pints tour."

"Ha, that's funny. You're funny. I forgot that about you."

"Where are you? Where are the guys?"

"Off talking to some blokes — that means men — in togas."

"Togas? Where are you?"

"A beer festival in Les-es-ter-shire-shyre."

"Where?"

"I don't know, I can't say it right. Babe, I think Rob's a virgin. Isn't that cute?"

"Um, I guess. Did he tell you that?"

"No, but he tried to tell us a kinky story about how he slept with some chick and he kept getting the position wrong, like he didn't understand how it all works. It was strange."

"Well, Andy, get the man laid. You're a good wingman."

"Maybe. Anyway, I can't feel my toes anymore."

"You're that drunk?"

"No, it's that cold. My snot's frozen." Between my shivering and re-hashing of the night's events, it dawned on me that we hadn't taken any post-sun shots of the castle. "Shit. I have more work to do."

"There's no chance those shots'll be blurry. Good luck, babe. Love you."

I walked back into the bar to find a ring of half-dressed men gathered around Harry while Rob peeked in from the outside.

"Harry, Rob, we have to take nighttime photos. Come on."

"Oh, let's let Rob stay and talk. Just you and I can go. It'll be romantic."

"Um, okay," I said, stifling another nervous giggle.

"Rob, Andy and I are going to go take some shots. See you in the morning."

I leaned in to Rob's ear and pointed to a group of four ladies chatting in the corner of the bar. "Hey, they're cute. Why don't you go over there and talk to 'em?" I said while giving him a slap on the ass to egg him on, like I was his football coach.

He jumped. "Hey, Andy! I don't think so. I'm not drunk enough. And I don't need the help," he added, returning to the circle of men.

"Suit yourself there, Robbie."

Harry took my hand and we started towards the castle, but just before the door closed behind us it swung back open.

"I'll go with you too," said Rob. "I don't want to skirt my duties."

Cockblocker. "Oh goody."

We reached the castle after a lengthy debate regarding its location, which turned out to be a straight shot from the bar. My vision was hazy, the tips of my fingers numb; the movement of the camera in my hands was akin to an inner tube navigating stormy waters. It was reminiscent of the first time I did a photo shoot on my own. I had been working for a tabloid and fought my way through a group of sleazy, screaming paparazzi to get a shot of the *Sopranos* cast leaving a late-night talk show. As though the camera had been slathered in butter, I dropped it three times, and when I was able to keep it in my grip the pictures came out looking like I had taken them while running a marathon. I thought my skill had improved, but an evening of drinking and frostbite brought me back. On both occasions I managed to fail completely to get a shot of the target, and I could have sworn the castle extended the same finger to me as my fellow paparazzi. Rob, Harry and I passed around the camera like a hot potato, uttering "you try" or "no, *you* try" with each toss. We quickly discovered that not one of us could hold the camera steady and we had trouble keeping the tripod upright. Artsy and focus-free photos of the castle would not be a hit at *Adventure*; we needed another day. In a mood where I already found everything amusing, I called Millie.

"Millie, we aren't going to be able to make the train in the morning."

"How will you get back here?" Millie asked.

"By train."

"But you just said you couldn't make it."

"Well, we will go ahead and take one at a different time. We had an extra day between this shoot and Nottingham anyway. We'll just go straight there tomorrow evening."

"Okay, will the trains do that?"

"If not, we'll just overthrow the driver and reroute it."

"That's a terrible—"

"Kidding, Millie. We'll be fine. I have to go."

I looked over at Harry and rolled my eyes at another conversation with Millie that you wouldn't believe without hearing it firsthand. He took my camera, told me to model, and began shooting. I struck various poses, thanking the alcohol for the courage to do so. I tried silly, sticking out my tongue in childish ways; sultry, pushing my lips forward in a pouty Angelina Jolie fashion; and playful, where I was merely me, smiling over my shoulder. Whether I turned my head, twirled my body, or raised my arms, I felt flat-out self-conscious and wondered whether I looked as awkward on the outside as I felt on the inside. My mind racing, two thoughts came to the fore: one, I had to remember to delete those pictures; two, I couldn't be alone with Harry.

Chapter Twelve

I woke early to guzzle a steaming cup of coffee, dark as the night sky and thick as tar, and sort myself out before I'd meet the boys to take some final pictures around Leicester. Each morning I awoke with a splitting headache that one-upped the one from the previous day. I was flirting with Harry, telling sex stories with strangers, and taking amateur photos: I wasn't doing enough to prove I could thrive without my family's protective coating and Brandon's help just minutes away.

I was disheartened by the idea that my success in life thus far, whatever it had been, was due to my family's interference and Brandon's affection. I was also motivated by it. The next shoot on deck was in Nottinghamshire (pronounced as spelled, with the first H silent and substituting "sure" for "shire"), the home of Robin Hood; and it would be special. For the first time in my career, I would run a full-blown photo shoot on my own: an entire set with models in costumes, made-up and posing as I directed. With live subjects, I had one chance, several hours to obtain the perfect shot and seal the deal — after all, there's a certain unprofessionalism to yelling, "oh, fiddlesticks, we failed to get a good shot, let's try again tomorrow" after a shoot or telling my boss, "sorry, you'll have to pay for a do-over." This was a genuine opportunity to showcase my talent, propel my career forward; and I would not let Henson down. And I would not let me down.

That night, we hopped on the train headed to Nottingham. With the possible career-changing event at the end of the tunnel, the shaking of the railway compressed my stomach, which was already wrenched and overflowing with butterflies. I couldn't enjoy the view outside, as it was nearly dark and the English countryside wasn't exactly lit up like the Vegas Strip. I had decided that preparation would be the perfect distraction. I opened my notes to review the research I had done earlier, ready to dive in and continue planning the shoot logistics.

"Right, then, an important moment," said Rob. "We must decide if we're going for the Errol Flynn, Sean Connery, Russell Crowe, or Cary Elwes Robin Hood."

But instead, I acquiesced to distraction by discussion of hot Robin Hoods past.

"Sean Connery — a better Bond than Robin," Harry said.

"Too true," Rob said. "But does it matter? He's Sean Connery."

"And we can't discount Russell Crowe," I added.

"We'd never discount Russell Crowe," Rob said dreamily. "I mean, he's a, uh, a spectacular actor."

"Will the costume designer be prepared for all of these?" asked Harry.

"Probably not. *Adventure* wants traditional," I responded.

"Cary Elwes it is," we all agreed in unison.

We left the train in a residential area where both sides of the surrounding roads contained long, continuous rows of attached three-story brick homes. The color, a dull and consistent brownish-red combination, made it look as though someone had finally found a use for Crayola's Indian Red and Burnt Sepia shades. The low-sloping, shingled rooftops created a continual dark brown line of triangles in the form of a skyline, interrupted only by a chimneystack on each roof. One might have trouble locating one's own home in the continuous line of nondescript buildings were it not for the sole demarcation: the front door. With no garage doors in sight, parallel-parked cars packed in like Legos occupied every inch of the pavement in front of the homes. We walked through these lovely neighborhoods until we arrived at our hotel. Too tired for another night of drinking and too uneasy to do anything else, I turned in moments after we checked in.

The three of us reconvened in the fresh, chilly morning and took a walk through the city center. It was similar to an outdoor mall in Anytown, USA: a few roads cut off to motor traffic, lined with shops and restaurants. The architecture I saw ranged from medieval, ornate brick buildings with hexagonal windows and cylindrical towers to contemporary, plain square structures. And though I saw some shops that could have been stunt doubles for my neighborhood Gap, the abundant use of brown stones and signs containing the words *Ye Olde* were constant reminders that I was in England. That and I still had yet to see an Applebee's.

Still early in the day, few people milled about, save in the cafés and coffee shops. Though it was not a dynamic cosmopolitan city, the charming surroundings announced Nottingham as a popular attraction for tourists who dared step beyond the Thames River and the gates of London.

Stopping only for pasties (pronounced *past-ies*, like they had happened before, not *paste-ies,* like the nipple stickers), pastry-sized treats with a crisp, flaky crust and filled with processed and inauthentic veggies, meat, and cheese, we arrived at our destination: Sherwood Forest, the legendary meeting place of Robin and his merry men. And it was precisely as the name foretold: a forest. Well-delineated walking trails wove through the rows of gigantic trees, some full and leafy and others just trunks with bare branches.

"You alright with forests then, luv?"

"Dammit, Harry! You had to put that out there. Now she'll be thinking about it."

As if I hadn't been thinking about it. Similar to certain patches of the park where I lived, in which you couldn't see the forest through the trees, à la *The Blair Witch Project*, I would not have come to such a place if it were not daytime, if I were alone, and if I were not being paid to be there.

"Nope, all good, boys. Let's just get out before dark."

Rob was able to secure us a spot on a wide-open patch of green stamped in the center by the Major Oak, a 1,000-year-old tree with a stump seemingly fifty feet in diameter and a top so full and verdant it created an umbrella of greenery that practically touched the ground on all sides. Rob, Harry and a small team of workers from *Adventure* began to create a scene around nature's props. I watched in wonder while providing my own input as we transformed the traditional forestland into a movie scene and everyday Joes into our movie stars.

First, the nobleman: a man with a mustache, maybe 6'3" (the man, not the mustache), in black tights covered by billowy brown pants gathered just under the knee. On top, a royal blue velvet vest with tacky gold buttons over a full white blouse with puffy sleeves swaying in the breeze. And, his fairer half, the noblewoman: a long-haired lady, enviably skinny, in a flowing floor-length tan dress with embroidered trim around the neck and bust line and a wreath of purple flowers pulling her hair back from her face. They stood together, her hand in his, as though they were strolling through the forest. Directly overhead in the trees, peering down on the couple with a mischievous grin, was Robin Hood, bracing his bow and arrow, ready to steal the satchel of change hanging from the nobleman's finger. And finally, Robin's merry men lurking in the forest all around. It was surreal.

"Rob, how well is Robin fastened to that tree?" I asked.

"He asked not to be fastened, as you call it. Says he's spent a lifetime climbing trees."

"No. No. That's not gonna work," I said. "I will not be responsible for killing Robin Hood. I want him strapped."

Harry and Rob took care of attaching Robin Hood to the gigantic oak tree while I finished preparing. Awake, alert, and running on adrenaline, I began to shoot. I rearranged the models. I shot different angles. I adjusted the lighting. I shouted directions; people listened. It was my shoot. It mattered not that I was thousands of miles from anywhere I felt comfortable and worlds apart from my family and Brandon; I was doing it and it was life-altering in a magical way.

"Robin, point the bow a bit more toward the ground. It's too high."

"You got it, boss."

He called me boss. I smiled and returned my attention to the scene when I heard rustling in the tree. A lot of rustling.

"Robin, how are you up there?" I asked as I shot.

"Oh, a little wobbly, I'm afraid."

"Well, you're strapped in, right? You should be fine."

"Not exactly."

I whipped my head to Rob and Harry for an explanation. "He refused to have the strap put on," Rob said.

"He refused the strap-on?"

"Sorry, he refused to be strapped in."

"It wasn't his choice," I said.

As we spoke, out of the corner of my eye I saw a restless Robin trying to prop himself up on the branches.

"Okay, let's just take a few more while everyone is living."

I snapped a few more pictures, but Robin wasn't able to get a firm hold on the tree. I demanded, again, that we attach him with some kind of rope. But before Rob and Harry could make it to the tree, we heard the leaves shake violently and watched the branches being tossed about, followed by the words "OH, SHIT!" and an intense yelp. Mouths agape, we watched as Robin tumbled headfirst into the fair maiden below. *CRASH!*

The most rewarding day of my professional life, ruined by a rogue Robin Hood. We rushed over to him although the I-fucking-told-you-so part of me was so angry it wanted to let him stir in pain for a bit. But I didn't. Harry and Rob took care of calling an ambulance, as I still had no idea how that was accomplished in the UK. Robin went to the hospital and was treated for a few sprains. "Luckily" he had landed on the noblewoman and a pile of brush. The woman fared pretty well too; she walked away with some minor bruising. I called Mr. Henson to advise him to notify the insurance company as a precautionary measure. Although I honestly felt the blame belonged to Harry, Rob, and Robin, it was my shoot. I had decided to hoist Robin into a tree; it was my responsibility to ensure he didn't fall from it. It really had been progressing flawlessly until then.

I sat on a bench, my back slumped and my head lowered, watching the workers remove the lights and the extras return their props, and tears filled my eyes. Harry threw one arm around me and took a seat.

"Oi, look here. You got some stellar shots!"

"Oh good, save them. We'll probably have to provide them to the prosecution."

"Oh, Andy, don't be so dramatic."

"She can't help it, she's—"

"Yeah, yeah, Rob, I know, I'm American. We're all batshit crazy. Let me see the camera."

Unenthused, I grabbed the camera and lazily thumbed through. My eyes lit up and I sat up just a tad straighter with each flip. Harry was right, some of the shots were fantastic, including one killer action shot: being a complete professional, or a colossal idiot, I had still been shooting when Robin fell, and happened to capture the most amazing facial expression mid-fall — a cross between horrified and callous — as he attempted to grab the satchel, for dear life. Looks of pure terror covered the faces of the nobleman and woman as Robin hung in the air, milliseconds from using them as a buffer between him and the ground. The men around the perimeter were all lunging forward, their faces also expressing horror while trying to save Robin and the maiden. It was classic. The near-catastrophe aside, the day had been quite successful.

"I suppose you want to call Brandon, yeah?" asked Rob. "Give him a ring, we'll meet you at the pub."

"Oh, it can wait until tomorrow," Harry said. "We've celebrating to do. Besides, you don't want to walk there alone, do you? It's getting dark. Come on, luv."

I certainly didn't want to walk alone, but I opted not to call Brandon for a different reason: I didn't want to run to him. And I didn't want to run to my parents. I didn't need their validation that it was acceptable for me to feel proud of what I had accomplished. And what if they weren't as delighted for me as I was? They'd trample on my elation. I was on an Andrea high and I wanted it to last.

"She should share her big news with her bloke first," Rob said. "Celebrating can wait."

"He'll still be happy for her tomorrow. Let's go before the adrenaline wears off."

I looked over at the boys: Harry to my right, an outstretched arm, his hand reaching for mine, and Rob to my left, hands on his hips, tapping his toe in a pissed-off, slightly effeminate pose. Whether it was the distance between Brandon and me, the liberation I felt from being detached, or the perfect width of Harry's shoulders, I chose to go with Harry.

"I'll call Brandon tomorrow. He'd be at work now; I'm sure he's busy." I took Harry's hand and we ran off to the bar.

Before I had had the chance to absorb the ambience of our dinner destination, The Belching Turkey, and not a minute after we had taken off our coats, Rob again brought up Brandon.

"Do you miss him, then?"

"Rob, why have you become Brandon's cheerleader?"

"I'm just trying—"

"Of course I miss him, but I accomplished something huge today, thousands of miles from him, all on my own—"

"Ahem."

"No, Harry, you get no props. You maimed Robin Hood." I turned my attention back to Rob. "Why are you trying to take that from me? This has nothing to do with him."

"I'm not taking anything from you. But isn't one of the points of being in a relationship that you have someone to share these exhilarating moments with?"

"Well, yes, but—"

Harry interrupted. "Can't you let her enjoy this as a personal triumph? She just said it has nothing to do with Brandon."

Rob and Harry took over the conversation, again tossing my relationship to and fro.

"I'm not saying she shouldn't be proud of herself. She did a bang-up job today. But if she shared it with Brandon she would get additional support, someone else to be proud of her accomplishments."

Trying to get a word in, I said, "I have you two..." But they didn't hear it, too focused on their own theories about my love life. I sat back in my chair, looked at the menu, and ordered a drink while Harry and Rob rambled on.

"Maybe she doesn't need that validation," said Harry.

"I don't mean it as validation, just celebration."

"She came here to be independent. That means not running back to Brandon every time something wonderful happens like a little puppy excited to go out for a pee."

"A what? I'm just saying it's nice to share these things with people you love, to know you have them on your side."

"Then frankly, she should call her parent—"

"Alright, enough!" I interjected. "I'm not sure why you two have again taken it upon yourselves to provide running commentary on my relationship. And my family. But I didn't ask. Let's just try to enjoy our night. We — sorry, I — accomplished a lot today. I ran my first live action photo shoot. And I was the fortunate recipient of oodles of dumb luck." Which was the truth about what happened that day: I lost control of the shoot but got lucky. I decided to celebrate the outcome, but the more I thought about the day the more I knew it had been something of a fluke. I could just as easily have obtained no usable shots and a whopping wrongful death suit. And that was why I didn't call anyone back home.

"Yes, of course. I'll buy the next round," said Harry.

"I'm sorry, Andy," Rob added.

"It's fine. Let's talk about something else."

We tried to continue our faux celebration but the thick grey clouds that hovered overhead outside made their way to our table, so much so that I left early, sick of attempting to participate in the stilted conversation. After having to practically chain Rob and Harry to the table, I walked back, alone, to our hotel. But when I say "walked" I don't mean a stride typical of those meandering home from a pleasant evening on the town. I mean at a speed that should have been a run but was a walk only because running seemed foolish. It was a power-walk, similar to what people who exercise do, only they do it in workout attire. I did it in high-heeled boots. I felt like a chicken, my arms pumping and my hips bobbing from left to right, and I most certainly looked how a bobblehead doll would if it was a "bobblebody" doll. And this marvelous display did not take place on the sidewalk with the sane folk; I ran-walked down the middle of the street, zigzagging through cars, convinced that anyone who wanted to kidnap me would decide otherwise when they saw that I looked like a mental patient.

Upon my safe return to the hotel, I put aside the aesthetics of my walk and allowed myself to be thrilled at yet another victory(ish): I had "walked" home alone at night in a foreign place. Between that and the professional leap forward I had taken by running a live photo shoot, I went to bed proud and eager to discover what personal feats I would accomplish, or what happy accident I'd run into, at our next stop: Liverpool, Merseyside, England.

Chapter Thirteen

"You know, you two didn't have to check in on me last night. I can do some things on my own," I said to Harry and Rob as we boarded the train departing from Nottingham.

"We wanted to make sure you didn't sprain your ankle walking so fast."

"Or get a concussion from bashing head-on into a parked car," Rob added.

"Yeah, well, I just wanted some exercise. All this beer's going straight to my ass," I said, a thinly veiled cover-up for my behavior, which there was no chance they bought. "How late did you two stay out?"

"Long enough for three girls to offer Harry their phone numbers."

"So five more minutes?"

"Thereabouts, yes."

"Gonna call any of 'em, Harry?" I asked, secretly wishing for a negative response.

"Not likely, no. Two were quite dull and the other, well, she was a minger, wasn't she, Rob?" I felt relieved. Not because I had a chance with Harry — I didn't, and didn't want one — but because I still had months left with him and I was not interested in competing with a girl who would fight me for his attention and interfere with our dynamics.

We stepped off the train in Liverpool and walked several blocks in the direction in which Millie had claimed we would find a castle. We walked through the city center alongside office buildings and department stores, the kind you would expect to find in a substantial metropolis: Debenhams,

Marks & Spencer, The Disney Store, Boots Pharmacy, and the like. People wearing three-piece suits and business-casual attire scurried around, cell phones attached to one ear and coffee in hand; it was as though I were walking through the downtown area of any major US city. The scenery did not appear to be home to an ancient castle, as the ones I had seen so far were tucked into trees or in more tranquil areas of town. However, every city is unique, and I refused to think I knew England well enough after viewing only several blocks in a few cities to say with certainty that there was no castle in the middle of this large, vibrant one. With each passing Starbucks, however, we became more dubious. Without any better ideas or a backup route, we continued using Millie's directions.

As it turned out, three sharp minds such as ours should have known better, certainly by the fourth city on the trip. But despite all the knowledge we had gathered about Millie, we followed her instructions and, as suspected, didn't come upon a castle. We saw commercial buildings, a statue of Queen Victoria, and a sign for the Queen Victoria Monument. No castle. We stood in the center of a place called Derby Square with four fingers to our foreheads, as though shielding our eyes from the sun, and looked around in all directions for a castle. Nothing. No buildings in sight that even resembled a White Castle.

I looked at the boys, who wore blank, dumbfounded expressions. "It takes a shrewd businessman with an eye for detail to put Millie in charge of our trip," I said.

"Well to be fair, I think there was once a castle here," said Harry.

"When? During the reign of King James? Great, Millie used the Bible to plot our route," I said. "We'll have to ask someone." I looked around and saw a pub across the way, its door ajar. "There, The Whispering Pig looks like it's already open. We'll ask the bartender."

"Oh, no, sweetie. I won't ask for directions in Britain."

"Fine, Harry. Rob?"

"Sorry, Andy. I'm with Harry."

"Wow. That male I'd-rather-die-than-ask-for-directions thing is transcontinental."

"No, it's fine, don't go, Andrea. We'll just call Millie, she'll sort us right out," said Harry, taking his cell phone from his pocket, baiting me.

"Okay, okay. Fine, I'll go in alone. I'm sure they'll expect that the American tourist has no idea where she's going." Of course, in Britain the question "where's the castle?" seemed as ludicrous as "where's the ocean?" on a pier in California, but my macho pals left me with no alternative.

I added a touch of color to my lips, pulled the ponytail out of my hair, and walked into the bar hoping to find a cute, helpful little old man I could charm with a hair flip and a giggle. Instead I found a young man with biceps too large for his T-shirt, tending bar between photo shoots.

I put my elbows on the bar and leaned up against it, trying to pull off "cutesy."

"Um, hi. This is sort of embarrassing, but can you help me and my friends out there find Liverpool Castle?"

He looked back at the other bartenders and smiled, then turned back to me and said... something. Well, his lips were moving and sound emanated from them, but the only words I understood were "...who and... TARD..." — followed by raucous laughter, as though the whole conversation had been played over a loudspeaker in front of a crowd.

During my short time abroad, I had learned that not all English accents were created equal. On one hand, there was Harry: eloquent, intelligible, with soft As that sounded like they were followed by a W. On the other extreme was this bartender. His accent was thick and he spoke quickly, like that mumbling character in *Trainspotting*. I was fairly certain his comment wasn't helpful, but I didn't understand him well enough to know. I wished I weren't so desperate for an answer. Bravely, I asked him to repeat himself, but a tad slower, because "I didn't quite catch the middle thing."

"Not. Without. Dr. Who. And. His. TARDIS. Was. That. Slow. Enough. For. You?" The laughter that remained from the first response grew exponentially.

"Oh, okay. Cheers."

I walked out the door three inches shorter than I had walked in, my proverbial tail tucked between my legs whacking me in the face from left to right, and still without the location of a castle.

"How'd that go for you?" Rob asked, though the answer was clear.

"Just smashing. He told me I'd need a tardy-something and a Dr. Who to find it. I don't know who or what the hell that is but I'm quite certain he was making fun of me."

"So letting your hair down didn't get us directions?"

"Funny, Rob."

"Dr. Who is a British TV character who travels through time and the TARDIS is his time machine," said Rob. "And yes, he was taking the piss — sorry, making fun."

"Sorry, luv. I'll translate: There's no Liverpool Castle anymore."

"Dammit, I should've known that reference. Brandon watches that show. Hmm, to be honest, I'm surprised this didn't happen earlier with Millie planning the travel. Of course, you two are British. Why don't you know there's no castle here?"

"Yes, it's very realistic to think we'd know the location of each and every castle in Britain. There's only what, one or two hundred thousand?" Rob said, looking at Harry, their shoulders shrugging uselessly in the air. "I guess we'll just have to go to the Cavern Club."

"Maybe later. For now, let's go to the cathedral instead. Liverpool must have one of those?"

"I imagine so… we don't seem to have a shortage of them, do we?" said Harry.

On the way to the cathedral we passed by the Hard Days Night hotel, a luxury inn inspired by the iconic band that sang a tune of the same name. The exterior was tan and decorative, with columns running along the outside of the first floor and lines of windows across the two floors above. Each member of The Beatles, immortalized in bronze, hung out on the second story, looking down upon the hotel's visitors. Much of the interior decor was seventies retro and pictures of The Beatles — old, young, candid, performing — hung on every wall.

Coming off our success from the previous shoot, and wanting one to go well on purpose, I devised a plan. I sought assistance from the Hard Days Night hotel concierge, looking for a Beatles cover band I could hire for a day. After all, it was the musical legends that had emerged from Liverpool, not a picturesque church, that would drive tourists here. The concierge mentioned that Beatles tribute bands play the Cavern Club virtually nightly and that I should have no trouble finding one for my shoot. It was settled: I would do what was necessary to make The Beatles the VIPs of my Liverpool spread.

The Cavern Club was the concert venue where The Beatles' legacy had begun. From the outside, it looked like a dumpy old bar, exactly what you would imagine when you think of a place where wannabe bands play in the hopes of being discovered. Old, glowing, orange neon signs reading

THE CAVERN CLUB highlighted the two entrances to a shapeless, industrial-looking red brick building with hundreds of fliers for live gigs stuck to the door and the surrounding area. On one side of the club was the wall of fame, an entire façade composed of bricks, each engraved with the name of a band that had played there. In front of the wall stood a bronze John Lennon, leaning in a leisurely pose against a post. The day we arrived, at least a dozen groupings of flowers lay at Lennon's feet, which I imagined was a regular occurrence for that game-changing musician.

Walking in, I was surrounded by brick walls in a multitude of colors from red to black, extending up through a low, arched ceiling, as though I were in a wine cellar. The stage was in my direct line of vision, the back wall of which looked like a large multicolored map of the United States, each "state" containing the name of a band whose music had graced the Cavern Club since its opening in 1957.

Preparing to talk to a manager, we overheard a conversation among the members of Hey Dude, the Beatles tribute band set to play that night. I approached the man who aspired to be Lennon and talked with him about starring in a shoot for *Adventure.* After a word with the others, he emphatically agreed, declaring that the band was "right chuffed" to be a part of the magazine. We set the shoot for the following day near Liverpool Cathedral.

With hours to kill, we did some perusing of the Liverpool city center, but spent most of the day at a café arranging approvals, gear, props, and incidentals for the shoot, ensuring that all members of the band would keep their feet planted on the ground. As the evening approached, so did my jitters about what would happen the next day; my mind battling the myriad things that could go wrong, and some that couldn't. Lightning would strike and we'd electrocute Lennon, even though we wouldn't plug in the amps. Ringo would poke his eyes out with a drum stick, even though he had been playing the drums since age three (and it is impossible to poke your eye out with a drum stick accidentally). McCartney and the fourth guy, what's his name, made it through my nightmares without a scratch, but it scared me to not be able to think of what could go wrong with them.

I was mentally fixated on an early dinner and bedtime, but Rob and Harry were "keen" on spending the evening at the Cavern Club. I admitted that a drink would help me relax and acquiesced to the proposition that, with virtually the entire world left on my list of places to see, I might never get another opportunity to visit that particular landmark. Therefore, after a quick but fantastic curry dinner at a nearby Indian restaurant, we went to the Cavern Club and parked ourselves at one of the tables in the back. The first band we saw kicked off the night with '60s classics: The Who, The Stones, Bob Dylan. I had always been a fan of more contemporary music, but as with most things, Harry and Rob were on the same page in their admiration of classic rock, especially that of The Beatles.

"How does anyone with the ability to hear not love The Beatles?" was their consensus.

"Oh, no, you aren't on the Rolling Stones side of the argument, are you, Andrea?" Harry asked.

"No, I don't like them either. And I think they've overstayed their welcome."

"I agree, they're rubbish," said Rob. "But I've never met anyone on neither side of the spectrum. There's two types of people; those who like The Beatles and—"

"Our enemies," Harry said.

"Precisely, my good man," Rob said as they clanked beer glasses.

"I just don't get the hype," I said.

"Because you have no sense of context. They played melodies no band had yet played, wowed the entire universe with them, and changed music forever. For the better." Harry spoke with intense passion. His eyes lit up and he gestured with his hands and nearly rose all the way out of his seat a few times, just to express the extent to which music and travel, or whatever it was he was explaining, invigorated him. "Is that not impressive enough for you, Andy?" Pondering his general energy and verve, I missed the Beatles specifics. But Harry was certainly impressive enough.

"Well, to be fair, Harry, they hardly displayed the musical prowess of Carly Rae Jepsen or Nicki Minaj," said Rob.

"Okay, easy there. I didn't say I liked computer-aided pop music either."

"You might as well have done."

"Well, The Beatles will come on any moment and you'll listen intently with me until you realize the genius," said Harry.

Against no odds, The Beatles — well, Hey Dude — took the stage after a short intermission, opening their act with "Happy Just to Dance with You."

"This one's not in my Beatles top twenty, but it'll do. Shall we, my luv?" Harry asked, extending his hand.

"What, here?"

"Yep, here, now. Excuse us, Rob, we'll only be a second."

Harry and I took what little open space there was around our table and created a dance floor for two. He pulled me in close and sang the words into my ear.

"Before this dance is through," he whispered. "I think I'll love you too..."

Alarmed that Harry would feel my heart pounding its way through my chest at warp speed, I tried to pull back and keep some distance. I looked around at the bar patrons, whose eyes were on us, in order to avoid looking into Harry's. "There's really nothing else I'd rather do, I'm happy just to dance with you." I tried to listen to the parts of the song that Harry labeled as "genius" as he gave me a play-by-play while we danced, but my thoughts roamed to whether I was doing something immoral. *No, it was just a dance.* It *was* just a dance. *But then, why am I sweating?* The song came to an end and I turned away from Harry abruptly to walk back to our table, where Rob sat with his head in one hand and a shot of Jack in the other. Harry pulled me back to him to continue dancing to "Love Me Do." I wiped the sweat from my brow and yielded to the dance, but Rob wouldn't have it.

"I'm bored. Can we put the danceathon to rest?"

"No, but you can join us," Harry said.

"I'm not much of a dancer."

"Who cares? Neither were The Beatles. Neither am I. Come on, Robbie. Come out of your closet," I said, sincerely attempting to include Rob in the revelry.

"My what? Closet? Why would you say I'm in a closet?"

"Just an expression, luv," said Harry. "Let your hair down."

The three of us danced around, me like a pogo stick with appendages and Harry and Rob with rhythm and smooth moves, singing every line of every Beatles tune. Rob had tricked us: he was quite the proficient dancer, and I was wonderfully surprised at how he metamorphosed into a suave dancing machine from his usual awkward, uncomfortable persona. Bit by bit, the crowd around the bar joined our three-person dance party and we turned the Cavern into a disco. I observed several couples dancing together lovingly and thought about how much I wished Brandon were there; he would have enjoyed the scene. He didn't love to dance, but he loved to be in the middle of a party.

While the band changed songs from "Back in the U.S.S.R." to "She Loves You (Yeah, Yeah, Yeah)," whether a traditional dance tune or not, I noticed the smiles on everyone's faces expand, caring nothing for the rhythm of the music or how they looked trying desperately to stay in time with it. Harry tried to teach me a move — any move — resembling something other than a back-and-forth sway or an up-and-down hop. I ended just as crappy a dancer as I began, but the amount of pleasure I derived doing it eclipsed any self-consciousness I might otherwise have had. Our own hard day's night came to a close after "Twist and Shout," when my feet couldn't take another moment of mobility, my stomach was as sore from laughter as it would be had I just completed *Abs of Steel*, and even the minimal "dancing" I was attempting was impossible. We retired to our respective rooms to get at least a few hours of rest before another day with The Beatles began.

Chapter Fourteen

Liverpool Cathedral was a massive rectangular structure of dull red to sepia with a tower in the middle extending high above the building. Eager to begin shooting, I walked inside and stretched my neck like a giraffe to peer at the several hundred-foot–high ceiling and looked around at the large, glorious windows.

I heard Rob and Harry yell from outside. "Andrea, do you want us to accompany you? I believe the crucifixion appears on a shard or two of glass."

Holy shit, how about that? I had walked right in. With a tip of my hypothetical hat in celebration of myself, I went in further. "If you want to, you can. But I'm good, thanks." I could only imagine the level of Rob and Harry's astonishment, a mere fraction of my own.

I walked around, snapping strategically. The reality that the architecture I had seen thus far, all of which contained an impossible amount of detail and ornamentation, was made by human hands made me feel insignificant, compounded by how physically small I felt in a room with ceilings too high to see. With each new castle, each new cathedral, I was witnessing incredible feats of human achievement. I stopped in front of a window depicting Jesus hanging on the cross with soulful-looking mourners kneeling in a circle around him. The rays of the sun shone through the glass, the reds and the yellows sparkling in the light. I focused intently on Jesus' expression and those of his onlookers. They weren't scary: sad, maybe, but also peaceful. I had spent years being afraid of something not in the least bit frightening. *Sigh.* What a surprise. I watched a woman light a candle and say a prayer; I followed suit. I lit a candle in memory of Harry's and Rob's parents and then looked up at Jesus. *They let Jews do this, right?*

I quickly wrapped up my shots of the Cathedral, itching to get to the day's main event: the Beatles concert. Several blocks from the Cathedral, Rob and Harry had set up a partial replica of an outdoor stadium and a minimalist stage with the help of a props team assembled and sent to us by Millie, Claire, and Gemma; we would add concertgoers in production. Hey Dude showed up in authentic Beatles garb, took the stage, and the "show" began.

I snapped picture after picture of Hey Dude while they played a few tunes for us, mimicking the motions of the celebrated Beatles. I was so taken that, while the camera stayed in focus, I lost mine, and my imagination began to fill in the sights and sounds of a dancing, cheering crowd in the background.

I rearranged the band several times for a variety of poses and backgrounds, entering and leaving the stage, taking bows and rocking out '60s style. As they shifted positions, Harry would walk over to the stage to chat and offer direction, but mostly with Ringo. Harry's hand touched Ringo's waist as he pointed them to the positions I requested. I couldn't make out their conversation, but it appeared affable, as Harry tossed his head back laughing multiple times. I watched Harry move the way men watch large-breasted women run: in slow motion. I tricked myself into wondering whether he actually moved that way. Was he flirting with Ringo? Not possible. Honestly, who flirts with Ringo?

While Ringo and Harry chatted it up, the band moving ever so slowly into new stances, the clouds rolled in, threatening yet another aggravating English rainstorm. Annoyed but not willing to make enemies, I tried to gently push the shoot along.

"Guys, we really have to keep moving. Harry, get off the stage." Harry saw my demeanor transforming from excited but controlled to freezing and short-tempered, so he tried to mitigate it.

"So sorry, darling. I'm such a huge fan, you know. And Ringo there is an encyclopedia of Beatles factoids. When we finish I'll make it up to you." He kissed my cheek tenderly and shot me a smile during which a sparkle bounced off his front teeth. If Harry had been female, that kiss and smile would earn him Tiffany jewels and Gucci leather goods.

"I'm going to the loo, be right back... in case anyone cares," I heard Rob say as I saw him walking off the set out of the corner of my eye.

Lost in Harry's eyes, it took me a moment to realize I was hearing a ruckus. People had begun to gather on the surrounding streets, screaming.

"Um, Andy. Andy! Look over here. Andy!" Rob was calling out from across the road, followed by a conglomeration of yells from various voices.

"OH MY GOD!"

"HOLY SHIT!"

"I THINK IT'S REALLY HIM!"

Loads of people were congregating to form a mob on the other side of the street and the yelling grew louder by the second. *Did my shoot look that real? Everyone knows John Lennon is no longer with us, right?* I couldn't figure out what was happening.

The Lennon character of Hey Dude quickly leapt up.

"Andy, sorry, we have to go. Now. Boys, let's go. Let's go now!"

"Wait, what's happening?" I asked.

"It's Paul and Ringo. They're across the street."

"Okay, that's fantastic. We can take a look. But I'm not done with my shoot," I said, eager to catch a glimpse but trying to maintain focus on our task.

So as not to miss a good, or even once-in-a-lifetime, photo op, I turned around to take some shots of the real Beatles, reliving my paparazzi days, when Hey Dude threw me a figurative left hook.

"No, you see, we're in a tad bit of trouble with them."

I nearly dropped my camera. "You're in trouble with The Beatles?" Apparently I hadn't thought of every possible catastrophe.

"Well, we might or might not have made a few recordings and sold them without permission. Really must leave now. Thanks for the gig."

"Wait, what? They know you?"

"Um, yeah, they do. BOYS! LET'S GO. Don't worry, you can use the pictures, darling. Cheers. Bye."

Hey Dude's Ringo shouted out to Harry as he joined the rest of his band running away, "I'll call you, mate."

Through the banshee-like wails across the street and the pandemonium of the crowd surrounding the real McCartney and Starr, all I heard was the sound of the fake Ringo's drumsticks hitting the floor as the band took off. The crackle of thunder shuddered through the air and the rain came down hard, like little fists to finish off my beating. I looked up at my empty set being pummeled by droplets. Rob was nowhere to be found, Harry was staring at me with his face cloaked in pity, I never did catch a clear glimpse of Paul McCartney or Ringo Starr, and another shoot was ruined.

****

"Hiya Brandon, it's Rob. So, I don't want to alarm you, but I'm pretty sure he fancies her."

"What? What is that, British speak for 'they're having sex'?"

"No, if I thought that was happening, I'd say 'Brandon, I think they're shagging.' But I don't think they are. There is some heat there, though."

"On both sides or just his?"

"Can't say, really. But most likely just his. She talks about you."

"Anything good?"

"Some things, sure. She said you make dinner for her sometimes."

"That's it?"

"No, I think she said she really liked the dinners you prepare."

"Anything of substance?"

"Um, yeah. Let me just think."

"Never mind. I don't want you to work that hard."

"I'm joking, she has talked about you substantively. But you have to understand, mate, she's having an adventure. She's figuring out a new country. And she's shot two live photo sessions on her own. For the first time, I gather."

"She has? That's fantastic. She didn't tell me that."

"I'm sure she will do. She's enjoying her away time, isn't she?"

"Yeah, maybe too much."

"Why don't *you* call *her*?"

"I don't want to bother her."

"You don't want her to *know* you're bothering her, actually."

"You say it your way, I'll say it mine."

"Brandon, aren't you two engaged-ish?"

"Yes."

"Then maybe you can stop worrying about bothering each other when inquiring about each other's days. Just a thought."

"Thanks, doc."

"Anytime, mate."

"Keep me posted if you see anything strange. Like him running out of her room naked."

"Yeah. Sure. Will do."

"I wasn't serious."

"Oh, whoops."

"That's not a possibility, right? Right, Rob?"

"Don't know. Will keep you updated. Must get back now. Cheers."

****

I was helping to remove the lights and take down the equipment when Rob appeared from the void. He looked at the scene, stunned. "It's really pissing it down now, isn't it? Did you see Starr and McCartney? Fantastic sighting! Where did everybody go?"

"Funny story," I sighed. "Why don't you tell him, Harry? He may not believe me."

Chapter Fifteen

I lay flat on my bed, staring up at the ceiling, distraught and confused. I wanted more than anything to hear his voice as it soothed and warmed my body like hot chocolate on a torturously cold February morning.

"Hi Brandon, it's me."

"Hi sweetie! How's it going?" he asked, with genuine enjoyment at hearing my voice.

"Oh, okay, I guess."

"It's nice to talk to you when you're not drunk or hung over."

"Yeah, it's nice to spend a day that way."

"So how're the shoots? I hear you're... wait, never mind. You tell me."

I turned over onto my stomach and perked up, placing my elbows out and my chin in my hands. "Huh? You hear what?"

"Nothing, I was thinking about something else. Tell me how it's going."

"Well, part of it was great. I did shoots with people in costumes, scenery, and props. It was unreal." I swung my legs from side to side as my heels kicked my own butt, excited to talk with Brandon about my accomplishments and tribulations.

"That's incredible, babe. A real step forward. You should've called me earlier."

"I was going to... but... they keep getting ruined. I wanted to call you when I had a real success under my belt. Anyway, it's been hectic..." Then the comforting feeling I typically got from talking with Brandon evaporated. *What does he mean by 'should have'?* "And why do you have to add something I *should have* done to an accomplishment I just told you about?"

"What? What are you talking about?" he asked.

I stood up from my bed and paced back and forth in my hotel room. "I just told you about a major career move and you turned it into something about you. That I didn't call you to talk about it."

"I don't know where that's coming from, honey. It would have been nice to get a call from you right after, that's all."

"How do you even know you didn't?"

"I don't, I guess. It just, uh, seemed that way by how you said it."

"Well, anyway, I shot live scenes — twice — of course, each one got a tad screwed up."

"How?"

"Well, Robin Hood fell out of a tree and Paul and Ringo came after my Beatles."

"I don't follow."

I didn't have the heart or the stomach to illustrate the details. "I'll explain later. I'm tired. I have to go back to shooting inanimate objects."

"I am so proud of you, Andy. You should call your parents and share it with them too. I'm sure they'd be thrilled."

"There you go again with the 'you should.' I will call them when I want to."

"Okay, don't get defensive. It's just that I was talking to them and—"

"You were talking to them?"

"Yeah, just because it had been a few days since I heard from you."

"Wow, I can't even be 5,000 miles away and be away."

"Is everything okay with you, Andy?"

"Yeah, it's fine. I'm fine. I'm gonna go. I'll call you soon."

"Okay. I love—"

"Yeah me too, Brandon."

I hung up the phone and thought about all the things I had done during my life to avoid feeling as suffocated as I did then. I never left plastic bags around my house, part of my plan to pack away everything that could be construed as a weapon. I feared suffocation. I was terrified of writhing around, trying with all my might to grasp a breath of air while stuffed in a bag where there was no air to be had. Despite my continual efforts to ward off suffocation from strangers, though, I felt it from Brandon. I put my head down and breathed in hard, but air refused my attempts at inhalation. I took short small breaths in, but without the sufficient amount my head became light and the open space around me gripped and squeezed me as though wringing me out to dry.

After a few moments of the deep breathing of a phone sex operator, I was able to regain lung capacity. I looked at my phone and prepared to dial my parents. But my fingers were too heavy. My stomach felt queasy. Having only just been able to breathe in a regular pattern, I had no desire to feel the strain of my parents' 'support.' I'd call them another time.

I walked down to the lobby of the hotel and suddenly felt a hand on my back. I jumped. "HOLY SH—!"

"You alright, luv?" It was Harry.

"I'd be better if you didn't sneak up on me. But, yeah, I'm okay. Thanks."

"You sure? Your face is even paler than usual and now slightly green."

"Yeah, yeah, I'm fine."

"Did you call Brandon?" Rob asked.

"Yes, okay. I called him! I fucking called him! Anything else I can do for you? What about you Harry? You need anything?"

"Call didn't go well, then?" said Rob.

"Wait, how did I get dragged into this? I didn't tell you to call him," said Harry. "I don't care if you ever call him. You should call your parents, though. It seems like it's been some time."

"Oh, man, you've gotta be kidding me."

"Well you have quite a stick up your arse, don't you?" Rob said.

"Do tell us, what's up your bum, luv?"

"Nothing," I said. "Let's go back to London."

"What about Manchester?" Rob said, like *man-chest-a*.

"Well, Manchest-a will have to wait a day or two. I'm sure we can get that talking houseplant Millie to rearrange it for us. We'll probably end up in Manchest-a, New Hampshire, though."

"New Hamp-shure?" Rob mimicked.

"Sorry, lads, I'll speak British: New Hamp-shy-er," I said.

I tried to sleep on the train back to London. I tossed and turned as much as one can do in the limited space of a pre-indented, 90-degree-angle seat. I had greatly wanted to *want* to call Brandon and my parents to talk about my shoots, and about the paradox of being gratified by shooting live action but frustrated that laws even Murphy hadn't thought of kept getting in the way. Why did things keep going wrong? Why couldn't I talk to my loved ones without the strangulation effect? Why were the kids in the seats behind me playing a card game with no rules other than to scream at ungodly decibels? I had no clarity. Teenagers to my left were singing their favorite songs, none of which even approached a melodic tune. Harry and Rob wouldn't stop talking. Their voices grated my patience. I learned that Harry liked gladiators, Tony Curtis, and horror films. Rob also enjoyed Tony Curtis flicks, but hated horror and shyly slipped in a beloved rom-com or two. When I questioned him on his assertion that *Last Tango in Paris* was the best film of all time, he said he meant *Tango and Cash*, "because I like films about dancing and money." I didn't think he had seen *Tango and Cash*.

When we reached London, I left the train and the boys and went straight to the tube; I wanted the fastest route home so I just walked right on — alone — my march toward independence clearly advancing. I didn't look around; I didn't second-guess it. When the reality of what I had done set in, I huddled up into a seat looking around quickly, like I had just stolen something. But as I watched the variety of people around me, I felt more at ease. People in fancy duds, some in homely duds, and some in barely any duds. Young. Old. Ancient. But they were all there for one purpose: transportation. Not to cause trouble, not to tie me down and steal my money or my dignity. Just to go from one place to another. I kept my eye on a couple of travelers who looked as though they had no good on their mind (it was a gift I had to be able to tell at a glance), and I doubted I would ever be as comfortable as the ladies in front of me who were sleeping through the ride. But really, it was quite easy.

It also helped that I spent some of the time looking at the Hey Dude pictures through my camera, which I held in such a way to keep out of the other passengers' view so as not to become a target. I found them to be pretty outstanding, if asked to speak honestly. As I had managed to do in Nottingham, in Liverpool I also captured wonderfully animated facial expressions against an inviting backdrop and could even envision a magazine that would feature those photos. Apparently not all catastrophes lead to failure.

Chapter Sixteen

⚭

"George, I called Andrea earlier. She didn't answer," my mother said, having assumed the predictable position in her well-worn arm-chair to re-grade papers.

My father put down his briefcase, took off his tie, and walked over to my mother to give her a kiss hello. "It looks like you graded those already, Annie. What are you doing?"

"I don't know if I was paying attention the first time. I miss Andrea. Why isn't she answering her phone?"

"I don't know. I'll send her an email. She prefers to correspond that way."

"Okay. What do you want to do this weekend?"

"Well, we have dinner with the Feinsteins on Saturday."

"Right."

"I was going to fix a few things around here. Didn't you say the dish-washer wasn't working?"

"No."

"Oh, was it the washing machine?"

"I don't think so."

"The barbecue?"

"No, George. Not that I'm aware of."

"I know it was something. Why can't I remember?" My father walked around the house shaking the tables and chairs to determine which, if any, wobbled. All were perfectly sturdy.

It was exactly the scenario I envisioned and agonized about: my mother and father sitting in the only two chairs they used in a house otherwise full of them, debating how to spend their time. They didn't go to the movies often, dismissing every trailer as "stupid" or "done before" — which might have been the case, but they had seen so few movies that there was little chance they had seen it done the first time. They didn't much care for concerts, because my mother complained that the music was too loud, parking was a hassle, and "I don't like to walk in swarms of people." My dad would garden, but more to yank loose ends than anything. Their cat, Squeaker, kept busier than they did by virtue of the variety of places she licked each day. My parents had a few friends they would visit from time to time, but a three-hour dinner in the span of a weekend is not the makings of a raging — or even geriatric — social life.

"I'll get dinner ready shortly, George."

"Oh, great." My father assumed his position in his usual seat, which had long been indented around his butt. He flipped on the television to the nightly news and leaned back. It was silent between them.

"You know, George. Maybe we should take a trip."

"Oh? Where do you want to go?"

My mother pushed a newspaper across the table toward my dad, folded open to display an advertisement from British Airways.

"Do you want to visit Andrea, dear?"

"Sort of. I was thinking we would just check in on her."

"Call her, Annie."

"I need to see that she's okay firsthand. What if she's not telling us everything?"

"That's silly. Why wouldn't she tell us everything? Besides, you know we'd certainly find out if something was wrong with her."

The topic of my parents coming to visit me had never been on the table. I knew it wouldn't happen, and talking about it would have been intolerably frustrating. My mother was more afraid to fly than I was, and figuring out currency exchange? Fuggeddaboudit.

"Annie, if we go we should tell her, but I still don't think it's a great idea. You've never been on a plane before. That flight's almost ten hours. Are you sure?"

"I don't know. I don't understand air travel."

"Why don't we go somewhere closer? San Francisco?"

"I don't want to go to San Francisco. We can drive there. I want to see Andrea. I think I can make the flight. You can prescribe me sleep aids. I'll be okay."

"Andy would not be thrilled if we went to England. She wants to be on her own right now."

"She won't know. We'll just show up, make sure she's okay, and leave. It'll just be a long weekend."

"You won't want to tour around on our own too, honey? It seems a bit of waste to travel all that way for a long weekend."

"Oh, right." It hadn't dawned on her to have a motive other than spying on me. "Well, sure, if there's time. But Andy is the priority."

My mother grabbed a pen and paper to begin preparing a checklist of the things she needed to do in order to take a trip of that magnitude: 1. Buy luggage ("our carry-on won't suit the two of us, will it?"); 2. Buy sweaters ("it's cold there, right?"); 3. Buy back-up umbrella ("what if ours gets stolen?"); 4. Call the teacher's aid; 5. Stop the mail; 6. Find someone to watch the cat ("we can't take Squeaker, can we?"); 7. Exchange currency ("they won't take my dollars, will they, George?").

My mother sighed after glancing at her list. She had overwhelmed herself with things to do, and though I would be abroad for a few more months her natural anxiety fooled her into believing it all had to be accomplished in record time.

"Oh, George. Maybe it's not a good idea."

"Let's at least sit on it for a bit, Annie. We have some time."

Chapter Seventeen

Perhaps it was unrealistic, but outside of Heathrow I had come to expect the entire country of England to be paved with cobblestone and coated with scenic vegetation. I was, therefore, disappointed when we came upon Manchester's city center: lackluster, industrial, ordinary. I had also just come from Liverpool, which was mostly cosmopolitan, but somehow thought maybe Liverpool was the black sheep, the one city in England that could not be a backdrop for a Jane Austen story. That said, Liverpool was fairly attractive; the office buildings were somewhat cold but still appealing. In Manchester, I stood in the center of a city that could have been anywhere — anywhere with a severe scent of oil and a six-to-one ratio of people to walking space.

Judging only by the few streets I traveled, which I acknowledge is an unfair barometer for the value of an entire city, especially one as large as Manchester, I wanted little to do with this one. I'd seen this city: it's in Southern California, only there it has sunshine. Regardless, we continued on our way to find the castle Millie had plugged into our route, fingers crossed. But, as with all situations that began with Millie, the possible endings were numerous, mysterious, and somewhat frightening.

When we turned the corner onto the road that would allegedly lead us to the castle, there was no castle. There was no structure of any sort. Dirt. We came upon dirt. It dawned on me that we had brought this upon ourselves, given our now-comprehensive knowledge of the person who had planned the trip, by not double-checking Millie's work.

"Well, this is an impressive piece of land. Andy, give us your camera," Rob said.

"Wait, this can't be it; there's no way she did this. Twice. I'll call Millie." I started walking further down the road, looking hopelessly under rocks for a castle.

Because my state of being could consistently be described as "on edge," I typically walked just a few paces in front of whoever was walking with me; that way, that person I was with could keep an eye on me. Brandon hated it; he constantly reminded me that he enjoyed walking to places together and that he could keep track of me fine — better, even — if I stuck by his side. My view was that I could be a few paces ahead and we would still be together, though he failed to see the (il)logic. I mostly walked likewise with Harry and Rob and as I stepped away to call Millie, I quickly went from two steps ahead to many, and the sensation that I was completely alone. I turned around to see the two boys immobile, a few blocks back. Rob had his hands on his knees, his head lowered between them, convulsing; had I not known he was laughing I would have thought he was choking on an apple core. Harry had been chuckling slightly, but once Rob's laughter went airborne he had caught it and gasped for air between guffaws in unison with Rob. I walked back to them and tried to make out what they were saying between the laughs, tears, and intermittent high-pitched howls.

"How... could... this... happen... twice?"

"What's... the date... on the... maps... she's... using?"

It certainly was beyond bewildering that we could be sent twice to locations where castles no longer stood.

"Hi Millie, it's Andrea. Where are we supposed to go?"

"To the castle, right?"

"To which castle?"

"There's more than one?"

"According to Wikipedia, about nine, actually. And you sent us to one that's no longer standing."

"Wiki-what?"

"Nothing. There's no castle here. Again."

"Oopsie."

"Was that *oopsie*, Millie?"

Once the word *oopsie* left my lips, the sound of the laugh-cry bellows of the boys became considerably louder.

"Yes, apparently I made a little mistake," Millie said.

"Ah, just a tiny one. If you could let us know which castle the magazine would like us to shoot, we'll just trot along over to that one."

"I don't know."

"Can you call Tom and ask him?"

"Afraid I can't."

"Why not?"

"He's on holiday."

"But he must have his phone?"

"I don't have his mobile number."

"How's that possible, Millie? You know what, never mind. I'll give it to you. Please keep trying to get a hold of him; we're going to start shooting them all."

"Good thinking."

"Yes, it's a very efficient solution to shoot all nine instead of the one we're supposed to shoot. Just keep calling him. Please." I gave Millie Tom's cell number, virtually certain it would make no difference; we'd be done with the entire shoot before she learned how to use it.

"Okay, boys, we're doing a castle tour through the glorious city of Manchester. I'm not going to ask for directions again. We're gonna shoot them all."

"Even this one?" Rob asked.

"Yes, this one's going to be the cover, smart-ass. Let's go."

Rob and Harry wiped their tears and eventually regained their breath.

"Unbelievable. Just unbelievable," Harry said.

We went to three castles that day and shot some pictures. They were not "proper" castles, though, as Harry described them; most were just piles of rocks and sand, monuments to where a castle once stood; without a drawbridge and a moat, I feared we were wasting our time. We finished the shooting day early so we could do more research before continuing the search for a photogenic — or even actual — castle to exhibit this already congested, noisy, bustling city of Manchester.

The most crucial decision of the day thus turned to our nightlife. I had requested that something different be placed on the agenda, but after we mulled the limited options, and on the heels of a superb night of dancing in Liverpool, the unanimous decision was to go clubbing.

"Okay," I said. "But I wanna see every drink as it's poured. I don't want to take a chance that some scumbag puts something in mine." Trying to turn a night of the same into a night of something new, I offered an option. "Ooh, let's go to a gay bar! I've only ever been to one."

"No. No. Absolutely not."

"Why not, Robbie Rob?"

"Because, hot, sweaty men. No. Not doing it. No. What do you think, Harry?"

"I don't mind. Gay or straight, both work for me."

"See, Robbie. Either one works for him. He's mature."

"I don't want to be hit on," Rob said.

"Well, I don't want to be hit on either."

"I'm looking at you lot, and I don't think either of you ought to worry," Harry said.

"Thanks, mate."

"How very kind of you."

Although it was meant to be a joke, from where I stood, Harry was right on target. When we had left London for Manchester, I was so focused on my foul mood and my yearning to complete a photo shoot that didn't blow up in my face that I hadn't thought about bringing attire for a night on the town. My stressed-out nature and always-be-prepared mantra came in handy, though: I had dressed in layers. Hidden beneath my jacket and jumper, I wore a black t-shirt, at least snug enough for one to recognize I was female. However, paired with my loose-fitting jeans, boots and minimally made-up face, I still felt like I could star in the one-act play "wilderness girl goes clubbing."

We breezed through dinner at the hotel's café, where I sampled the traditional English feast of bangers and mash for the first time. It was a tasty arrangement of sausage, mashed potatoes, and gravy made from God knows what, and every bit as "lovely" as Rob and Harry had suggested, probably due to the copious amounts of butter and whatever other lard-filled substance had been used to create it. I continuously pondered the effects of heart disease on the British populace as I ate my way through England's signature cuisines.

After dinner, we followed our concierge's recommendation to a popular nightclub near the city center. I walked in and was instantly transported back to freshman year at UCLA and the countless nights I had spent at clubs exactly like that one, all of which ended at 11:45 so I could heed my parents' curfew. A giant dance floor lay in the center of an enormous room with a second floor that was shorter so the non-dancing public could peer over the banister and watch, or spit on, the dancers if they so chose. A constant stream of colored lights swirled around, the vapors of smoke from smog machines created a hazy ambience, and girls in barely-there clothing shook everything they could that jiggled, mostly alternating between T and A. A bunch of tarts, as the Brits would say. An uncomfortably loud, mismatched techno-rap mix of sorts, spun by what must have been a hearing-impaired DJ, completed the scene.

After a stop at the bar, the three of us began our stint on the dance floor. I pointed Rob toward groups of girls, scantily clad, dancing lasciviously with each other as a sneak preview of what was in store for the men watching should they accept an invitation to dance. Harry also nudged Rob, who threw back a shot and reluctantly walked over to them. Harry and I danced too, but were mostly voyeurs to Rob's awkward attempt to strike up conversation with the slutty women. After a series of what appeared to be, "What?" "Huh?" and "Sorry, I don't understand," the drunken ladies threw their arms over Rob and began to grind against him, rolling their hips around his nether region. Uncomfortable with the forward displays of sexuality, Rob tried to maintain some distance and dance in front of them in his own space. The women tolerated none of his prudish antics: they sandwiched him in, one rubbing up against him with her backside and the other awkwardly shoving her crotch into his butt. The whites of Rob's eyes protruded as he looked down in horror on what these women were doing to him. He noticed how oblivious they were to everything around them, just grinding away and sliding their hands up and down his body. He clenched his lips and attempted to turn his face away, as though he was being whipped rather than seduced. After a song and a half, he was finally able to squeeze out from their collective grip and scurry over to the bar, where I met him for a shot.

"Downright vultures, they are," he said, straightening his shirt and running his fingers through his hair, smoothing the ones pulled out of place by the voracious women.

"Yeah, Rob. I saw. But a guaranteed lay."

"They're frightening." He seemed genuinely traumatized.

"Come on, Rob. I'll dance with you."

I tried to pull Rob out of his wallflower act and back to the floor, but he wouldn't budge.

"Okay, never mind. I'll stay with you for a bit."

As we stood with drinks in hand, we people-watched and drank, solidifying our hangovers for the following day. We watched a beautiful woman dancing with her friends, fending off suitor after suitor. Rob labeled her an "uppity bitch."

"Maybe she just wants a night with the girls," I said.

We observed the men who watched her, scanning her from head to toe, a slight lull at her cleavage, with lecherous grins. I felt for her. She paid them no mind, as though she wanted to be left alone, but she had no chance against the pack of wolves eager to pounce. Despite that girl's popularity with the male species, however, the most popular person in the club by a landslide was, of course, Harry. Women ravaged him, sliding their bodies up and down his. Men danced around him, scrutinizing and imitating his moves. He was at ease dancing with each and every type of person; nothing fazed him. I admired Harry's outlook and I found myself studying his demeanor from time-to-time as if he had been sent to me as an example of how enjoyable life could be if I worried less.

As I looked on with slight envy at the merriment in which Harry was engrossed, and noticed the room slightly swaying on its way to spinning, a gentleman I couldn't clearly make out requested the honor of a dance.

"Do you think that's a good idea, Andy?" Rob said into my ear.

"Oh, don't be such a tight-arse. It's just one dance."

I took the gentleman, who I named Dancer Bob, up on his offer, which I attributed in part to my desire to have as gratifying an evening as Harry appeared to be having and in part to the unseemly amount of alcohol swimming though my blood. I followed Dancer Bob's lead to the floor, leaving Rob to stay in his comfortable position as a hermit.

The dance began innocently, with me and my uncoordinated limbs bouncing around at a distance in front of my partner, and him laughing and doing the same. Neither of us made any attempt at conversing: the noise level was too great to talk at any distance and I had no inclination to lean in close enough to speak into his ear. I was content just to dance. Apparently feeling that one song was an adequate introduction, during the second one Dancer Bob put his arms around me and pulled me in to his chest. We danced together closely, and I attempted to move my hips like the other women. To no avail, though, my moves were robotic and I was going to have to live with it. During the dance, I felt a mysterious tapping on my back.

"Come find me when you're done," said Harry.

"Or me," added Rob.

I waved them off.

"Who are they, your chaperones?" Dancer Bob asked.

"Just some friends."

Dancer Bob pulled me into him so that I was so close my face could not escape his breath, which was warm and reeked of a whiskey-smoke-and-beer concoction. I felt vomit rising through my esophagus. I tried to plant my hands in his chest to push him away, but he held me in tight. I pushed harder, but despite my attempts to shove him off he tilted his head and leaned in for a kiss. I got a good look at his dirty, cracked, wretched yellow teeth as he opened his mouth in preparation. I wrenched my head backwards, fighting to keep everything of his off of everything of mine.

"Oh come on, you cock tease. Just give us a kiss."

"No!" I said trying to wriggle my way out of his grip, like a ten-month-old in the arms of an over-coddling aunt.

His hands were pressed hard against my back, compelling me to succumb. With the putrid smell of his breath wafting through the air between us, I knew I was moments from passing out. I had little time. I reached into my pocket and grabbed the pepper spray. Before my lips hit his, I screamed, "I SAID NO!" and, with the reflexes of Jason Bourne, gave his tonsils a pepper-spray cleansing. I continued screaming like a banshee to gain attention and assistance, but the sound emanating from my mouth was no match for the volume of the music. While he leaned over to cover his lips, I kneed him in the groin. Now completely overtaken by adrenaline, as he cupped his balls and grimaced in pain, I sprayed his face and ran away.

I darted out of the bar and walked briskly down the street, jittery and paranoid. I looked from right to left so often and so quickly that whiplash seemed inevitable. Everyone I passed was ominous. I shied away from a pack of men smoking outside a coffeehouse; I crossed the road to avoid a group of teenagers in tracksuits and hoodies, my finger on the trigger of my trusted spray all the while.

As I passed a corner market, a group of construction workers engaging in late-night drilling whistled at me.

"Oi there, whatchyoudoin' all alone?"

"Yeah, we'll keep you company, doll face."

Nothing like a holler from a sleazy construction worker to begin a list of things no more attractive when said with an English accent. I've never understood why men yell at women from across the street or honk at us while driving by — is it our reaction that so strikes their curiosity? I often wondered what those men would say if we took them up on the offer. Had I said, "Yeah? That's great. I'd love your company, sir. Drop those suspenders and give me a cuddle!" my guess is they'd have shut up pretty quick and returned to their work like the cowards they were. Of course, I couldn't risk the opposite, so I would never put it to the test. The wise move would have been to keep walking as if they didn't exist; they were vile, but most likely harmless. With my confidence at an all-time high and my blood alcohol content not far behind, however, I turned toward the crotch-grabbing workers to give them a piece of my mind. I walked backward down the street, intending to scream "buzz off, you assholes!" but instead I ran into someone whose hands grabbed my ass.

I instinctively turned around, took out my spray, and went to town on the jackass.

"Stop! Stop! I'm blind! I'm blind!"

"Then maybe you should keep your hands off of strangers' asses, you dick!"

"No, I'm blind. I'm really blind. I dropped my cane."

"Oh, shit. Oh god. Oh shit. Oh, I'm so sorry," I said, through the background of roaring laughter from the construction guys, none of whom came over to help me or the harmless blind man I had just coated in pepper spray. I picked up the cane and handed it to the man as his friend ran out of the adjacent market.

"What are you doing, you stupid bitch? He's blind, for fuck's sake."

"I know, I know. I mean, I didn't know. I thought he was trying to molest me."

"Stupid cow."

I walked slowly the rest of the way to the hotel, my fingers finally removed from the pepper spray trigger and my body soaking in the effects of another night of drinking.

When I finally reached my destination, feeling alone and melancholy, I called Brandon.

"Hi honey," I said, my voice dragging and cracking in pain.

"Hey. You okay?"

"I'm sorry for getting upset when we last talked."

"Thank you. I am trying to give you space; I'm just not all that good at it yet."

"I appreciate the effort."

"You sound sad. Everything okay, Andy?"

"I don't know. I was walking home alone—"

"You were alone?"

"Yeah, listen—"

"Why were you alone?"

"The boys left. Listen, B—"

"Rob left you alone? He's supposed to watch you."

"What? No he's not. He's just my colleague. He can go off on his own."

"Well, sure, right. Of course. I just think it would be nice if he made sure you were okay."

"I'm fine, Brandon. You can't always watch over me."

I instantly felt awful at how concerned Brandon was, how helpless he felt, all amplified by the physical distance between us. He couldn't see me to confirm that I was okay. He couldn't hold me in his arms to comfort me. I decided not to tell him about the foul-breathed, snaggle-toothed dirtbag who had tried to molest me. He would worry too much. As a loving boy-friend — hell, just as a man — he already feared being defenseless against those forces out to harm me; he didn't need specific cause for concern above the general ones he had about me traveling abroad. I told him I had left the club alone because I was tired and then pepper sprayed the hell out of a blind man who thought I was someone else while fending off dodgy construction workers.

"Oh, man, Andrea. Well, at least you react quickly."

"I know, but I feel terrible."

"Sure, but you have to take care of you. It sounds like you reacted rationally, actually." When used in that context, the word *actually* means *surprisingly*.

"Gee, thanks. I guess so."

"Just, please try to be safe."

"Are there times I don't try to be safe?"

"Andrea, I'm your boyfriend. Give me a little room to worry for chris-sakes."

"Yeah, fine. Just please try not to abuse it. How's everything there?"

"All is good here, babe. Uneventful. I miss you."

"You too."

We chatted an additional fifteen minutes or so and I hung up feeling better, finally, and fell into a deep sleep.

****

"What the hell, Rob? You left her alone?"

"I'm sorry, mate, I don't—"

"Don't call me mate, you prick. Why did you leave her alone?"

"I didn't know she was alone, did I, Brandon? When I left, Harry was still there. I thought she was with him."

"That's just as bad. Your job is to keep her away from danger *and* Harry."

"You know, at some point you are going to have to trust her. She's actually quite self-sufficient."

"I told you, this isn't about not trusting *her*, it's about not trusting the rest of the world, including you."

"Oh sod off. Someday you're going to have to give in to the fact that you can't control everything. You can't just throw money at a situation and make it better."

"Maybe, maybe not, but this one I can. Or at least I thought I could. I need you to watch her, Rob."

"Yeah, yeah, okay. Is she alright?"

"Now she is, yeah. But it sounds like she had a traumatic evening."

"Bollocks. I'm sorry, man."

"Whatever. Please keep your eye on her."

"Okay, mate. I know."

"Thank you. She means the world to me."

"Yep, got it."

****

Coffee was again my greatest ally to combat my pulsating forehead as I met up with the boys the next morning to continue researching castles in Manchester and decide what to shoot.

"I'm sorry you went home alone, Andrea."

"How did you know I went home alone, Rob?"

"Um, I didn't. I said I'm sorry *if* you went home alone."

"You were alone? I thought you left with Rob. When did you leave?" Harry asked.

"I don't remember. But I had a rather uncomfortable run-in on the dance floor with an overly aggressive brute who needed major dental work."

"Oh, ha. Yes, we're British, we don't have dentists. Ha, ha."

"No, Rob. That's not what I mean." He saw in my expression that I was serious.

"I'm sorry, An—"

"No, it's okay. Then I pepper sprayed the hell out of a blind man."

"That was rude," Rob said.

"You what?"

"Nothing. It's fine now," I asserted.

Rob and Harry both muttered to themselves under their breath, clearly feeling bad that they had left me to my own devices. But I was fine, surprisingly fine; what's more, I was impressed with how I had handled myself (in the club, mostly; not as much with the blind man). Most importantly, I had lived to see the next day, a day during which we devoted hours to the search for a castle in Manchester, England.

"You know what? Let's shoot the frickin' cathedral."

"The itinerary says castle."

"I know it does, Rob, but Millie typed up the itinerary. She might've just misspelled cathedral."

"Fair point. Let's go."

The Cathedral was by far the most impressive building we had seen in Manchester. It was caramel-colored and, like the castle in Liverpool, had one tower that rose above the building. The top corners of the tower each came to a point; several large hexagonal windows with a rounded arch marked the front, a Union Jack flew overhead, and a large gold clock sat in the middle. The body of the cathedral was long, extending back hundreds of feet, and much shorter than the front tower; viewed straight on from the back, it looked like a railroad car emerging out of a tall building.

As with the other cathedrals we had visited, the ceilings reached such heights that, though you could tell they were replete with garnish, you couldn't make out any actual detail without a zoom lens. Of course, I had one. Though it was resplendent in every sense of the word, I enjoy taking pictures of living things infinitely more than I like shooting inanimate objects. With cathedrals and castles, one can obtain incredible close-ups of the most spectacular artistry, such as detailed flower arrangements in stained glass, the faces of angels painted on the ceilings, and geometric shaped engravings in wooden pews — but I have always been more satisfied by the expressions people wear while playing or posing. Capturing a detail of a building is nice, but it lacks the pizzazz of halting a moment in the life of a living creature.

The boys and I continued what had by then become customary: I took pictures while Harry and Rob took notes and surveyed the surroundings for interesting angles and the buildings for appealing and unique features I might have missed. While pointing out a distinctive detail atop a column, Harry put his hand on my shoulder, turning me to face toward him, cornering me under a buttress.

"Darling, I feel awful about last night," he said in a low tone, almost a whisper. I could feel his breath on my face and saw the sheen on his hair created by the natural light streaming through the windows.

"Um, it's fine. It really is."

He gently brushed away the hair that fell into my face and looked deep into my eyes.

"It's not. We should have been there for you."

I didn't know what was happening. *Why was he positioned like he was going to plant one on me? Why hadn't I moved away yet? Did he use under-eye cream?*

By the time I had finished with my inner Riddler routine, he said, "Don't worry, luv. I certainly won't leave you again," and kissed me softly on the cheek, then backed away.

My phone rang and I shook my head as if coming out of a dream, in time to see Rob rounding the corner. "I think we're done here," he said.

"Oh perfect, Millie's calling." I answered it. "Hi, Millie."

"Hiya, Andrea. I got a hold of Tom. It wasn't a castle; you were supposed to shoot the cathedral."

"Millie, it's been three days. We shot several castles and the cathedral already."

"Then why did you ask me to call Tom?"

"We asked you three… never mind. Sorry, our screw up."

"Where would you all be without me?" Millie asked with infuriating sincerity.

"Efficient and finished. I have to go."

"Wait, Andrea. Tom also said he got you tickets to a rugby match. They're at the will-call window."

"Rugby, you said?"

I looked at the boys who were vigorously shaking their heads, "No!"

"I don't think we want to go to a rugby match, Millie."

"Okay, but Tom says it's for the best team in football."

"It's football?"

I looked up again at the boys who were now just slightly shaking their heads, as if still deciding.

"That's what I said, rugby."

"Millie, football is not the same as rugby."

"It's not?"

"No. Is it football or rugby?"

"Oh, I don't know. He said the team was Manchester United."

"Manchester United?"

"Football," Rob and Harry clarified.

I wondered what the chances were that we would end up at a ballet. "That was nice of Tom," I said. "Did he mention any particular reason for the game?"

"No, I don't think so. He said, 'tell them I said to have fun.'"

"You don't *think* so? Whatever, okay, Millie. We're gonna go. Thanks."

I turned back to Harry and Rob. "Boys, we're going to the soccer, I mean football, game!"

The news, which I thought was fantastic enough to be greeted enthusiastically with high-fives and chest bumps, was met with shrugs. I didn't understand it: two boys — two *British* boys — football, free tickets, Manchester United, and "okay, I suppose we've nothing else to do"? I would have thought a Brit shunning a football game was some sort of misdemeanor, like badmouthing the monarchy or drinking a beer cold. Neither Rob nor Harry had ever been to a football game; neither even enjoyed sports. On the way to the match, we discussed this unlikely ambivalence.

"I quite like crew, actually," said Harry, which made sense given his preppie appearance, though I may have been judging based on an Abercrombie and Fitch ad where models who resembled Harry were rowing. "I don't really like choosing teams," he added.

"I'm more artsy, I guess. I can watch sports, but to me, they're all repetitive until the last few minutes." There was something about Rob's explanation that made sense, but it stripped every sport of its gamesmanship, all the action and strategy that propel the teams to the last few minutes.

I felt otherwise; I enjoyed watching sporting events, although until that time I had attended only a few. "It's too dangerous; sports fans are no better than gangbangers," my mom had said (many times). Brandon and I had gone to an ice hockey game on our second date. I knew nothing about the sport, but I have always found pleasure in activities with a spirited crowd and the rush of competition. My mother and father had begged me not to attend, telling me tales of people who had been killed after being whacked in the head by a wayward puck or pummeled to death by belligerent fans pissed off at a referee's call. I too was scared of such scenarios, but went with Brandon anyway; it must be that love conquers all fears. Or at least some.

We took a bus to Old Trafford. I had learned the name of the stadium on the bus ride over by listening to a group of lads talk about the game. The boys were all dressed in various shades of red and chanting the Man United fight song in unison. During the ride, one of the rowdy fans sat up on his knees and exclaimed, "Oh, boys, we've got an enemy in our midst." They then began to chant "you're going down, you wanker," as if someone on the bus played for the opposing team. I looked around and laughed, taking in the scene, elated to be part of the camaraderie.

We walked up to the ticket windows and stared across the field. WE'VE GOT BALLS was written across the rooftop of the opponent's side bleachers. I took a picture of it and texted it to Brandon with the caption: *Look babe, I've finally got balls!* At *my first game of footie. Boys aren't excited but I'm right stoked! xoxo*

"Right stoked?" asked Harry.

"Yes, I'm mixing English and American. And don't read my texts."

"Why don't you send one to your mum too?"

"Because my *mom* will just tell me all the things I need to worry about while I'm here." And I was afraid I hadn't thought of some of those things yet. Then I became fearful of not being fearful enough, adding a whole new dimension of fears. Talking to my mother brought fears into focus; I needed the opposite. I had come to learn that if I didn't allow myself to stop and think too much about the obstacles or perils of a situation, I could get my brain to zoom in on the bull's-eye, the end goal, instead — as I did with my camera. But there, in the stadium with a tightly packed crowd of burly men, most of who had moved past drunk without saying hello before they even entered the place, there was plenty at the fore that could go wrong. However, I felt secure with my pepper spray snug in my bag, which I planned to hold closer to my chest than I would a friend's child. That is, until the security guard — a 300-pound bald ogre with armpit stains who was a tad too thrilled to give the women pat-downs — pulled the spray out of my bag.

"Can't bring this in to the game, dear." Before I could beg and plead for my security blanket, the oaf continued, "oi, you're sitting with Man United but you're wearing Manchester City's colors. I'd watch it if I were you. Carry on." Then something I hadn't planned for happened; something horrific: the ogre tossed my pepper spray into the trash. I watched it swish down the can in slow motion and I heard "boys, we've an enemy in our midst" echoing in the background. *Shit, they were referring to me.*

We walked to our seats and I was immediately taunted. A pack of men together yelled, "you support a load of shite!" a few times over. Not exactly the team spirit I had appreciated about sporting events.

"Oh, no, not really. Just an unfortunate coincidence," I shouted. Tucked away in a closet that would impress the editors of *InStyle*, I owned one powder blue item. Just one: a powder blue cashmere zip-up I had picked up one day at a sale and I wore it on the only day of my life it seemed that it would get me killed. *Curse this unflattering color!*

I took off the sweater, but had only a tank top on underneath. I mentally flip-flopped between death by hypothermia and death by disorderly soccer fans, and chose the former, thinking it would be quicker.

"That's right, sweetie, take it off."

"Oh, she's a stripper too!"

I couldn't win. Harry and Rob, trying with little might to stifle their laughter at my shitty luck, were of little help besides their offering to leave. I felt compelled to stay and enjoy my one chance to see a soccer game in England, certain that the crowd would turn to a different target when the action on the field began.

For a while it worked. The audience paid attention to the game, which was fast-paced and exhilarating. I cheered extra loud along with the Man United fans to blend in. Our seats located just a couple rows from the field, I could see the determined looks on the faces of the players and the beads of sweat accumulating in their hair and gliding down their cheeks. I tried to involve Harry and Rob in the action, but they were lost in each other's words about almost anything else — music, films, judgments of other people in the stands. For me, the spirit of the crowd was contagious; I reveled in it. I screamed the fight song along with the fans after Man United's first goal and jeered Man City and the ref when it was their turn to score.

The game was tied one-to-one at the beginning of the second half. Only a few seconds in, the crowd jumped up and roared, celebrating another Man United goal, putting them in the lead. But the clamor soon stopped as the referee and the linesmen gathered at the sidelines. They disallowed the goal, declaring that the player had used his hands to send the ball into the net. The fans immediately began to yell: at the ref, the goalie, the situation, and each other. Though my sweater sat neatly under my butt, some teeny-bopper shit-head pulled it out, lifted it up, and yelled "enemy here, boys!" Food started flying from behind us toward the field.

"Boys, we should go," I said.

"Ah, it'll be fine. Happens all the time at these dos, doesn't it?" said Harry.

"I don't know, but it doesn't feel right."

"It's all part of the ambience. It'll be over in a minute."

I looked closely at the faces of the screaming fans. Veins protruded sharply from their necks and their faces were beet-red as they used every vocal cord to scorn anyone who agreed with the ref's call. I saw real venom in their eyes, and it didn't appear to be moments from subsiding.

"I realize nothing sways you, Harry. But I'm just not the same. This is scary to me. Let's go. Rob?"

Rob sat quietly but looked around like a terrified puppy crouched in the corner of a room. The Man United team circled the referee. We saw their hands flying up and heard a multitude of artful expletives. The crowd's yelling grew in proportion to the length of the pause in the game. People were becoming violent. Next to us, fans of each opposing team had begun yelling at and pushing each other. I then had a horrific vision of the Channel 4 News anchor breaking through the fifth rerun of *Friends* for the day:

We interrupt your programming with breaking news — an American photographer touring the UK was killed today during a brawl at a Manchester United soccer game while wearing Manchester City's colors. As we understand it, her pepper spray was taken from her upon entering the stadium. If only they'd let her keep it, she might have lived to see her photographs be printed.

And that was it for me. "Boys, we're going."

"Oh, Andy, it'll be fine," Harry said, rubbing my back. "I'll take care of you." It was the one time that Harry's hotness couldn't melt through my terror. Like a snowball rolling down a steep incline, the ring of fighting fans multiplied. Security fought vigorously to break it up.

"Look Andy, security's here. What are you afraid of?"

Being trampled to death as everyone stampedes for the door. Being punched in the eye by someone with bad aim and ending up blind. Being struck by a candy apple and ending up in a coma. "A lot of things. I can't stay. You haven't watched one moment of the game anyway."

"Okay, Andy, we'll go."

I grabbed my sweater, put it in a ball, held it close to my chest, and bolted. I ran all the way out of the stadium, ducking and dodging the airborne snacks: crisps, popcorn, ice, the works.

So I hadn't yet made *all* the strides I had wanted to in my anti-fear campaign. I finally stopped running when I felt safely away from the stadium; it felt like about a mile. While breathing heavily and waiting for Rob and Harry to catch up, I received a call from Tom, who had been watching the game on TV and saw the melee. He wanted to ensure we were alive and confirm that we had had "the good sense to take some pictures of the scene" since I was shooting the game anyway. I hadn't. While thinking of the million and one ways I might die, it hadn't occurred to me for a second to take a picture. I hadn't even brought a camera, other than the crappy one on my cell phone, fearing something would happen to it. I wasn't a journalist and I didn't know that Tom wanted pictures of the game. "So, the tickets weren't just perks, huh?" I apologized profusely, but Tom was less than thrilled. Goddamn Millie, I thought before coming to the realization that, as the photographer, I should have had my camera — I should always have my camera.

I longed to leave Manchester that night, but it was too late to catch a train and I had to take evening pictures of the cathedral anyway. My remaining activities would consist only of a few shots of that landmark, a load of sleep, and some type of prayer to whoever or whatever was responsible for my living to see our next destination, Stratford-upon-Avon, Warwickshire County, England. In pictures, it appeared to be precisely what the doctor ordered: tranquil and serene. Stratford is famous for birthing the man whose prose has melted women's hearts, dazzled people's minds, and set the bar for romanticism beyond reach: William Shakespeare.

Chapter Eighteen

My trip from Manchester to Stratford was not the first occasion where packing more than one bottle of pepper spray proved a fortunate fluke. After college, I had taken a covert road trip to Las Vegas on which I brought three cans — all were needed. One of them was accidentally thrown out the window of the car when two of my friends thought it would be a hoot to toss it around the back seat in a game of keep-away and a surly bouncer guarding a dance club, basically a cousin of the squeeze-happy Andre the Giant I encountered at the soccer game, took the first backup. Luckily, I had packed a third in a friend's luggage, which I remorsefully used on a cabbie who became a tad too friendly with my ass while helping me with my luggage. I wasn't sure whether I would need my backup during my UK trip, but merely knowing it was there provided the comfort level of a belt and suspenders gripping and holding up an ill-fitting pair of jeans.

We walked through Stratford-upon-Avon's main road, High Street, a quaint path of shops and restaurants that looked like adjoining cottages. The "cottages" showed little variety: they had either white or light brown façades with dark brown trim and vertical wood strips striping the front, and low-hanging, wood-shingled roofs, or red bricks and no distinctive markings other than the windows. We walked past Shakespeare's home, a building that looked much like the shops on High Street: a two-story structure with a painted exterior the color of lightly toasted bread and the same dark brown wooden stripes that decorated the shops. Both stories contained lines of windows, the panes of which were tiny diamond-shaped glass mosaics merged into larger square panes.

The river Avon flowed through the middle of this charming town and a brick path lined each side, caressing its curvatures. Rowers paddled gracefully across the water and under a grey cobblestone bridge, their boats leaving rippled wakes with artsy reflections in the various colors of the rowers' clothing. The 360-degree view revealed luscious greenery, seemingly farther-reaching than England's borders. I snapped picture after picture, if only to create my own postcards of this magical place.

On our way to Trinity Church, we passed by an impressive structure: the Royal Shakespeare Theatre, where the world-famous Royal Shakespeare Company performs. It was a huge square building of blood-orange brick, connected to a cylindrical structure. A red- and white-checkered trim lined the top edge along with rows of decorative windows, rounded at the top. A group of men with well-defined biceps stood chatting, their chiseled pectorals pushing through their spandex tank tops while their muscular thighs and, ahem, *packages* bulged through their pants of the same material — a material that should never be worn as the sole covering of one's bottom half. Especially not men... on a cold day.

"Blimey, looks like it's a bit chilly for those men, doesn't it?" said Harry, subtly pointing 'down there' and garnering gossipy snickers from Rob and me.

"Oh dear, blimey indeed," I said. "It's a spandex/shrinkage combo! Too bad Gemma's not here, she'd offer up her de-shrinking services."

While considering the sad effects of weather on the male genitalia, I suddenly became creative. Ideas do come to us in the strangest ways, and sometimes at the most unexpected times. This one began with the notion that a few of the men had some compensating to do, and ended with the thought that I did too — compensation of a different nature. In Manchester, I had failed to snap many photos worth the price of a camera cartridge. I would make up for it in Stratford, using these confident, brawny men to help. I walked directly into their circle, trying not to let my eyes fall where they were naturally being pulled. I learned that they were, as I had thought, players from the Royal Shakespeare Company taking a break from their rehearsal of *Hamlet*. After a pleasant conversation, they pointed me to the director, who politely took time out of his day to have a chat. After minimal persuasion, he agreed to allow us into the rehearsal, but mentioned several times that we must keep quiet so as not to disturb the actors. We were beyond fortunate to obtain behind-the-scenes access to the Company's rehearsal, and I hoped that Mr. Henson's pleasure with this shoot would eclipse his disappointment with my trip to Manchester. I planned to shoot the Trinity Cathedral too, as required to deflect the *rogue photographer* label slowly appearing on my nametag.

The inside of the elegant theater was an oblong room, with a large, round stage in the center. I set up a camera in the middle of the orchestra section, which contained several rows of plush red chairs assembled below numerous rows of seats, the uppermost of which were bleachers. Several wooden planks extended out like arms from the stage through the orchestra-level seating, providing a road for the players. I imagined that sword-fighting scenes took place on these extensions, making the drama of the fight even more compelling by setting it only feet before one's eyes. While the actors rehearsed Shakespeare's celebrated tragedy, I traveled around the room, camera in hand. Rob and Harry barely assisted, as they were caught up in the performance. I requested aid several times, but they couldn't tear their eyes from the scene. I didn't mind picking up the slack on this shoot, however, because Rob and Harry had been there for me when a stained-glass window and ghost stories scared me out of doing my job at the beginning of the trip. As I focused the camera on the target of my picture, my brain achieved the same focus. I heard nothing, but saw clearly.

Until a deafening *BANG!* rang out from a faux cannon, followed by a *THUD!* from several players dropping to the floor.

"AAAAHHHHH!" I screamed, startled by the sudden noise and the flicker of light. With my scream, I fell backwards into Rob, knocking him backwards into a tumble of his own over the bleachers.

My scream and the echo from Rob's fall set off a chain reaction: the guy holding the matches for the cannon got frightened and fell off the rafter, but not before the match he had been holding lit the ropes, which took only milliseconds to be devoured by flames. After taking the ropes, the fire spread to the curtains — which was the moment everyone's brain caught up with the scenario.

"Oh, crap. Oh, shit. I'll call 911!" I yelled, still without the knowledge of whether 911 was England's emergency number.

Harry calmly made his way toward the stage to assist with the exit plan. "What for? What the hell's a 911?" he asked.

"You don't have 911?"

While Harry and I debated the emergency phone number, the actors and crew grabbed props and made their way to safety.

"I don't know what you're talking about, Andrea but it's time you exited the building."

"Don't you have an in-case-of-emergency number?"

"Yeah, sure, it's 999, but they've already called it."

"Okay," I shouted, heading for the door. "Rob, look for a fire extinguisher."

"There aren't any here," said a voice from the crowd. *No fire extinguishers? Don't these people have mothers?*

Hamlet and Polonius ran out the door, their swords clanking and swaying in tow. Only in England.

In Ophelia's rush to save her child, who had been sitting on a high chair in the bleachers, letting out a staggeringly high-pitched shriek that could be heard even above the commotion and that was slightly more terrifying than the flames themselves, she fell and yelled for someone to save her child. Harry showed Rob to the exit and ran to the child. As if he were wearing a cape and a giant *H* on his chest, he swooped down, saved the child, grabbed Ophelia, and exited stage left.

We stood outside and watched firefighters work to save the world-famous Royal Shakespeare Theatre from utter destruction by putting out the fire I had helped cause. I questioned whether rigor mortis would set in around my mouth, causing it to remain in its open state. *A fire? Really? This my mother was right about?*

Chapter Nineteen

"Oh my god, George, come quick. There's been a fire in England!" my mother said as she flipped on the morning news.

"Oh, Annie, stop being dramatic. There hasn't been a fire," my father said, wearily walking downstairs to prepare his coffee.

"No, come in here. It's on the BBC News."

"BBC? Since when do you watch the BBC?"

"Since Andrea left. It's quite good!"

"*Quite* good? Annie, what's—"

"George! I mean it. There's been a fire at the Royal Shakespeare Theatre. Isn't Andrea in Stratford? We have to go to England! Oh, here it is, listen—"

"We've just received word that there has been a fire in the world-renowned Royal Shakespeare Theatre. We don't know yet the extent of the damage or whether there are injuries. We will keep you posted as we obtain the details."

"Oh, no, George. What if she's hurt? I don't want to wait to find out. She might be frightened. I need to know she's okay."

"Call her, Annie."

"I did. It went straight to voicemail. I have to see her. Don't you want to see her, George?"

"Of course I do, but we will find out if something is wrong, you know. She's not alone."

"I don't care; I don't trust them. Let's go!"

My father thought for a minute while watching the tears fall from my mother's eyes. She stared at him with a frightening intensity, as though waiting for him to decide my fate.

"Alright, Annie, let's go to England. I'll call the hospital and make arrangements for my patients. In the meantime, please keep calling Andy. Can you get us tickets?"

"What? Of course I can. Go take care of your work." Of course, she couldn't. My mother had no idea where to start. My father knew that, but he often played this game to get her to learn new things. She turned on her computer and, with quaking fingers, entered "planes to England" in the search bar. But as always happened when my mom used the Internet, she gave up after seeing too many choices. She wanted just one answer to pop up so she could click the mouse three times, say "there's no place like Stratford," and arrive at her destination. But as everyone above the age of two knows and appreciates, the magic of the Internet is the quantity of information it provides. Therefore, instead of picking one or several from the variety of options, she picked up the phone and called her well-traveled friend Sally for step-by-step instructions on how to travel to England on a moment's notice.

"George, I got us tickets. They were two thousand dollars, but we're on a flight that leaves in three hours."

"Two thousand dollars?"

"Is that unusual?"

"Yes, yes it is. Keep searching."

"Oops, no can do. I bought them already. Sally said it's more expensive when you book last minute."

"You don't say. Okay, honey. Three hours? We have to leave soon!"

"That's okay, I have two bags already packed."

"What?"

"Yeah, I didn't know if we would want to go, so I packed bags and stuck them in the closet."

"That probably explains my missing blue sweater. Honey, where are we going to stay?"

"Oh, crap, I forgot about that."

"And we need to get to Stratford from London. Do you know how to do that?"

"No, but I thought you could figure it out en route. You're always using your phone for that stuff."

"Annie, did you call Andrea again?"

"We can try her again on the way there. Let's go. We're going to miss the flight!"

My father was furious, but his fury paled in comparison to my mother's hysteria. He changed his clothes and followed her out the door. On the way to the airport, he made numerous calls trying to book a place to stay and figure out how to get to Stratford when they arrived. Luckily for them, my parents lived close to the airport, so time was not an issue. But security was.

"We all have to take our shoes off? What type of place is this?"

"Annie, don't make a fuss. You'll get us in trouble."

"Okay, I just don't understand why I have to take my shoes off."

"In case you're hiding something in them."

"Huh? People do that?"

"Put your bags with your shoes on the machine, Annie."

"I don't want to, George. What if someone else takes them on the other side? I want to watch them as they go through."

"No one will take them. Annie, you have to abide by what these people tell you. This is serious business and now we're holding up the line."

As expected, security picked up my mother's toddler-sized travel bag and motioned to her. "Come with us, Miss."

"Not without my husband."

"Annie, go with them. I will wait for you here."

My father had set off the security alarm three times, having failed to remove the change from his pockets, the belt from his pants, and the metal case on his belt loop in which he kept his cell phone. My mother continued her protest as security took her into a room where they stuck their gloved hands in her bag and tossed away lotion after lotion.

"You can't take bottles of liquid this large on a plane," they said.

"What? Why?" she asked.

"And you can't take scissors, either."

"They're part of my first aid kit."

"Is that a lighter?"

"Yes. I need it to light my candle in case the battery in my flashlight dies."

"Have you ever flown before?"

"No, why?"

"No reason. Look, Miss, we're taking the scissors, the candle, the lighter and the flashlight."

The security officer continued to sift through the bottomless pit that was my mother's carry-on, as well as her earthquake survival kit, her first-aid kit, and her caught-in-a-mine-with-a-serial-killer kit.

"Christ, lady, is that pepper spray? You can't take this on board."

"Can't I check it in my luggage, officer?"

"You could have, but there's no time now. Let's move it along."

Once the security agents finally let my mom go, she met back up with my dad, her carry-on a solid ten pounds lighter than when she began and her ego equally deflated.

"George, they took my pepper spray."

"Of course they did, honey. You can't bring that on board. We should have put it in your luggage. Anyway, we'll get more if we need to."

I am more grateful for having been 5,000 miles from that spectacle than I am for the invention of coffee and men like George Clooney. I would have experienced a shame similar to that of showing up to junior high wearing only a training bra and granny panties. Ironically — or expectedly, in my family — I was enduring a similar humiliation. Concurrent to my mother's run-in with the authorities, I was having one of my own.

Chapter Twenty

Sirens blaring, four policemen arrived at the Royal Shakespeare Theatre, dressed as they do in the movies: navy blue jackets buttoned up to the fold of their chins; shiny silver badges pinned to their left lapels; matching loose-fitting pants stuffed into tight black boots laced up to their knees; thin, silly-looking black hats rising three feet above their heads; and long sticks rocking back and forth at their sides in the holsters that American policemen use to stow guns.

"What's all this, then?" they asked, surveying the scene.

I watched the bobbies (a British term for policemen I had learned while anxiously waiting to be hauled away by one) question everyone present and contemplated how I would explain what had happened while biting through my fingernails (which was unfortunate because, as I looked down at my fully-formed nails, I realized it had been many days since I engaged in that anxious behavior). From afar, the interviews appeared to last thirty seconds and all concluded with a finger pointed at me. The police finally followed the fingers in my direction.

I explained that I had been startled by the cannon fire, and then explained the succeeding domino effect of absurdities (leaving out the 26 years of parental angst underpinning my paranoia).

"No one else was startled at the cannon, officer? Really?" I asked.

"Well it wasn't a genuine cannon, was it?"

The policemen requested copies of my pictures and walked away from me slowly, their heads shaking. It was exactly how I imagined my parents would react if I were to tell them about this incident, minus their inevitable "I told you so." Hence, I didn't plan to tell them.

The damage to the theater was minor, especially in contrast to what could have been. I heard someone say he could have it "properly fixed in days." If only my feelings had fared as well. I was grief-stricken: another shoot up in flames, this time literally. I walked around trying to apologize to *Hamlet's* cast and crew even though uttering the word *sorry* seemed shallow and unhelpful. But lacking a general contracting license or a time machine, it was all I could think to do. A few of them appreciated the sentiment but many were too angry to listen; after all, as one of the actors so bluntly reminded me, "sorry won't fix our theatre now, will it?" About the time my apologies became more annoying than thoughtful, I joined the boys to go back to the hotel.

"You okay, Andy?" Harry asked.

"Huh? What?" I was in a daze, ignoring the people and the splendor surrounding me.

"Andy, you alright?"

"Oh, bloody fantastic, as you would say. I'm going to bed. Are you two okay?"

"We're fine, Andrea. Why don't we go shoot the cathedral?"

"What? No. Not today. Maybe tomorrow. Let's leave it standing for one more day."

"Oh, Andy, don't be so hard on yourself."

I looked through Harry, my eyes glazed over.

"You know what Shakespeare would say?"

"I don't know, Rob, something like, I much prefer it if you didn't burn down my theatre," I replied.

"Well, maybe. But also, what's past cure is still past care."

"I really don't know what you said. And I don't understand your behavior. You both are acting like nothing happened."

"Well, we're fine, aren't we? No one was harmed—"

"And life goes on, doesn't it?" Harry added.

I couldn't recover as quickly as Rob and Harry could. Without so much as a wave goodbye, I walked into my room and started changing before the door had time to close behind me. I longed to be comfortable. My skin felt too tight, like I had stuffed myself into a dress two sizes too small. I threw on baggy pants and a tent of a T-shirt — attire that wouldn't cling to me if I gained a hundred pounds. I fell onto my bed and stared at the ceiling. I turned on the telly, but my eyes didn't focus — or were too focused for me to see the big picture.

I stared through the screen and wondered why my trip had turned into a comedy of errors. Why couldn't I get a shoot right? Why was I fulfilling the prophecy that I couldn't do anything without my parents' or Brandon's help? What would I do to turn this trip around? Be a better photographer? Through the limited view of a thumbnail thus far, my pictures were turning out great, including the *Hamlet* rehearsal. What I still lacked was confidence (beyond the lens) and bravery. I had come to England to become strong and self sufficient — but how?

I reflected on the people in my life who exemplified grace under pressure. Brandon was at ease with the world in a way I had always admired. Sure, he was overprotective of me, but he was comfortable in his own life. I recalled the evening we had spent together when Los Angeles had a large earthquake. After the initial quake had subsided, Brandon calmly moved around the house: he grabbed a flashlight, turned off the gas, scooped up his cat, and relocated us to a safer environment. I sat in the doorway, paralyzed aside from my trembling, as useless as Weight Watchers to a supermodel, waiting for Brandon to save me. And then there was Harry and his actions during the fire: I saw him again in slow motion, expertly taking care of everyone and everything with time to spare, never losing an ounce of composure. I wanted to be like Harry. I wanted to be stress-free, assured of my abilities, impervious to the countless possibilities for failure, danger, or harm. Picturing how I wished I were like Harry, I realized I wanted to be *with* Harry. Maybe his nonchalance would be infectious. Would I be able to catch confidence? What about self-adoration? Were these traits contagious? I hoped so. I got up out of bed and tiptoed down the hall. No real reason for the tiptoe, other than the subconscious thought that I should hide what I was doing from someone.

The light from Harry's room shone under the door, casting a shadow in the hall. I walked closer and heard laughter. I thought it was the television. I tried to distinguish the voices on the TV from Harry's. Was he with someone? I heard a girl's voice. But I soon heard her singing. I heard a man's voice. Was he with a man? The man started singing too. A familiar tune — *Mamma Mia!* He was watching *Mamma Mia!* I heard laughter from another voice. It was Rob. Just Rob and Harry and a late-night viewing of a mediocre play portrayed miserably on the big screen. Rob came to the door to let me in.

"Hey guys, can I come in? Can't sleep."

"Come in, darling. You alright?" asked Harry.

"Lonely."

"Did you try calling Brandon?" asked Rob.

"No. I can't talk to him."

"You could've been hurt."

"I know that, thanks. But I don't want to explain that... I failed... again."

"You didn't fail," said Harry. "You got us good shots."

"I also got *Hamlet* postponed for a week so they can rebuild the stage. Oh, and the special effects guy? He'll need a week too... for his sprains to heal."

"See how well that worked out," Harry said, trying to lighten the mood. "You really are just so down on yourself. You got some fantastic photos."

"I know. I don't know how that keeps happening." I had still been shooting when the fire erupted, before my brain caught up and I realized the place could burn down. Apparently one can capture interesting and photogenic facial expressions from people who think their lives are in danger. The magic of catching one moment in time on film is that it doesn't matter what other moments are happening around it. Merely looking at a snapshot of my day, no one would know that I helped set the stage on fire just moments before, or that minutes later firefighters would swarm the theater and douse it with water to save it from devastation.

"It keeps happening because you're a good photographer," Harry added.

"I can take a picture, yes, but I'm also getting lucky. And unlucky."

"Welcome to life, Andy. That's how it works... for us all."

"Harry's right. And Brandon's there to comfort you. He won't judge you."

"I don't understand this, Rob. Do you know him?"

"What? Huh? No, of course not. Don't be daft. I just think you wouldn't be in a relationship with someone who would judge you."

I tried to process Rob's words. True, Brandon wouldn't judge me. But he would know how much trouble I was having. And he'd worry. He'd think I couldn't be independent. He'd think that when I got home I would need to install padding on the walls.

"Would you feel better if you called your mum?" asked Harry.

"I don't know. I just don't want to prove them right — that without a leash, dog tags, and an ankle bracelet, I'm doomed to fall prey to a catastrophe. My god, if I tell them there was a fire, my father will create some sort of extinguisher belt and have it surgically sewn to my body."

"Sexy."

"Do they have an issue with fires?" asked Rob.

"I can't even get into it. Harry, can I stay in here?"

"Sure you can, luv. Rob, you want to stay too, have a bit of a sleepover?"

Like a teenager cockblocked from his chosen babe, Rob threw his hands down, pushed himself up, said no, and briskly stormed out, slamming the door behind him.

"What's up his bum?" I asked.

"His bum?"

"Yeah, I'm trying to fit in."

"I think his bum is fine. He's just knackered."

"Knack—?"

"Tired."

"Got it."

I lay down in bed next to Harry, keeping a friendly distance. He continued to exude a subtle scent of Irish Spring. We watched television, late-night *Seinfeld* reruns.

"Are these new here? Do you want me to tell you what happens?" I joked.

"Oh, sod off," he said, lightheartedly smacking my arm, a move I reciprocated and which slowly evolved into a back and forth play fight.

Laughing at Jerry and lying with Harry was an instant panacea. It was easy. I was comfortable. Happy. And when the room went dark, I was shaking. I felt exactly as I had the first time I hooked up with a guy my freshman year of high school: feelings of ecstasy and apprehension jumping in and out of my body. And, similar to high school, when I waited patiently for Jeff's embrace, too timid and unsure to make a move of my own, I deliberated whether I would turn away if he did.

"Goodnight, luv," said Harry. I heard the rustling of sheets and I felt him move in toward me. The minty scent grew stronger as his lips came toward my face. A lump developed in my throat and the anxiety was palpable. I felt his breath hit my nose. *This can't happen.* I tucked in my chin and moved my head back slightly. He kissed me squarely on the forehead and turned over. A thick cloak of silence covered the room.

Facing away from Harry, I lay wide awake. *Was he going to kiss me? Was I going to kiss him? If we had kissed, what would have happened next? He's probably a good kisser, he's so tender. Wait, it doesn't matter. Brandon, I love Brandon. I really do love Brandon. And if I don't, I need to break up with him. Would one kiss be considered cheating?* My willpower around Harry was growing thin, and my head was clouded with visions of me perishing in flames — which, contrary to my normal delusions of disaster, could actually have happened that day. But I wasn't the cheating kind. I looked back over toward Harry; the moon's light, peeking through an open sliver of the curtain, hit his hair. *Why doesn't his hair move when he sleeps?* He was like a robot programmed to be the perfect man. But he wasn't perfect. He was convenient.

****

"Oi, Brandon. She's staying in Harry's room tonight."

"Hello? Who's this?"

"It's James Bond."

"Huh?"

"Who do you think it is? It's Rob. Andrea's in Harry's room."

"Wait, what? Are you joking?"

"Do you know *anything* about comedy? How would that be funny?"

"It wouldn't."

"Right."

"What's she doing in Harry's room?"

"Don't know. Sleeping, hopefully. He invited me to stay too."

"Okay, would've been nice if you'd stuck that detail in earlier. Why is she in there?"

"Well, you see, there was this fire—"

"A fire? What? What the hell's going on?"

"It's a tad crazy. I'm sure she'll tell you."

"I wouldn't be so sure. Is she okay?"

"Yeah, she's okay."

"Why didn't she call me? Did she say?"

"She's embarrassed."

"Embarrassed?"

"Well, she sort of *caused* the fire, didn't she?"

"I don't know, did she?"

"Sort of. So she feels like a failure, doesn't she?"

"I don't know, does she?"

"She does."

"Why aren't you helping her more?"

"I can't stop the world from spinning, you know."

"I know. But a fire? Christ, couldn't you have stopped it?"

"Yes, I suppose I could have, had I been born with the ability to see the future. But alas, you hired a copywriter, not a fortune teller."

"It just feels like you could have done *something*."

"I did. I let Andrea be Andrea. And you know what? It worked. We survived a calamity that could have happened to anyone, and we got some amazing photos."

"Yeah, okay. Think I can call her now?"

"Ooh, I wouldn't disturb them."

"WHAT?!"

"Well they're sleeping, aren't they?"

"I don't know, are they?"

"Right, must teach you the art of the rhetorical question."

"Or, you can just make a statement. Anyway, thanks for the call, Rob."

"Yep. No problem, Brandon. Cheers."

****

Just as I was knocking on sleep's door, the light from my phone signaling a call caught my attention; it was Brandon. Something must be wrong, I thought. He had calculated the time difference accurately many times before and it was much too late for a "what's up" conversation. I answered it right away.

"Hey, you ok?" I whispered, trying not to wake Harry; but failing.

"Yes, I'm fine. You alright?" Harry replied.

"Shush," I said to Harry, but Brandon replied. "Why are you shushing me?"

"I wasn't, I was, uh, sneezing. Are you, is everything okay?"

"I just told you I'm fine," Harry repeated before he turned toward me and noticed I was on the phone. "Oh, blimey, sorry," he whispered.

"Yeah, I'm okay. I just thought I'd call and say hi," Brandon said.

"At this hour, Brandon?"

"Hiya, Brandon," Harry said, before I cupped his mouth and shook my head, "no."

"Who's that?" Brandon asked.

"Who's what? Oh, can you hear the TV? You know I watch TV when I fall asleep. Why are you calling so late?"

"Just wondering what you're up to."

"Sleeping. What else would I be up to?"

"Nothing, nothing. I didn't think you were doing anything. I just thought you're normally up at this hour. So... where are the boys?"

"What, Brandon? Sleeping. We're all sleeping. Goodnight."

"Okay. But let me tell you one more thing—"

"Yes, Brandon?"

"I love you."

"Me too, goodnight."

I hung up the phone feeling like a two-timing philanderer. Harry and I hadn't done anything, but I was sure there was no eloquent, innocent way to say, "don't worry babe, I'm just in bed with the hottest guy in England, possibly Europe, to be comforted after escaping the fire I started."

"Well that's unfortunate," Harry said. "Next time I have to be hidden from someone's boyfriend, I hope I get a shag out of it."

"Ha, ha. That's not helpful. You know this would have been tough to explain."

"Of course, luv. Night, night."

The loud creak of a showerhead resounding through the room shook me out of slumber and, thankfully, a horrible nightmare: I was sword-fighting on the roof of a burning building. The structure weakened below me as I stepped closer to the edge, throwing my sword left to right until my only choices were to jump to a neighboring rooftop or stay and fight a knife-wielding, 300-pound sorceress. I awoke with a heavy heart. That any thought of betraying Brandon had fluttered through my head, for even the duration of a tweet, was sickening. I was thrilled and relieved that I had done nothing wrong, that I hadn't acted rash or stupid despite my loneliness and despite my sadness. *How did Harry get up so early without an alarm clock?* I thought further about my robot theory as I left his room.

I took a long shower, savoring the feel of the hot water and the peace that accompanied it. I enjoyed a large cup of coffee and a scone. I had learned to appreciate scones as bagel stand-ins. I walked downstairs to meet the boys for a quick walk to the cathedral on our way out of Stratford and found Rob still in mid-tantrum.

"Have a good night then, kids?" he said in a grumpy, sarcastic manner, as if we had gone to a party and left him at home to babysit a Pekingese.

I couldn't comprehend his immature, passive-aggressive behavior. What was he so angry about? He hadn't been left out of anything; he was invited to stay in Harry's room too. And what did he care? People generally act that way for one reason: jealousy.

Oh. My. God. Rob fancies me, I thought. *Wait, does Rob fancy me?* Holy shit! That must be it — he does. Why hadn't I seen it before? I thought back and analyzed the signs: he continually pulled me away from Harry; he wouldn't let me be alone; he wouldn't hit on other women. But then he didn't actually hit on me either, I didn't think. It was hard to tell because Rob was just generally awkward. And he was always reminding me to call Brandon. Then again, maybe that was a sly way of detecting whether I was still in love with Brandon or ready to move on.

Harry, not willing to play Rob's games, replied as if Rob's question had been genuine. "It was pleasant, yeah. Slept like a baby."

"And you, Andy?"

"Barely a wink."

"Oh, is Harry a snorer?"

"No." *Of course not, only mortals snore.* "Just thinking a lot. Glad to be alive today."

"Oh, don't be so dramatic," Rob said.

"You know what, I'll meet you both at the train after I take shots of the cathedral. I wanna be alone."

"You sure you'll be okay?" asked Harry.

"Yeah, it's morning. There are people around. I'm fine."

Rob and Harry went to have a "spot of tea" at the station while I wandered off to snap the cathedral. With questions about Rob and Harry swirling around my psyche, I didn't want to see either of them. I wanted some time to be with only me, my lens, and my target.

The Holy Trinity Cathedral was a remarkable structure alongside the river Avon, nestled in foliage and swaddled with trees resembling weeping willows. Like the other cathedrals I had seen on my trip, its exterior consisted of a camel-beige tower with an old English clock, topped with a pointed spire that extended high above the square building. A copious configuration of stained-glass windows, all retelling the story of the life and loss of Jesus Christ, lined the interior walls in colors more luminous than a new rainbow cascading over a valley after a storm. Marble columns and arched walkways supported the colossally high ceilings and a huge organ made up the second story along the back wall, providing the soundtrack for the churchgoing public. Unique to the Holy Trinity was William Shakespeare's grave and the accompanying shrine: a large, cordoned-off section of the main hall with a decorative wooden tomb, candles, and statues of the literary master.

The shoot went fine, considering it consisted of an immobile 13th-century landmark; it would have been exceedingly difficult to ruin that one. I walked around to several nearby parts of the city to snap the cathedral against its lush landscape and admire its venerable beauty — but I with less animation than the inanimate object itself. I had spent the last few days in one of the most splendid, charming little towns I'd ever hoped to set foot in, and during most of it I had felt like a lonely failure. I was sad: sad that I had let myself destroy my only few days, perhaps ever, in Stratford-upon-Avon. But since I had watched the Royal Shakespeare Theatre and possibly my career and relationship go up in flames, owing only to my cowardly ways, I was eager to leave the city I was coming to view as an unlucky hex to find what awaited me in our next destination: Oxford, Oxfordshire County, England.

Chapter Twenty-One

"You know, George, the damage to the theater doesn't look that bad," my mother said as she and my father sat in Stratford-upon-Avon's train station, watching the news on a television anchored to the wall.

"Yeah, you're right, it really doesn't. That's a relief. I'm curious how close Andrea was to it, though."

"Hopefully not too close. I think I've been pretty clear about fire danger."

My parents continued to watch the screen, hoping for additional information, but the volume was muted. Consequently, they discussed what a shame it was that such a magnificent theater was now cordoned off with police tape and condemned, while blissfully ignorant of the cause.

"So, George, how are we going to find her?"

"Let me look, her location must be in one of her emails." My dad flipped through email after email on his phone. "Oh no, it looks like she's leaving Stratford this morning to go to Oxford."

"Honey, it looks like she's leaving right now," my mother said.

"How do you know that, Annie?" my father said, his nose still buried in his cell phone.

"Because, she's right there. George, oh, George!" my mother said, hitting my father on the arm and beginning her customary panic.

My parents had arrived in Stratford at the same time I was leaving for Oxford.

"Oh hell, really?"

"What do we do?" she asked, scanning the station for a place to hide.

"Let's go behind that wall, wait for her to board. When they start walking back to their seats, we'll sneak on." They scurried across the room and cowered behind a wall, like thieves who've spotted the police on their tail — thieves with large, clumsy luggage, that is.

As I stepped onto the train with Rob and Harry, my parents studied my maneuvers, waiting to creep out and board at the last possible moment.

The conductor yelled the final call while my parents were examining the train, working out where they could go and remain incognito.

"It looks like they took seats in the back. Okay, let's go. Let's go now!"

They started to run for the train, but my father stopped short. My mother's momentum was too powerful and her focus too intense to notice that he had stopped, so she smacked right into him, knocking her luggage over. "Shit, sorry, George," she said as she fumbled to pick her luggage back up.

"Wait, Andrea's walking forward."

"Honey, we have to get on or we'll miss it."

I had turned back, thinking I had dropped my coat, but noticed that Rob was holding it.

"No, she's going back. We're okay. Let's go."

My parents made it onto the train seconds before the doors closed. They fell into the closest seats, exhausted from the ordeal and unable to stand against the swaying of the train leaving the station.

"Wow, that was a close one," my father said.

"I know," my mother responded. "This is not going to be easy. But at least we know she made it through the fire."

Chapter Twenty-Two

Oxford. Merely pronouncing the word requires an uppity, over-emphasized English accent. *Ox-fid. Ox-fud.* I tried saying it several times but couldn't do it without pretending I was British. And from the moment my left foot met my right stepping off the train there, I could tell it was a distinguished, classic city that deserved the respect of the accent it nurtured. Its indoor equivalent would be a large parlor room in an old mansion with dark oak lining the walls, burgundy sofas, and ornate antique furnishings placed atop a richly colored floral rug.

As a result of starting a fire in a globally revered theater, taking pictures of people wanted dead or alive by The Beatles, and catapulting Robin Hood from a tree, in Oxford, I would shoot nothing with a pulse. I stuck to my itinerary, which included Oxford Castle, built in approximately 1071; provided it didn't crumble to the ground from decay the day I shot it, it was the ideal target.

En route to the castle, feeling somewhat melancholy about not divulging my full experience to Brandon, I called him.

"Hey honey, so glad you called. How's it going?" He again sounded genuinely appreciative that I had thought to call him.

"Okay. A bit crazy."

"Crazy, how?"

"Oh, I don't know. Not sure if I got any usable pictures in Stratford."

"I find that hard to believe."

"Oh, thanks Bran. I don't know, I was trying to shoot a Shakespeare rehearsal and, well… I just don't know if it went okay." As per usual, I had overthought the conversation before it happened and couldn't come clean. I was embarrassed and humiliated. I had failed and was too proud to tell him. Or I was too proud to tell me. Who was I trying to impress? I knew Brandon was similar to Harry, calm in a crisis situation. But this was a crisis situation about me, and I was far from home. Very far from home. I couldn't decide whether he would be easygoing and calm me down, or become more anxious than I was and make it worse. I became certain that Brandon would take the next flight to England for a rescue mission. What I wanted him to say was that it would get better. That I would do better. But I didn't know whether those were the words he'd use to comfort me. So I continued to speak to him with shallow language — "it's all fine" — to disguise my continual mishaps and my true feelings.

"Well, I'm sure your photos came out better than you think."

"Yeah, maybe. I miss you, Brandon." It was a phrase that felt good to get off my chest. It was true; I missed him with every ounce of my being. And I was glad that I felt that way — that was how I was supposed to feel. If I didn't miss him, I might have had to exchange the "not now" for a "not ever," and I hadn't at all decided that that was the route I wanted to take.

"You too, sweetie." *Darn, I should have told him.*

I hung up not only wishing I had told him about my trip but also hoping for the things I was embarrassed about to stop happening; then there would be nothing for him to save me from. I had to continue to focus on what was crucial: my pictures. I had a portfolio of England to continue creating, and I was determined to take award-winners. I looked at my surroundings and succumbed to them. I began shooting everything I saw, maybe to include in the magazine or maybe for personal benefit. It didn't matter. My inspiration and determination increased in proportion to the number of pictures I snapped.

We strolled through Christ Church University, part of the Oxford University conglomeration of buildings. I looked at it with astonishment; the word *wow* dove continually from my mouth without prompting or forethought. I had been fortunate to attend a college with a pretty campus; it was clean, with old brick buildings and natural life; it was lovely. But it wasn't stately. Christ Church looked intelligent, like you had to have invented something just to be entitled to fill out the application. There were long one- and two-story biscuit-colored buildings set in a square surrounding a massive, immaculately cared-for lawn. The tops of the buildings had a fluted trim, like an archetypical castle, with rows of rectangular windows, some rounded and some triangular at the apex. The middle building of one of the long ones stretched up to a tower with a rounded dome capping it off at its zenith. I had never before seen a picture of such a glorious building, nor had I visited anything in the same hemisphere of magnificence.

As we toured the campus, Harry reminisced about his college days.

"Harry, I can't believe you went here," I said, my jaw maintaining its open, awestruck position through the tour.

"You know, Oxford isn't the be-all, end-all of universities. We have plenty of nice ones in England," said Rob, defensively.

"I know, Rob, and I'm sure yours was lovely. But this is absolutely unreal."

"You know, I notice it now, but I really didn't think about it while I was here," Harry said. "It was college. We had to study. We had to figure out who we were. We hadn't the wherewithal to stop our shenanigans, look around, and say, 'now that's a spectacular building.'"

With such short attention spans and a preoccupation with socializing and the opposite sex, the young don't often study the buildings through which they pass. Except me. I've been enamored with photography since I was ten; even then, I often paused to scrutinize a building or examine a rose bush. On school field trips, I was always the one holding up the class. *Andrea, I know you want to take pictures, but you have to keep up.* My desire to take pictures often battled my fear of being left behind... and it sometimes won. At parties, I was an annoying little fly, buzzing around people's heads, constantly flashing photos. *Andrea, just go one night without a camera, please! You're like Big Brother!* I couldn't do it, or rather I wouldn't. What would I miss if I stopped snapping? What would I want to remember later in life? If any of my friends ever ran for public office, though, I'd have to host a picture-burning bonfire.

After I finished drooling over the University and the surrounding city streets, silently cursing my parents for birthing me in America, we came upon Oxford Castle, a proper medieval castle. Up close it looked exactly like I had imagined all castles would, before I came to England and laid my eyes on the variety of them. It wasn't glamorous like Nottingham but more prison-like, like the Tower of London. It had taupe-colored brick walls stacked like a winning Jenga pile, as though the removal of one block would cause the rest to come tumbling down. Naturally, my mind wandered to the place we Californians cannot seem to avoid when faced with any building (or piece of furniture, or vase, or glass of water too close to the edge of a table) that appears the slightest bit rickety: earthquakes. If an earthquake were to occur at Oxford Castle, we'd perish for sure. I doubted the structure would withstand even a small one. I had no idea whether England sat on or near fault lines, though. I looked around briefly for what I might duck under or run to in the event of a quake before realizing that it was an exercise in futility; I was powerless in the event of a tremor. But rather than dwell on the unlikely and unpreventable, I knew to move on, buoyed by the hope and likelihood that it wouldn't occur. Dwelling on all of life's possible catastrophes was becoming a thing of my past. I walked along the castle snapping pictures, some directly of the building and some through the thin rectangular openings in the side wall, which I imagine had been used to insert cannons and fire arrows during wartime.

"Did you call your parents, luv? It seems like it's been some time, hasn't it?"

"Harry, why are you always reminding me to call my folks?"

"I don't know. Maybe because I didn't have parents that really cared growing up and I think you should take advantage of the fact that you do."

"Well, first off, I think I do. But sometimes I think I'd be smarter or more worldly or something if I'd grown up without parents."

"No, you'd feel unloved. I grew up unbelievably envious of my friends who had close relationships with their parents. To know there is someone who is always looking out for you is a treasure, Andy. You should thank them every day that they bother to love you enough to annoy the shite out of you."

In what had become typical Rob fashion, Rob jumped in with a comment about my boyfriend. "He's right, Andy. And you not only have parents who think the world of you but Brandon too. From everything you've said, you have a right protector in him, don't you?"

"I don't want a protector. I want a partner. I don't want chaperones. I want parents. None of them will allow me to grow up. You want to know why I didn't tell Brandon about the fire? Because he'd be on the next flight to the UK."

"Maybe. But what's wrong with that inclination?" Harry asked.

"Nothing's wrong with that *inclination*. It's the *action* that's the problem. I would rather hear him say, 'babe, if you want me there, I'll be on the first flight out. But I know you can do this on your own. You're doing a great job.'"

"How do you know he won't say that?" Rob asked.

"Because I know him. And my parents, man, if they knew about the fire, I'd be locked away in my room for the rest of my life, allowed only to the bathroom."

"Well, maybe the kitchen too, to be fair," said Rob.

"Oh, no, not the kitchen. Fires happen in there."

"They just love you," Harry said. "Maybe they don't love you the way you want them to; but you can't decide *how* they love you. Sometimes you just have to be glad *that* they love you."

I didn't agree; for our relationship to work, my parents had to love me in a way that worked for us all. But Harry and Rob didn't understand my suffocation — how could they? Their lives were so drastically different. Regardless, Rob and Harry made enough sense for their advice to stick.

"Okay, I'll call them."

After completing a circle around the castle, I sauntered away from the boys to find a bench. While meandering, I looked out at the world and saw the wisps of bright, white clouds strewn across the sky like cotton balls spread into Halloween cobwebs; I snapped a picture of the exquisite setting and found peace.

Chapter Twenty-Three

My parents had been walking around Oxford Castle, continuing sur-veillance for Operation Andrea, as I took pictures. They hadn't a care for the grandeur of the building or the landscape; their eyes focused solely on me.

"She looks good. Her hair's a little frizzy, though," said my mother. "I can't believe you forgot the binoculars, George. I'm dying to see what Harry looks like up close."

"Well, I can't believe you didn't put them in the bags you packed weeks before we left."

They took seats on a nearby bench beneath the trees, keeping a safe distance from the castle to monitor my situation.

"Wait, she's walking away from the castle. Where's she going?"

"Oh my god, she's coming this way. To these benches!"

"Honey, quick, go into the castle."

"We can't. We'll lose her."

My parents looked around for a place to take cover as I walked in their direction, but they were in an open space.

"Let's go over to that park. We can hide behind a tree."

"Hide behind a tree? Annie, I'm 6'4", 280."

"Hmm. Look, there's some brush over there. We can duck behind it."

Chapter Twenty-Four

I sat down on the bench, took a deep breath, and dialed my parents' home line, figuring it was early enough to catch them before they left for work. They didn't pick up, though; I got their answering machine. I called a second time and again got the machine. I knew their routine. They should have been home. Concerned, I called my mother's cell phone.

Chapter Twenty-Five

My mother jumped up when she heard her phone ring. "Oh, crap, George, that's Andrea," she whispered. "What if she hears our phone?"

"There's a lot of people around. It could be anyone's phone. Andrea knows we're always home at this hour. You have to answer it. She'll worry."

"I don't know what to say. You answer it."

"Annie, it's your cell phone. Answer it."

Chapter Twenty-Six

"Oh, Andy, hello! You're not hurt, are you?" my mother asked, faintly.

"What? I can't hear you," I said. "Why are you whispering?"

"Oh, I uh, I have a sore throat. I asked if you're hurt."

Her first words to me after I had not spoken to her in days. Not "how's it going?" or "we miss you," but rather whether I was injured.

"No, mom, I'm not hurt. Why didn't you answer your home phone?"

"Oh, it's, um, it's not working. So you're staying safe?"

"Yes, mom, I am. And I'm getting some very lovely pictures."

"Oh, that's great. How's Harry? Anything happening there?"

"What? I have a boyfriend. Brandon, mom. I'm still with Brandon."

"Oh, I know. I just thought—"

"Don't you want to know how the shoots are going?"

"You told me already. You're getting lovely pictures, you said."

"Yeah, okay. Can I talk with dad?"

"Sure, honey. Stay safe. And have fun while you're there. Don't worry about Brandon."

Every time I spoke with my mother she made less sense to me. But talking with my father was a relief. We spoke for about fifteen minutes, during which time I provided him with more detail than my mother had requested about where we were and what we had seen, thrilled that he cared about my career and wanted to hear about England's majesty.

"It sounds like a wonderful trip, darling. Where are you off to next?"

"Bath."

"Oh, when are you going?"

"Tomorrow."

"And how will you get there?"

"By train."

"Oh, fantastic. Is it an easy route?"

"Yeah, everything's pretty easy to figure out here. Besides, Harry and Rob know the geography well."

"Great. How long do you think it will take?"

"What? Dad, what's with the questions?"

"Oh, nothing. I just like to know what you're up to."

"Okay, well, I have to go now. Love you."

I hung up and walked back over to the boys.

"You didn't tell them, did you?" Harry asked, offering me a cheese sandwich while snacking on one of his own.

"Nah, I didn't want to frighten them." And they would never change their opinion about me if I never gave them reason to. Harry and Rob shook their heads in displeasure, but I knew better than to allow my parents to be right about the fire.

After a lazy afternoon spent discussing the status of our trip and how we would present it in the magazine, we went back to the castle. Lit up at night, covered by shadows, it was both haunting and striking. Although the shadows created an eerie ambience, they also made for some spectacular pictures. I was sorry I hadn't spent more time at the previous landmarks at night, examining their auras as illuminated by the evening's hues. We had gone out for a quick drink after the photos, but I turned in early. As I drifted off into slumber, I thought about how Rob and Harry had grown up sans parents and the consequences that had had on their lives. Harry didn't worry about anything; he loved everything, as he had never learned to be selective. Rob, well, he didn't know how to love. And me, with suffocating parents, I was too scared to love. Was there anyone who had it right, I wondered?

I awoke early the next morning and sent some pictures to the ladies in London for them to continue assembling, with a list of which landmarks we would feature and how we could arrange them. The email, addressed only to Claire, read: *Please be careful with these; you're probably the best person to handle them.* I would ultimately do some editing work using Photoshop and

Illustrator, but to ensure the ladies did not become experts on *EastEnders*, their favorite soap opera, I had to keep them occupied.

I spent the remainder of the morning enjoying the brisk air on my face and sharing the time with my good friends: a cup of coffee, a book, and a daydream. *What if I just stayed in England?* England was stimulating. It was a photographer's dream. Regal surroundings at every turn and stylish people in well-fitted coats and tailored boots, eating at cafés — well, in London, anyway. Outside of London, there were quite a few mingers, a word I had learned from Harry and Rob for unattractive folks. Similar to what I had found in the United States, outside of a cosmopolitan city people appeared to care less about fitness and fashion and more about comfort. Of course, most people, whether or not they are conventionally beautiful, have unique characteristics that are fascinating to capture on film. But Londoners were so stunning and the city so vibrant that I believed I could live there. I was putting down my book to succumb to my daydream and feel the warmth of the coffee lining my throat when I saw Rob and Harry walking up the road to join me. My dreams turned to a few short-lived flashes of living in London with Harry — that is, if he would stop nagging me to call home. I wondered if I could live without Brandon if it meant not returning to my parents.

I thought about Rob, too. His mood had changed dramatically since the night I spent in Harry's room. Maybe he did have a crush on me. Maybe he was lonely and just *thought* he fancied me. And what had I been doing in Harry's room anyway? I hadn't done anything other than permit a few untoward thoughts to play around in my mind, but that I had even thought about kissing someone while I was in a relationship with Brandon was gut-wrenching. It felt like an emotional affair, albeit a half-assed and one-sided one. I wasn't certain whether my feelings for Harry were genuine or whether I just felt them by virtue of being away from Brandon, and so close to someone so goddamn good-looking with an accent that could melt butter in the polar ice caps (dammit, there I went again). I understood why so many actors screwed their co-stars while away on a movie set, regardless of the adoring partner waiting for them at home. It was loneliness causing a void, and coupled, for me, with the possibility that that void could be filled by someone as attractive and charming as Harry. But I didn't take Harry up on it and I was confident — nearly confident — that I wouldn't if given the opportunity. Three more months, though. Was I playing with the fire my mother was so sure would kill me?

I consistently felt guilty about the series of half-truths I had told Brandon about what was actually happening in England, the sheer volume of screw-ups and mishaps due either to my personal failures or to the eloquent idiom "shit happens." I wasn't giving him the chance to support me. My parents — well, I knew what they would say, how they would react. With Brandon, I was merely projecting and guessing. My head was too crowded with rhetorical questions and *what if* scenarios. While my daydreams teased of a permanent life in England, my rational side conjured up an alternate scenario: *maybe I should leave now.* I thought about calling it quits and going back to the studio to snap photos of color-coordinated families, or being brave in an easier way and capturing celebrities leaving Los Angeles nightclubs, hoping to get the crucial scoop on whether they had left underwear out of their attire that night.

What I wanted most was something, a pill or syrup, to stop the swirl of questions, an antidote that would allow me to just be. At home, when I got too caught up in questions and decisions, Brandon would be my guide. He was rational, and he knew how to deal with the fact that I, well, wasn't. *God, I miss him.* I couldn't wait to see him. And once that thought hit my brain, I felt the calm typically associated with slipping into one's own bed, exhausted after a painfully long day of work. I had clarity on that issue. Dependent? Maybe. But I knew Brandon could help me stop my head from moving at warp speed in every direction. With that clarity, and the thought that he was only a week from visiting me in England, I smiled into the distance. Soon I would be able to throw my arms around him and feel the heat of his chest against mine. I could hardly stand to wait.

"You alright, luv?" Harry asked, pulling me out of the reverie.

I looked at their faces: Harry's, sparkly and carefree, and Rob's, serious but tranquil. "Yes," I said. "It's a new day. Let's go to Bath."

Chapter Twenty-Seven

Bath: a city whose name refers to pools of water originally used for public orgies — I mean, bathing. Bath is in Somerset, England, located on natural hot springs. Our assignment was to photograph the Abbey as well as the Roman baths. I had read that Bath was a sprawling city, but as we walked through the center it appeared compact. And beige. Very beige. The city was a virtual tract of monochromatic buildings atop cobblestone streets. It wasn't unattractive, just redundant.

One of the baths was below street level, somewhat like the dance club we had visited in Manchester. We walked around the perimeter from the upper level and looked down on it. The water was the dark green of an unkempt, algae-filled koi pond, but the layer of steam tiptoeing across the top helped disguise the water's filth. I had read that the water still passed through the same pipes the Romans had constructed eons ago. *Astounding.* I could imagine the aristocrats bathing in this opulent landscape: the large outdoor pool surrounded by columns, decorative gold shrines, and bronze statues; peering up at the stars overhead as well as the adjacent Abbey. If Hugh Hefner had lived during Roman times (and he didn't, right?), this probably would have been his backyard. I was somewhere special, no doubt about it.

Harry walked around enthusiastically, marveling at the baths as he did with just about everything. His carefree attitude despite his lot in life, which some would label as tragic, was admirable and probably what drew so many people to him.

"Oh, this is fantastic, don't you think? I would definitely join in an orgy here."

"Of course you would, and you'd probably be invited by the king himself," said Rob in a tone meant to be simultaneously inaudible and audible.

"What was that, Rob?" Harry asked.

"Oh, nothing, nothing."

"Can't you just picture it?" Harry continued with outstretched arms. "A large party with poolside pitchers of wine brought by servants, a musician playing the harp, and loads of naked people. Glorious."

"Oh, sure, if I was allowed in."

"Come again, Rob?"

"Oh, I said, it'd be wicked."

Harry and I walked through the bathhouses, taking photos and enjoying the scene, while Rob continued on his unexplained passive-aggressive warpath.

"You okay, Rob? You seem to have a muttering problem today," I said.

"What? Nonsense, I'm fine."

"Okay. You seem a tad pissed off though."

"Well, if you don't like my mood, why don't you stay with Harry for another night and leave me out of it."

"Oh, okay, I was clearly misguided. You're chipper as a mortician."

I decided to leave Rob alone to let him pull out whatever was plugging his arse; his desire to talk about it while not actually talking about it was dreadfully annoying. I would not allow his sour mood to trample my positive one: I was in an amazing setting and Brandon was coming to England in a week to spend two weeks on vacation with me, just the two of us. I couldn't have been happier.

Chapter Twenty-Eight

My parents walked through Bath's city center a few minutes after I did.

"Honey, she really does appear to be fine. Maybe we should go home. What if she sees us?"

"Oh, now you're worried she'll see us. Annie, she won't. Not with you in that stupid hat. You know, I never tell you this, but you look ridiculous."

"Well what about you? Standing in the open like that, exposed for your daughter to see."

"Honey, I'm not exposed. We're keeping a good distance. Look, she's walking over to the Abbey. Let's follow her."

"Wait, she's turning around."

"Shoot, she probably wants some pictures of the bath from over there."

"Hide behind that column."

"Again with the tall, thin objects. I'm a large man, dear."

As Harry, Rob and I looked around and snapped pictures of the Abbey and city center, my parents were searching for the proverbial — or an actual — rock to hide behind. They ran around the bath looking for shelter, one after the other, as if they were in a Disney cat-and-mouse crusade.

"What if we wind up in her picture?" my father asked.

"Let's just hope she's not zooming in."

"Oh my god, I'm going to fall into the bath."

"Don't fall in! You'll definitely be in her picture!"

"And she'll come over here."

"Sonofabitch, now I'm gonna fall!"

"No you won't, I got you."

"Where is she? Can you see her?"

"No, I can't look. I'll lose my footing."

"Go there, behind that shrine."

My parents dove and ducked behind a shrine of a Roman goddess and peered around the corner.

"Phew," said my father to my mother, breathing heavily. "I think we made it."

While cowering behind the sculptures, where I would venture a guess they felt hopeless and undignified, my parents came to several realizations: that I was doing great; that I was confident behind the lens and at ease with Harry and Rob; and that it would be disastrous if I saw them.

"Maybe we should go home. She doesn't need us."

"Yeah, maybe we should. God, if she knew how absurd we looked right now."

"Well, it's a good thing she won't. Let's have some lunch and head home in the morning." It still hadn't occurred to my mother to stay and tour England with my father.

Chapter Twenty-Nine

That evening Harry and I wanted to continue basking in our lovely day, but Rob continued basking in self-pity. Harry and I had to drag him out after he had a fantastically unattractive tantrum behind the closed door of his room while we waited in the hall.

"I've nothing to wear, I'm not going," Rob said in the tone of a petty, incensed teenager.

"It doesn't matter what you wear, Rob," I said.

"Yeah, look what Andy's been wearing the whole trip."

"Thank you, Harry. Rob, we just want to see your sparkling face, the one we saw several days ago but for some reason has disappeared."

"I don't feel well."

"You'll feel better with a pint, mate."

"You and Andy will leave me, and I'll get stuck talking to tossers and mingers."

"Rob, we won't leave you," Harry said. "This is silly already and I won't stand for more. You coming out or not?"

Rob finally opened the door slowly, looking quite dapper in well-fitted jeans and a green button-down shirt with thin black and white pin stripes.

"See look at you, you're dashing," said Harry.

"Perfect. Where are we going? The Horny Hen, perhaps?" I asked.

"Oh, you think you have us all figured out, don't you?" Harry joked.

After a few drinking games at the local pub, The Dainty Hippo, I was well on my way to wasted. With Brandon's visit just around the corner, I couldn't stop talking about him and how ecstatic I was to see him soon, in England. Although Rob usually cheered on discussions about Brandon, he stayed oddly quiet while I babbled on and on about how I was excited to finally have sex and eat in a restaurant that didn't serve food straight out of a vat of oil.

"Andrea, don't you want your parents to visit you too?" Harry asked.

"Nooooo. No, I do not. They are not good travelers."

"Says the cowardly lion."

"Yeah, well, you think I'm bad? You don't know my mother. Anyway, it was important for me not to see them during my journey. They're so panicky for me at home and I think it would multiply to the nth degree if they were here."

"I thought you said Brandon was inhibiting as well," Harry said.

"He is, but he's insane about me only. He can deal with his own life just fine. My mother has trouble with everything."

I hoped that by the time Brandon came to England I would be wiser and braver and that he would, as a consequence, lighten his overprotective behavior. I knew I was making strides; whether he would notice it, take heed and adapt his way of being had yet to be determined.

While at the bar purchasing additional drinks for those of us already too drunk to stand, Harry ran into some people he knew. He brought us drinks before joining their table for a bit, leaving Rob and me to have our millionth drunk-to-drunk chat.

"How ya doin', Robbie Rob?"

"Oh no, it's drunk Andy."

"It sure is. You alright?" I said in a British accent.

"That's your accent? It needs work."

"Well, one can aspire."

"Yeah, I'm okay. But I was thinking…"

Uh, oh.

"I think, I mean, I'm fairly sure, I'm ready to go home," he said.

"What? You are?" The thought of losing Rob's company caused a giant lump to lodge in my throat.

"Yeah, well, you don't need me here anymore."

"What? Why would you think that?"

"Well, you're doing fine on your own and you have Harry."

"No, no, I need you. You're a huge help and, up until the last few days, really fun to have around. What will I do if I start shooting live objects again? I couldn't do it without you."

"You'd do fine. I'm just a crutch, Andy."

"No, I was wrong... I can't do it on my own. You've seen it, I burn shit down. I cause riots."

"That was a one-off. Okay, two-off. And you didn't do that on your own. It's just, I feel...I mean, I have feelings..."

Oh no — I *was* right about his feelings for me. But I wouldn't make him say it. He'd be too embarrassed. I decided to step in and help him out.

"You're falling for me, aren't you?" I asked at the exact moment Rob said:

"I'm falling for Harry."

"I knew it. Wait, what?" And then my brain heard what he had actually said. "Come again?"

Rob repeated himself. "I said, I'm falling for Harry. What did *you* say?"

"Huh, what? Nothing," I said, turning my face away, disgraced.

Then Rob's brain processed what I had said. "Falling for you?" And he laughed. And laughed.

"Okay, maybe I was wrong," I said. "But it's not that funny. Seriously."

Then Rob added some more laughter.

"You can stop now. I'm not that undesirable."

"Oh, I'm sorry. It's just that... I'm gay, you see."

"Yeah, I got that. Now."

"So falling for you would be, well, against God's plan."

"Yeah, I got that too. Harry, huh? I get it. I thought I was falling for him as well. But do you think he's gay?"

"I don't know, there are certainly things about him that blur the lines. For a while I thought he fancied you."

My cheeks turned pink and I stammered, "well, no, I. You think? No, I'm sure he doesn't. Right? No, he doesn't."

"No, you're right, he doesn't."

My heart sank a little.

Rob propped his head in his hand. "Anyway, I can't be in love with Harry. I'll get hurt, even if he is gay, which he probably isn't given my luck. I mean, wouldn't we know by now? Anyway, I need to go home, but if I do,

I lose money and burn a bridge with Mr. Henson, who I like and want to continue to work with. Brandon did pull a special favor for me to be here."

"Huh? Brandon? Brandon who?"

"Oh, bugger. I mean, crap. Bugger, shit."

"Rob, what are you saying?"

"Nothing. I didn't mean it."

"You said Brandon pulled a favor for you to be here."

"No, I didn't. I said—"

"Yes, Rob, you did. Tell me now what you meant," I said, tears beginning to well up in my eyes, obscuring my vision.

Rob looked at me with his head cocked sideways and a you-poor-dear-child expression. He put his hand on my back and lowered his head.

"What? What's happening? Tell me now. Do you know Brandon?"

More silence.

My voice got louder and I removed his hand from my back. "Rob, what aren't you telling me?" And then I heard it, *really* heard it. "Holy shit. Brandon? *My* Brandon? My boyfriend Brandon is paying you to be here?"

Rob nodded his head yes before he spoke. "Well, sort of. Yes. Brandon wanted someone to watch over you. Make sure you were safe."

I shook my head vigorously, as if doing so would rid my brain of this knowledge and make it untrue.

"Brandon went to Henson's wife and demanded that someone go with you. He offered to look through the resumes, and after talking to me and finding out I was of the homosexual persuasion he requested that I come along. Mr. Henson and the company barristers were going to do it anyway — they thought it was a good idea. So *Adventure* went along with it."

"Um, okay."

I let the information set while I stirred in my seat.

"Also—"

"Also? You're not done?"

"Nearly there. When Brandon found out that a handsome chap named Harry was coming along, he told me to keep you away from Harry and to hide the fact that I'm gay. He only did it because he loves the daylights out of you."

"No, no. That's not love. That's deceit." My temper flared more with each second as I processed the information. "And suffocation. And dishonesty."

"Alright, maybe. But with a basis in love."

"He shouldn't have done that behind my back."

Rob sat in silence, nodding his head.

I sat fuming as my eyes metamorphosed into faucets. I turned my anger to Rob, questioning his character. I looked at him harshly, squinting my tearing eyes, trying to stare into his.

"And you?" I asked.

"What about me?"

"What kind of person agrees to do that?"

"The kind of person that's looking for a job as a copywriter and is offered one while touring around the UK with a photographer reputed to take wonderful pictures."

"But you did what he asked. You lied about your sexuality and tried to keep me from Harry while shoving me toward Brandon, all of which is none of your goddamn business."

"Yes. But it was also not my business to judge Brandon's actions. I did it for the opportunity."

"I'm sorry. A professional tattletale is not a resume builder. I have to go." I got up and left.

"Andy, I'm really s—"

"Fuck off!" I yelled without looking back.

My focus during my storm-off was to locate the nearest pub — in England, always about twenty feet in any direction. Within minutes, I took a seat at the bar of The Choking Chicken and ordered a shot of courage in the form of Jack Daniels, chasing it with a pint of my pal Murphy, who makes a hell of an Irish Stout. I noticed a group of guys staring at me out of the corner of my eye as I tossed back liquor like I was in a contest. The guys cheered and slid another shot in my direction. I picked it up without a care as to what type of alcohol it contained, or what drug had been slipped in it, and threw it back. I raised my arms in victory as the men cheered. I threw some money on the bar and walked out the door. As I got up to leave, I heard the Neanderthals booing and screaming like the orangutans they were. "Oh, we're just getting started, honey." "Wait, baby. Don't leave without me, sugar."

I walked dizzily and alone to my hotel, cell phone in hand, too distraught to allow any fears to manifest. The smart plan would have been to call it a night, allow the alcohol to exit my system, and process the information with a clear head. Sadly, the alcohol that was flowing through my system didn't permit that sort of rationality; it mixed with whatever it does to exacerbate my anger and sadness and compelled me to call Brandon.

"So, Brando... didn't think England... I... make it?" Anger wasn't the biggest problem, though. I was a smidge too drunk to speak.

"What? Are you drunk? I can't understand you."

"Rob... you... hired, watch me."

"Honey, you sound like Yoda. What's happening?"

"Give me a second, will you!" I stopped dead, gripped my head with my hands and tried to collect myself, my thoughts, my words. As though the alcohol were leaving my body with each falling teardrop, it became easier.

"Didn't think I'd make it in jolly ol' England on my own, didja?"

"What? What do you mean?"

"Rob told me. I know it was your idea to hire him."

Brandon said nothing, leaving an awkward silence thick as setting cement between us. I imagined him hanging his head and putting his hands through his hair while searching for where to go, as I had seen him do before.

I continued. "Yep, I know all about your little plan."

"That prick."

"Not sure you have your finger pointed at the right person, Brando."

"Stop calling me Brando."

"How 'bout I just stop calling you."

"I prefer the Brando option."

"This isn't multiple choice," I said.

"Honey, I was just scared for you. I did it because I love you."

"Yeah, Rob said that."

"He did? Good."

"Yes, money well spent, pookie."

"I couldn't let anything happen to you."

"You should've told me."

"I know. But I thought you'd say no and I didn't want to risk that."

"You risked our relationship instead?"

"I didn't think I was doing that."

My head was spinning like a top. "Well, I don't think you had your lil' thinking cap on when you devised your scheme, Brandon."

"Look, let's work this out when I come there next week."

"No. I don't want to see you."

"Oh, baby, please don't say that. I just love you."

Hysterical is an understatement for my rant that followed. "You know how I resent my parents for smothering the shit out of me growing up. You know I flew five THOUSAND miles to get away from it. And, you know how hard every step of this journey has been for me as someone whose own shadow causes night terrors. But I wanted it so badly that I dared confronting all of the things that frighten me, sometimes several at a time. You took that away. By paying someone to look after me, you stripped me of any independence I believed I was earning. You continued the smothering I tried so hard to escape. Do you know me at all? Do you care about my wishes at all?"

"Of course I do, but I love you and would die if anything happened to you."

"You should believe in me."

"It's not you I don't believe in… it's everyone else."

"You should have trusted me to deal with it. I can't be under your watch every second. You have to know I'm strong. I have to know I'm strong. I… I have to go."

"Andy!"

I hung up out of breath, feeling as I had each time I awoke from a recurring nightmare in which intruders stuffed me into my trunk. But the masked intruders ruthlessly trying to take my breathing space and my life had become my fiancé. My boyfriend. My special love. I had spent a year with Brandon complaining about the stifling from my parents and telling him all the ways I sought to make myself a responsible, independent person including *finally* moving out of my parents' house — at the age of 24. He had heard none of it. I also recalled the story I once told him about going with Ashley to 7-11 for the first time without my parents. I was 13. It took until I was 13. I was so excited that my parents trusted me enough to go without them. On the way back, however, a row of bushes that lined the sidewalk appeared to move with Ashley and me. I investigated the scenario by tossing a plastic bottle into them. When the bushes yelled, "it's not nice to litter," I confirmed that it was my parents, undercover. When I remembered the story this time, though, I saw Brandon's face in the bushes, shrugging his shoulders and saying, "just trying out a Halloween costume, honey. What do you think of us going as George and Barbara Bush?" I felt betrayed. And mortified. And Brandon knew it. I didn't want to marry my parents. I wanted to marry someone who could love me while having faith in me and allowing me to breathe. I didn't think Brandon fit that description anymore.

Upset and irrational, I went to find Harry... but I ran into Rob.

"Where are you headed, Andrea?"

"Aren't you off duty yet?"

"You really should go to bed, shouldn't you?"

"Listen Rob, cat's outta the bag. I don't need you to look after me anymore."

"Andy. You're drunk and upset. As your friend—"

"My hired friend—"

"As your friend, I really think you should go to bed. Let me help you, won't you?"

"I don't understand. Is there anyone in England who has learned to make a declarative statement, or is there something about the shape of the question mark you all enjoy so much? I DON'T WANT YOUR HELP!" My decibel threw even me off. I was hysterical. I had no ability to reason. I was going to see Harry.

"Where's Harry?" I asked.

"What about Brandon?"

"I want nothing to do with Brandon, we're done."

"You're being rash."

"I didn't ask for your opinion. Do you know where Harry is or not?"

"I'm not helping you find him. You're on your own, just like you wanted."

"Fine. I located castles in Manchester, I can find Harry."

I left Rob and wandered through the hotel, possibly in circles, looking for Harry. When I was satisfied he wasn't there, I strode through the city streets until I came upon the first Roman bath we had seen and, curiously, I spotted Harry — with Rob. I didn't know how Rob had gotten to him before I did, but I was so snookered that he could've walked *with* me hand-in-hand and I wouldn't have noticed. I was desperate to eavesdrop, but I couldn't hear their conversation. I saw their blurry lips moving and their hands gesturing, but between the alcohol and the distance I tried to maintain I heard nothing. So I just watched.

****

"Andy's looking for you, Harry."

"She is? Is she alright?"

"Not sure. She found out that Brandon had me hired to watch over her."

"Oh, Christ. She's going to have one of those outlandish American shit fits."

"Yes, in the midst, actually. She didn't take it well. She broke up with Brandon and is now looking for you."

"Me? Why?" Harry asked.

"She's drunk and upset."

"Jesus. What a family she's got."

"Well, from what I understand, Brandon acted alone."

"Not exactly."

"What do you mean?"

"I'm here because Andy's parents used their pull with her boss to hire me to watch her. They wanted me to help make her think about other guys, put off the marriage, move in with them or something. I didn't care so much about that part of it."

"Wait," Rob said. "Brandon had me hired to watch her and *not* fall for her and her parents had you hired to watch her and fall for her?"

Harry nodded.

"Oh, shag a dog, Harry. You're joking."

"If only."

Talking over each other, Rob said, "At least Brandon knew that..." just as Harry said, "...and the joke of it all is..."

They both finished the sentence together. "I'm gay!"

Together again: "You are?" Then, in unison, "yes."

"Why does this keep happening?" asked Rob, rhetorically.

"What?"

"Nothing. Um, Andy thinks she might have feelings for you."

"Oh, the girl's just confused," Harry responded.

"Well, I guess being gay, then, you, well, don't have feelings for her?"

"What? No, you know I don't. Frankly, there's someone else here I'm after."

"Oh. Should I let you get back to the bar?"

"No, someone else *here*, that I'm after. Right here."

"Right here — oh, blimey. Really?"

"Yes, really. You seem surprised."

"Catatonic, actually. Have you seen me? Or better yet, have you seen you?"

"Yes, I've seen us both. And I'm thrilled with each of us... equally."

****

I watched Rob and Harry grow closer — physically closer. Harry put his hand on Rob's face. *What the?* Rob tried to look away, but Harry softly pulled Rob's head back toward his own. And there, next to the bath, lit up by the stars and the light from the lamps swirling with the rising steam, Harry kissed Rob, and Rob reciprocated.

My heart leapt into my tonsils and my jaw fell to the pavement. I looked around to find a comrade, anyone, for confirmation as to what I was seeing.

As it turned out, a few people were watching. I had turned my head back to the boys in time to see a petite older woman run up to Harry, swinging her purse at him and yelling. Assuming she was a bigoted homophobe, I got angry and leapt up to help them. As I got closer, I realized the female figure looked familiar. I got closer. Very familiar. Closer, still. And sounded familiar. *Is this some kind of joke? What the hell is my mother doing in England?*

Chapter Thirty

"You're not supposed to be gay!" my mother was shouting, still swinging her purse and tapping Harry like a five-year-old hitting his father on the knee.

"Who the hell are you, you mad woman?" Harry screamed. He tried to duck, but getting closer to the ground only helped my mother's aim.

Rob joined the fray, politely pushing my mother to get her away from Harry, screaming, "it's the 21st century, you homophobic bitch! Everyone knows it's not a choice!"

"No, he's supposed to be falling for my daughter!"

Rob stopped dead. "What? Harry, what is she on about? Do you have a girlfriend?" Upset at that notion, Rob grabbed Harry, put him in a head-lock, and turned to my mother, "Here, I'll hold him for you."

As Harry struggled to break free he said, "no, of course not, I am actually gay. Will you let me go and you, lady, stop hitting me!"

Stunned and dumbfounded, I emerged from the darkness. "She means me. He's supposed to be falling for me."

All three immediately stopped the brawl and looked up, leaving an angry silence between us all until my father ran up with a baguette in hand.

"Holy shit! I mean, Andy... what... what are you doing here?"

"Really, dad?"

"What do you mean? God, it's so great to see you! What a coincidence." Trying to continue the charade, he walked over and started to put his arms around me, but I wouldn't hug him; I held my arm out as a barrier but it flapped flimsily in the breeze.

"So, Rob and Harry, this is my mother, Annie, and my father, George. Annie and George, this is Rob and Harry. But you already appear to know Harry. Why is that?"

"What? What do you mean? We don't know these men. I was trying to push him aside. They were blocking our view of the bath."

"Mom. I'm drunk, I'm tired, and my boyfriend is an asshole. To top that off, you and dad arrive in Bath out of the clear fucking blue sky and start assaulting Harry. Why are you here? How did you know I was here? And what did you mean?"

"We just wanted you to be safe, dear. You've never been on your own before."

I looked around at the people gathered in a horseshoe around me — Harry and Rob, my parents — all wearing sullen facial expressions. I was in the middle of a spinning scene, as though I had vertigo. I didn't understand what had occurred, other than the fact that I had gone across the world but never left home. My two traveling partners were the eyes and ears of my parents and my boyfriend, none of whom thought I could go it alone.

"We're just going to go now," said Harry.

"Yes, shall we leave you to it, then?" added Rob.

Harry and Rob paused, waiting for a response, but we remained silent in our ire and they left.

And then it completely clicked. It was the explanation for why my parents had rarely called me and only sent sporadic emails while I was abroad. It wasn't that they were learning to trust me, or that they wanted to provide me with the space I had requested. It was because they had a camera on me in the form of a gorgeous British man. And it was the reason that Rob and Harry had taken the liberty of debating my relationship on more than one occasion — they were earning their keep.

"Yeah, mother, that's right. I've never been on my own. And whose fault is that? You never prepared me for the real world, so I go off into the real world to prepare myself and you hire a chaperone?"

"Our home may have been a little strict while you grew up, I suppose."

"It was a convent."

"I'm sorry. You're our only child. We couldn't let anything happen to you."

"Then you should have taught me to survive, not stopped me from living."

"Andy, we're so very sorry," said my father.

"Yeah, you guys are sorry, Brandon's sorry, everyone's sorry."

"Brandon? Why?"

"Oh yeah, the real kicker. Brandon hired Rob."

"He stole our move!"

"This isn't about plagiarism, mom."

"We talked about this before you left," my father said. "He told us that he wasn't going through with it."

"You plotted this together?"

"Well, we started to. But Brandon claimed he didn't feel comfortable with it and we didn't know if Mr. Henson would hire more than one person to go with you."

"Well, it looks like he changed his mind."

"How did Tom not tell us? I thought he told us everything."

"Well, he didn't. I'm so sorry you had to find out this way," I said with the sarcasm of Stephen Colbert praising the actions of the GOP.

"Maybe we were wrong about Brandon," my mother said.

"No, maybe *I* was wrong about Brandon."

"He just did it because he cares about you."

"I think you're confusing controlling with caring, as usual. Please don't stick up for him. You *all* made me feel like I'm inept, untrustworthy, and helpless."

"It's not that he doesn't trust you. It's that he doesn't trust everyone else."

"Yeah, that's what he said, too. You all don't have to be able to trust everyone else, just in my ability to deal with everyone else. And he didn't. And you didn't. It's unfair to me and gives me way less credit than I deserve."

My mother was silent. She understood Brandon's point of view, not mine.

"You know what, never mind," I said. "You should go."

"When will we hear from you again?" they asked.

"I don't know."

"You're right, Andrea," said my father. "We should go home."

I got hysterical again and started to walk away, screaming. "No, don't go home. Look around you. You're in England. Tour England, see London, it's amazing. *Then* go home. And get a life. Do something. Get a hobby. I can't be your hobby!" And I took off.

I ran through the center of Bath, pushing through groups of club-seekers and couples out for a late-night stroll. Another drunk girl thought she'd play a little game of you-go-left-no-I'll-go-left with me as I was running toward her, so I just stayed on my path and knocked her ass down. I collapsed on the steps outside my hotel and dropped my head into my hands, wailing and crying. Waiting for my arrival was Harry, alone.

"Oh, luv. I'm so sorry," he said, his rubbing my back. He kissed my head several times, tender as a mother to her child who had fallen off the jungle gym.

"I don't know what's going on," I said, gasping in between words.

"Well, Rob and I have spent a lot of time together when you weren't around. We've a lot in common."

"I don't mean about that. It's just, why did they do it?"

"What, luv?"

"They paid people to watch me. Brandon paid Rob to watch me."

"I know."

"You know?!"

"Rob told me just now, didn't he?"

"Seriously, you have to stop with the questions."

"Sorry. I mean, I just found out."

"I can't believe Brandon would do that to me. And I can't believe my parents would do that to me. I never thought they would go this far."

"Well, they love you, don't they... I mean, they love you, full stop."

"That's not an excuse to be conniving."

"I don't think they thought of it that way."

"Then they're fools."

"Maybe. But you do have to look at the rationale and not just the action. Intent is important."

"Okay, then. They *intended* to have me watched."

"You just need some time to digest."

"You know, life isn't as happy-go-lucky as you make it out to be."

"I know that."

"God, and to think I thought I had feelings for you too."

"I know," he said.

"You know?"

"Yeah, Rob told me that too."

"Oh, he's a real pal."

"He didn't mean anything by it."

"Yeah, yeah, no one means anything by anything."

"Look, you don't have genuine feelings for me. You're just a little lost. You're far away from home and on your own for the first time. It's natural to get a little turned around. And don't blame Rob."

I gave Harry as ruthless a stare as I could muster, eyes squinted and jaw clenched. "I blame you both."

"I mean it," he continued. "We didn't know you when we took the jobs. It was a chance for us to travel around England, take photos, and help assemble a reputable magazine. It was a good gig. We had no reason not to take it."

"But you didn't have to agree to hit on me to make me think about other guys."

"When did I hit on you?" he asked.

I thought for a moment, but struggled to come up with an instance that couldn't otherwise be rationalized as friendly. As I came up blank, he continued. "Everything I said about your parents over this trip, I would have said regardless of my 'job.' Andrea, we wanted the photo tour, nothing else. Unfortunately, one didn't come without the other."

I stared at his warm face and knew he meant no harm.

"And at the end of the day, we made the journey safer. Say what you will, but we did. You wouldn't have fancied a trip on your own."

I softened. Harry made sense. Again.

"I know. It isn't your guys' fault. I just don't know of anyone who would take money to chaperone while pretending they aren't chaperoning."

"I think, in our view, we took money to do a job. The rest was just something we would attempt when it was convenient."

"I thought you guys were my friends."

"We are your friends. Money or not."

I slowly collected myself. "I need to be alone. Go. Find Rob. Shag. Be happy."

****

"Hi Brandon, it's Rob. Listen, mate, I've got some news. Harry's gay. You've nothing to worry about."

"How do you know?"

"Well, see we were standing by the baths—"

"Of course you were."

"No mocking me, you dick. Anyway, we talked about you having me hired to watch Andy and he told me that Andy's parents had him hired to watch her. They wanted him to fall for her and make her think about other guys, put off the wedding, yadda yadda, and it turns out Harry and I fancy each other. Yay!"

"Andy's parents hired Harry to get her to leave me?"

"I don't think they were ready to let go."

"I knew they might hire someone, but not for *that* reason. They don't like me?"

"Maybe not. Crazy that."

"But Harry's gay."

"Pretty quick on the uptake there, aren't you? They didn't know he was gay, did they?"

"Can't you make a statement without asking a question?"

"Sorry. Clearly they didn't know he was gay."

"It doesn't matter now anyway, Andrea broke up with me."

"Well, you were a right wanker."

"Really?"

"We speak the same language. You know, a wanker — an asshole. What is it with you and her parents that you didn't trust her?"

"I trust her, I just worry about her. She's never been on her own, you know."

"I know. But that's why she came here alone. With what you lot did to her, she still hasn't been on her own."

"You know, if you thought I was an evil wonker—"

"Wanker."

"Wanker, sorry. You didn't have to agree to go."

"It's not my job to judge. I liked the assignment. I'll take some of the blame, but certainly not the whole pot. You're her boyfriend, nearly fiancé. *You* have to believe in her."

"Yeah, I know. I screwed up. I screwed up bad. I don't know what I'm gonna do."

"Give her some time, Brandon. I wouldn't give up yet. I will take Henson's money to continue our job, but I won't take anything additional. She's my friend, and I will look after her as I would any friend."

"Yeah, okay. You'll let me know if something happens, though?"

"That's up to her."

"Yeah, ok. Bye, Rob."

Chapter Thirty-One

The rain came down in sheets outside my hotel room window — "pissing it down" as the Brits say. My limbs were heavy but my heart was empty. My body wouldn't let me out of bed and my brain couldn't derive a good reason to get up anyway. I had arranged to stay an extra day in Bath and requested that Harry and Rob go back to London without me; I would be there soon. When I could lift my arms and head high enough to put a sweater over them, I traveled back to London. And then I stayed in bed there.

I had scheduled a two-week vacation to spend with my beloved boyfriend, but, disgusted by the sound of his name, I spent the first week alone under the covers. Rob and Harry tried to visit a few times, but I lacked desire to spend time with them either. I didn't hate them quite so much, as they weren't completely to blame, but for a while they'd be painful to look at — they were the faces of my parents' and Brandon's betrayal.

Brandon called a few times. At the beginning of the week, I didn't pick up the phone; I didn't even look towards it when it rang. By the end of the week, when the phone rang, I took the time to glance at it, pause, and then decide not to answer it. I knew the words "I'm sorry" were on the way but they just weren't powerful enough to solve anything. My mother and father called too, and when I saw their number I never hesitated: I just ignored them. I had no clue how I would handle my relationship with them from that point on.

I spent the time mourning, my only exercise being the twenty-foot jaunt between the couch and the bed, where only five days got me hooked on *EastEnders*, so much so that I emailed Gemma and Claire to apologize for asking them not to watch during the workday. *My word, that Jack Branning is attractive!* I tried to call Millie too, so as not to leave her out of the discussion, but she kept asking which end was east. My hair had merged into one large tangle, and I could feel my gut getting larger due to immobility. I looked through the three large photo albums I had brought with me — an occupational hazard, I guessed — and thought about my life at home: at the beach with friends (shielded by the sun's rays under an umbrella, hat, and glasses); bike riding with Brandon (I, wearing a helmet and knee and elbow pads while he looked perfect with no pads); at art festivals with Ashley (holding a buyer's guide to overzealous hagglers); at restaurants with my parents (all of us sitting near the bistros' fire extinguishers). The pictures captured hundreds of blissful moments of my life and they were all in front of me, reminders of what my life might have been at that very moment had I not decided to chuck it all for a tour of England. I missed each person that graced the pages as I stopped to say hello. I wondered what they were all doing at that very moment. Were they sad too? Did they miss me? Were they all together creating stories and inside jokes that I'd be left out of when I returned? My insides hurt and my skin was uncomfortable.

I looked out the window. It had rained every day. Every single goddamned day. I was certain there'd come a time when I would to go to sleep and wake up under water. What kept London from sinking, anyway? It wasn't raining in any of my pictures from home. I sighed as I watched droplets, more droplets, then some more fall from the sky, as if the Queen had lost a bet with God. I hated the rain. I made mashed potatoes from a box and ordered "takeaway," as they call it, almost every day; usually pizza from a well-known international pizza chain, fearing that a UK-specific pizza parlor would do to the pizza what their cafés had done to the bagel. I didn't like the pizza deliveryman. He became all too familiar with me after only a few days, feeling comfortable enough to declare (in the form of a question), "you really should leave the house, shouldn't you?" The question mark became an ugly, annoying mark.

The city had lost its majesty. I no longer cared that the most stunning architecture enhanced every turn or that I was in a place with impressive history and universal importance. Watching the buildings try to leave an impression through the blankets of rain was depressing. Stone everywhere, drab and lackluster. There were no convenient strip malls or cheap places like 99-Cent stores. And it smelled rancid. Rain mixed with exhaust and foul body odor from the sheer volume of people. Oh, look, another column — how original, I thought when I finally left the apartment one morning to go to Tesco (grocery store) after having shaken and scraped the last drop of shampoo from a bottle. *Why wouldn't they update this city already?*

By the end of the first week, I couldn't stop in front of a mirror long enough to look at my entire face. I was hideous. At Tesco, the lady behind the counter studied me, still in my pajamas, hair tousled in a Helena Bonham Carter *Fight Club* do: "Oh, having a bad day, aren't you? The ice cream is in aisle four in case you need it." *Thanks.* "Oh, but I don't need it, do I?" I repeated in a similarly high-pitched, over-emphasized English accent, adding under my breath, "oh, I'm so posh with my cute British accent, if only I could figure out how those toothbrush contraption thingies work." I topped it off out loud with the finale: "Yeah, I heard your conversation from before. The word is jaguar, as in jag-war. Not jag-u-are. Cheerio." Then I felt bad. *That was bitchy.*

I had nearly three months of my assignment left and I loathed the city in which I slept. My pictures were certain to be awful if my piss-poor attitude toward their subjects continued.

While continuing to browse my pictures of home, I picked up the phone. There was somebody I could call, someone who would understand my pain, listen to it, and then redirect my focus and push me to move past it.

"Ash… " I couldn't even finish saying her name before I began an alarming sob storm.

"Oh my god, hi!!" she shrieked.

In the midst of my tears, my voice box had closed.

"Hello, hello, Andrea? Are you there?"

I held my hand to my face; I was shedding more tears than London had shed rain. It was a painful crying spell so harsh it knocked the wind out of me. Breathing was a chore, speaking even harder.

"Andrea?"

"Yes… yes, I'm here," I said, trying to inhale in between bouts of tears.

"What happened? Are you okay?"

"I don't know."

"Take your time. It's okay. Tell me what's going on."

I slowly collected myself and rehashed the devious plot of my scheming family. How my parents had showed up. How they had hired Harry. How Brandon had hired Rob. How I had lost Brandon. If I hadn't lived it, I might not have believed it.

"THEY DID WHAT? Oh, good lord. Really?"

"Yeah, really."

"For fuck's sake, Andrea, I'm so sorry."

"Yes, everyone keeps telling me they did it because they love me."

"Well—"

"Don't you dare."

"I know, Andrea. But it's obvious that they do. I'm sorry, but it's true. They do an ass-backward job of acting on it, but it's a fact you can't deny. And before you say anything, I know that at this moment that doesn't make it any better."

"No, it doesn't."

"It will."

Ashley and I talked for over an hour. She said what I needed to hear. That it would be okay. That I would be okay.

"I know you're hurting about Brandon, and you will deal with him over time, when the pain goes away. But now, it's ass-kicking time."

"I know, you're right. Where do we start?"

"With you. Get yourself out of your disgusting *I Love LA* bedtime T-shirt that Brandon gave you, brush your mangled hair, and go outside." She was right: I had been wearing Brandon's T-shirt. For days.

She continued. "Go take pictures. You need to take pictures. It'll help. You're in England. You have no choice but to be in England for the next few months. You have a job to do. Do it."

"Okay."

"Don't say okay and then dismiss me. Say okay and mean it."

"Yeah, okay. I will."

"Remember, every picture you take gets you one step closer to shooting for *Vogue*."

"Right."

"I want you to email me the pictures you take today to prove to me that you took some."

"Ha, okay. Thanks so much, Ash. I needed this."

"Anytime. Look, I know this is going to be painful for a while. I know you're going to miss Brandon. But he isn't going anywhere. And your parents? Something tells me they learned their lesson. But you can't deal with them now. Give yourself time. You *will* get through this."

"Yeah, okay."

We sat in silence for a moment. I knew she was searching for a way to change the subject, but not so much as to seem disrespectful.

"So, Harry's gay, huh?"

"Sorry, Ash."

"Damn, we were all fighting for him back here."

"Well, Rob won. It's pretty cute, actually, and it makes sense."

"Well then, good for them. You okay?"

"Yeah, I'll be okay. Thanks again. I'll be in touch soon."

"No you won't."

"By email."

"Or unless you really need me, of course."

"I know."

"Okay. Take care of yourself, Andrea."

I hung up the phone with resolve. It *was* ass-kicking time.

I used the second week of my vacation to kick my own ass to be more productive than I had been during the first. I took walks. I brushed my hair and figured out myself how the toothbrush worked — I had become quite lax in my hygiene duties. I tried to find the beauty in England as I had seen it when I first arrived. Honestly, though, any lessening of the rain would have been a huge help in that regard. I tucked away my pictures of home in a closet and looked through the photos I had taken while in England, thinking about which ones I would recommend, how they would look on the page, what type of airbrushing and cropping we might do, what the captions would say, how the articles would read. I became excited and proud, very proud. If only I had looked through them earlier, I might not have wasted an entire week in bed, creating an Andrea-shaped indentation in it. Although it did become comfortably molded around my figure.

I traded my anger for determination. I daydreamed about the magazine I was creating, my name in the credits, all the people that might call me to license my photographs. The doors these photos would open, the call I would receive from *Vogue* to shoot a fashion show in Milan or a Gucci spread in Paris, the call I had envisioned since I was ten years old and first felt the significance of capturing life through the lens. Then I picked up my camera and snapped some shots outside my window: kids playing in the street; trees blowing in the wind; vendors cooking on the corner. I couldn't wait to get back to work.

After viewing the pictures of Liverpool, instinctively I grabbed my phone to call Brandon. I pushed three numbers of the fifty you have to dial to call the US from the UK and put the phone down. Beyond sharing my excitement of the photos, I didn't know what I would say, and the pressure of deciding was too great to bear.

Toward the end of the second week, I decided to shoot the inside of Westminster Abbey after nearly passing it by without stopping. It seemed utterly foolish to spend six months in England and admit that I had never thoroughly explored the inside of this supremely famous attraction — and for fear of tombs and stained glass, all of which can offer memorable and resounding beauty. I walked through the church portion, again snapping some pictures of the pews, and then turned out of the Abbey and walked around the perimeter. I passed the coronation chair — a large, carefully crafted wooden chair with a high back and decorative carvings — and the tombs of the A-list British men and women permitted to rest in peace in the Abbey. I saw a marble statue of Queen Elizabeth I lying serenely on top of her coffin, and the elaborate tomb of King Henry VII in the chapel bearing his name, the walls of which are lined with colorful banners of the knights of the order of Bath.

I perused the nave to view and snap more famous tombs, many of which had statues on top of them depicting the people that lay inside, all of which were ornate pieces of art. The nave was murky and damp, but that added to the ambience of solemnity, an apropos atmosphere to experience while walking past such notable individuals and remembering the important contributions they had made to the world. When people eventually walk by my grave, I hoped they would do so with gravity and serenity as they recalled the images I had donated to society. I dealt with the moist and grimy aura to absorb the scene in its entirety. And I enjoyed it.

When I got tired of being by myself, I called someone who had always appeared normal (whatever that means) and whom I thought I might be able to call a friend: Claire. We decided to go to dinner at a low-key Italian restaurant near my apartment. We met out front and shared an uncomfortable moment deciding whether to hug hello, as I did with my girlfriends back home, shake hands like we had just met, or merely walk in without any gestures, like acquaintances. After slightly leaning in and out for hugs multiple times, ultimately I put my arm around her and patted her back, like I was her mother.

We walked to our table and sat down, pulling our chairs out through the awkward silence, and opened the menus.

"This place looks good. I wish I had come earlier in my trip," I said, trying to break the gigantic block of ice between us.

"Yes, it does."

We talked about a few items on the menu as I searched my brain for something to say after our order was taken. I ordered the roasted chicken. And then the time had come.

"So... where did you grow up?"

"Essex," she answered.

Silence.

"Oh, do your parents still live there?" I asked.

"Yes."

Silence.

I took a sip of water while determining what to say next.

"How often do you see them now?"

"Once a month."

I was at dinner with a mannequin. "Have you always wanted to work in publishing?"

"Sort of," she replied.

Pulling teeth from a famished tiger would've been easier.

"Okay. What do you mean by that?" I prodded.

"Well, I want to shoot pictures; I don't really care what for."

"Well, you should come along with me, I'll show you a thing or two." *Damn. Please don't take me up on that.*

"Oh, I don't want to bother you."

"Okay, well, we are on a tight schedule."

The evening lightened up a little from that point, as Claire came to realize it would take two to converse, but the tone and tempo of the dinner continuously felt like I was interviewing her for a job she wouldn't get.

On the last day of my vacation, I continued walking the London streets, snapping photos of buildings I hadn't yet seen and new angles of buildings

I had, galvanizing myself for work the following day. I walked through a popular theater and shopping district, Covent Garden. It was bubbling with activity. In the Piazza, a man performed a solo acrobatics show to techno music played out of an '80s-style boom box. I stopped to watch him as he flipped in the air, split his legs into rather uncomfortable-looking positions, and did various other bendy maneuvers, many while balancing on chairs. The crowd that had gathered around him cheered loudly. Up the street, a violinist prepared to take a seat and play for the passersby.

Passing Andronicas, a small café in a tall white stone building with several tables in front, I noticed a couple sitting under an umbrella, gesturing and laughing like two stand-up comics telling competing stories. I stopped and watched, envious, certain that Brandon and I used to look the same when we were at a table together. Brandon made me laugh; it was what I fell for first. That and his beautifully sculpted arms, to be perfectly candid. As I walked to the door of the café, I saw that I knew the gesticulating couple. Apparently, even large cities become small towns once you get used to them.

"Hi, Rob. Hi, Harry."

They stood up and we shared welcome hugs.

"Oi, luv, you alright?"

"Hiya, Andy. Want to join us for tea? I mean, without actual tea, though, of course." I chuckled; it was an unfamiliar sound, weeks had gone by since the sides of my mouth had formed anything but an upside-down U.

"Sure boys, just for a minute."

I was touched by the way Rob and Harry seemed so utterly endeared. And I was sincerely delighted for the ecstasy they had experienced in finding each other. But their closeness left me lonely. They were so in tune with each other. I could never fit in. I told them about my previous week of shame, how horrified they would have been had they gotten just one glimpse of my appearance. I was also sure to mention that I had picked myself up during week two of my vacation and prohibited myself from the wallowing I had perfected during week one. I stood up to leave about twenty minutes after I had sat down.

"So, off to Warwick on Monday, then?" Rob asked. Warwick, pronounced like *war-ick*, leaving out the second W — another of the myriad examples of Britain's superfluous use of letters.

"Actually, I think I'll go with Gemma."

"Oh, Andy. You aren't on a shagging spree, are you?"

"No, Harry. But I just need a little bit of change." In reality, I feared the loneliness accompanied by the place of third wheel.

"Why not Claire?"

"Because it'd be like going alone. She's sweet but we really don't connect. I think I'll get to know Gemma."

"Okay, be careful." The words stung, and Harry saw the burn as it singed my face.

"Rob, she'll be fine." I nodded my head at Harry with a faint, approving smile.

"Great to see you both. I'll be in touch next week with notes."

Chapter Thirty-Two

Bright and early on the first Monday following my vacation-turned-staycation, I stepped onto the tube, energized by its rumbling sounds and the promise it brought for the day's new destination. I walked into the office eager to work, looking forward to sharing my day with someone new and to focusing my attention away from my despondency about breaking up with Brandon and from my somewhat dreary outlook on the world.

I slunk up to Gemma slowly, with a devious smile stamped from ear to ear. "Morning, Gemm. I have a stellar opportunity for you."

"Who is he?"

Seriously? "How would you like to come to lovely ol' Warwick with me?"

"Oh, I don't know. I've heard little about the Warwick men."

"There's a jousting event... "

"Oh, fantastic! I can find out whether armor has a penis hole!"

"Of course, we'll be taking pictures and not whoring ourselves out to men in medieval costumes, so it won't matter."

Mentally scanning her bucket list, she replied, "I've never done it on horseback either."

"Okay, but again, pictures. We're taking pictures. You know what, never mind, I'll take—"

"No, I know, Andy. I promise to be there."

"Groovy."

"For some of it."

"Gemma."

"Okay, most of it."

"I'll do it alone."

"Fine," she conceded. "All of it."

"Appreciated."

On the train to Warwick, Gemma and I did something I wasn't sure she'd ever done: we had meaningful conversation. In fact, she went a full five minutes without a comment about sex or the male genitalia, which must have been a record for her. I had been eager to learn about her family. I was sure she'd reveal something about her past that would explain her reliance on sex for icebreakers, salutations, and everything in between. But the story she told was about the most functional, cohesive family I had ever encountered. Gemma's mother was a teacher, blissfully married for thirty years to a barrister. Her parents still celebrated every monthly anniversary with each other, which they had done on cue through their entire marriage. She had two siblings, both of whom had gone into the medical profession and married people Gemma claimed to like. That was it. No traumatic experiences that would explain why her only interest in men seemed to be carnal pursuit. Apparently the sex fiend falls quite far from the tree.

After learning about Gemma's background, I understood even less about her constant, continual frat-boy discussion of sex and I couldn't help but wonder whether, through her family, education, and belonging to a society that for the most part acts differently, she shouldn't know better. But then who was I to judge? I couldn't even look around at people unafraid to drive their car in between two other cars and realize I should act the same. Despite having ten successful years of driving under my belt, I drove in constant fear that drivers in the adjacent lanes wouldn't see me and would careen into my vehicle, killing me in a heinous manner. I asked Gemma several times over the trip why she didn't believe in relationships, to which she responded, "I have relationships, loads of them. I don't understand the purpose of just one." She obtained whatever emotional support she needed through her family, her friends, and many, many men; she didn't believe that one man or woman could suffice. And there was something about her philosophy that made sense, until: "besides, one man couldn't know all of the sexual positions, now could he?"

Gemma walked around Warwick Castle with me as I took pictures, asking the questions of a sex-crazed child: "are we done yet?" (repeated over and over); and "do you think sex with the armor on will be too loud?" (repeated over and over). I promised her that if she remained patient, and quiet, we would go to the jousting event. She was also less helpful than the castle I shot — the castle at least posed for photographs. I missed Rob and Harry. On shoots, they helped me locate interesting shots and took notes. Gemma walked around unimpressed, as if the scenery were as uninteresting as a back alley, and jittery, as though she were merely killing time while waiting for a "real" friend to join her for dinner.

I tried to finish quickly, but it was difficult; the castle was exceptional and I wanted to capture every crevice. Warwick Castle, somewhat like the castle in Oxford, was very much the image of a castle as portrayed on television: an enormous structure of large stones the color of a Band-Aid, with several towers containing arched, rectangular enlarged "peepholes" running the entire length of the building, offering a slight sliver of ventilation for Rapunzel or other (real) prisoners to stick out their heads, or through which arrows were flung and cannons were fired during battle. The castle's tour guides and employees were dressed in medieval costume, the finishing touches to my imaginary transportation to the Middle Ages.

The castle sat adjacent to the bank of a river, snuggled in between trees and greenery on all sides, making it picturesque and imposing. Thick iron lattice portcullises marked various passageways on the grounds — in movies, the type of gate that's closed and locked by a swordsman on horseback immediately after the announcement of an enemy on the property.

Against Gemma's wishes, we walked into the castle and through its stately rooms. When we came upon one that housed a display of knights clad in various types of armor, however, I picked up my pace — I knew I'd see more of it at the jousting event, and I hoped to avoid Gemma's XXX-rated commentary.

"Oh good, I can plan my route," said Gemma approaching one of the knights in the exhibit to scope out how the armor all fit together.

I took Gemma's arm and pulled her away gently. "Gemma, let's go. I'm sure you'll work it out just fine."

We walked through several rooms that contained statues of the sorts of people who had once roamed the halls of the castle, portrayed as we would have found them hundreds of years ago: a blacksmith working in a shed, women embroidering flags, a countess entertaining guests and pouring tea in the music room. The costumes were authentic, the statues so detailed

I could interpret their facial expressions. Even the slightest imagination could have taken me to the point in time when these scenes were alive.

Gemma, much less impressed than I, sat in a huff while I explored the exhibits. Rather than continue and make us both miserable, I cut my visit short, confident I had obtained some nice photographs and that I could return the following day if necessary. Mr. Henson had requested pictures of the jousting event if we could get there in time, and, unless I wanted to see Gemma performing a tantrum instead of knights performing a joust, we would get there on time.

Because the only joust I had ever seen was done by Heath Ledger in *A Knight's Tale,* I was curious to witness a live one, even if it was just for show. We walked over to the field and grabbed seats in the rickety old wooden bleachers. While I wandered to the front for optimal photographic access, Gemma went to find a knight to get up-front genital access. I sat in the stands and prepared for the event, while she went to the stables to watch the knights mount up. She emerged with her hair tousled half an hour later, just before the horses came out of the gates.

"I've got the scoop on a major party afterwards."

"Looks like you've already been to the party," I said, detangling and pulling hay out of her hair.

"Oh, no. That was just hors d'oeuvres," she said, clapping her hands in quick, enthusiastic spurts like a madman about to watch his devious plot commence.

We heard the stampede of hooves in the distance and the bleachers began to tremble. I steadied myself and my camera to capture every exhilarating moment. The bleachers shook more violently and the sound of running got louder as a knight, the Duke of Worcester, emerged from the left on a shimmering white horse and a knight called the Duke of Wilcox on a regal, glimmering brown horse came from the right. Steel shielded their bodies from head to toe, concealing every inch, including their faces, ensuring zero vulnerability. As they closed in on each other, I imagined their facial expressions transforming from straight and serious into open and horrified, like Janet Leigh's during her stabbing in *Psycho.* I watched through my camera's eye and continuously clicked while the knights extended their long, pointed, lances at their targets: each other's hearts. The lances were festively decorated in the colors of the knight's coat of arms: the Duke of Worcester's draped in green and white, Wilcox's in blue and yellow. With Wilcox sporting UCLA's colors, I picked him to win. I didn't much care, but sporting events are infinitely more enjoyable when rooting for one side... and wearing the colors of the team whose side you're sitting on, as I had learned harshly in Manchester. The horses galloped toward each other and the knights stood up in their saddles to begin the attack. They let out deep, hearty yawps, loud enough to be heard through the chanting audience and the roar of the hooves. And then: a stunning blow to the chest from Wilcox to Worcester, hard enough to take him down and for pieces of the lance to splinter outward. Worcester fell to the ground and his horse galloped off. The Duke of Wilcox quickly jumped off his steed, stood over his opponent, placed one foot on Worcester's torso, and declared victory. The crowd went wild.

After the first joust finished, I walked through the stables to take some additional pictures of knights preparing for the following event. Gemma came along, but left me immediately to talk to a knight who she thought carried an exceptionally large "lance." When I returned several minutes later to where I had been, she was gone. I called out her name and a helpful man covered in a suit of armor that clanked as he walked toward me pointed left. "She went that away with Sirs Hollingsworth and Davenport."

"Thank you, my lord." I had always wanted to say that.

I returned to my seat in the bleachers, hoping Gemma would meet me there for the next joust. She never showed. In fact, after the final joust finished, she still hadn't. It was getting cold and it had long been dark. The lights covering the field wouldn't stay on forever, and frankly they weren't all that bright.

I walked to the stables and found only disrobing men, none of whom had seen Gemma — in the last hour. I wandered around the castle grounds; she wasn't there. I called her phone: straight to voicemail. *Why didn't I take Rob and Harry? They were at least paid not to leave me.* I was safe with Rob and Harry. Frustrated that I had made the choice to take Gemma, I took a cab back to the hotel. My leg bobbed up and down quickly and my hands shook during the ride. My stomach felt queasy. I called Rob, Harry, and Claire; none of them had heard from her. I was going to call Millie, but was already annoyed at what idiotic question she'd have in response, such as "who's Gemma?" or "did you check with Andrea?" Rob and Harry offered to come and stay with me, but I declined. Gemma was a big girl who would have to stand on her own; so was I. As a precaution, though, I called the police.

They said they couldn't do anything until she had been gone twelve hours, a rule I only sort of understood. In twelve hours, she could be dead; but less than that duration and she could just be hiding. And with Gemma, she probably was hiding, between the thighs of Sir Screwstoomuch.

I sat in my hotel room looking around, as if a clue of what to do next would fall from the sky. But I was powerless. And I had done everything I could do. Except wait. I tried to read; I couldn't focus. I tried to watch the television, but merely flipped through channels. I closed my eyes but my mind wouldn't allow sleep. At about 6 a.m., the hotel room door came bursting open.

"What a night!"

"Holy shit, Gemma, you nearly killed me!" I grabbed my chest and felt my heart sprinting to the finish.

"The armor does have a penis hole!"

"Well, I'm sorry you didn't crawl in it and suffocate."

"Well that's not very supportive. I came all the way to Warwick with you."

"Are you joking? You could have at least told me where your vagina would be working so I knew you were okay."

"I sent you a text."

"No, no you didn't." I looked at my phone again and flipped through the messages. She had in fact texted me: *Going with Sir Wilcox to a party, call his number if you want to meet up; my phone's dying. Tootles, Gemm.* "Oh. I see you did. Well, I still wish you'd called to make sure I got your text and knew where you were."

In my scrambling to call Gemma, Claire, Rob and Harry, I must have glossed over her message. "I'm sorry. I'm glad you're okay, Gemma. Let me sleep for another hour and then we'll leave."

My plan was to take Gemma directly back to London, without stopping to provide an opportunity for her to find another hole. But it was only eighty miles to Salisbury, my next stop, and it was a pain in the bum to go back to London first. I sighed.

"Gemma, do you want to keep going with me?" I said sweetly, knowing I had screwed up but very much against returning to London.

"I don't know, Andrea. You're a tight ass if there's ever been one. I don't need two mothers."

"I know. I promise I'll try to be more fun and I won't mother you."

"And you won't judge me."

"And I won't judge you." *I'll try very hard.*

"Well, alright then."

Although I had caused our mishap by overreacting and Gemma was a grown-up, at least physically, she had left me alone for a long period of time, tempting the fates for both of us, and waited hours to text me. I would not lose her again.

Chapter Thirty-Three

"So, George, I've been thinking since we got home... we probably shouldn't have gone to England."

"No shit, dear."

"Hold on, that's not fair. If you recall, I wasn't alone. We're both to blame."

"All I know, Annie, is that I never, ever want to see that look in Andrea's eyes again. She was so hurt."

"I know. And to think we caused it."

It was more than enough for my parents to witness the pained expression I wore upon running into them halfway across the world and discovering they had hired a chaperone to look after me to realize how horribly wrong they had acted. They had to discuss it for some time, though, before they grasped why that would upset me so much. To them, all they were doing was loving me the only way they knew how — which was what had to change. They had to continue to learn how to love me. They had to adapt to me growing up, to love me as an adult differently from the way they loved me when I was a child.

My parents ended up essentially taking the two-week vacation I had planned with Brandon. They toured the places they knew I had gone: Bath, London, Stratford-upon-Avon, and Oxford. My mother never rode the tube, but enjoyed her time abroad regardless. After two weeks in England, it was back to life as they knew it: work, television, dinner; work, television, dinner. Or so I thought.

They sat one evening on the couch, rather than in their standard arm-chairs, snuggled closely with their arms around each other. They talked about how proud they were of me, how much they had enjoyed watching me take pictures while they were stalking me in Oxford and Bath.

"She looked like such a professional, George."

"Yes, she sure did."

"That must be our influence."

"I'm not so sure, honey, but I would like to think so… at least mini-mally."

I too felt terrible for how I treated them. For yelling at them and for telling them I couldn't be their hobby. I never wanted to speak to my parents in such a manner, but discovering how they had watched me like I was a feeble bird who had lost its wings had been the breaking point. And as it turned out, my maniacal rant had worked.

"England is such a beautiful country. I'm so sorry that I never traveled before. We should travel more. I want to see Italy."

"Okay, honey, we'll do that. I'm going golfing with Jim and the gents this weekend. I'm thinking it's time to give that a shot."

"I think that's a wonderful idea. George?"

"Yes, honey?"

"I want to call her."

"I know you do. Let's give her space for a while. We screwed up pretty bad. Harry will still update us if we need him to, even though he won't take our money."

"I hope so. She'll be okay, right?"

"I think she'll be even better than okay. I think she'll be fantastic."

My father lightly pulled my mother closer and she rested her head on his shoulder. "Yeah, I do too."

Chapter Thirty-Four

Salisbury, Wiltshire, England: home to Stonehenge. Given the minimal amount of time I had been spending in each town, all I could really do was compare Main Street (often called High Street in the UK) to Main Street. Salisbury reminded me of Stratford: High Street was a continuous row of two-to-three-story shops that looked like homes, blocked off to auto traffic. I expected horse-drawn carriages to traverse these quaint cities but, alas, I was traveling in the twenty-first century; I was more likely to see a flying skateboard. Also similar to Stratford and other small British towns, a river ran through it. Pubs and cafés backed up against the river, providing a stunning and tranquil ambience for their patrons.

Salisbury Cathedral looked unlike the others. It was the lightest-colored of those I had seen, a cream or winter-white in most lights. It was also small, relative to most, but had a pinnacle that stretched high above. The interior felt and looked as all the cathedrals had: the unspeakably rich and dizzyingly ornate craftsmanship of the altars and choir areas, with carvings and engravings at every corner; the large rectangular stained-glass windows, richly colored and picturing the Virgin Mary; the high, complicated and lavish ceilings, some painted and some an intricate mix of wood, bronze, gold, and other decorative materials. Despite the similarity in functional features, each cathedral and each castle had a unique beauty that film could reveal better than words. This was part of what I found so satisfying about photography.

"Are you going to take pictures all day?" Gemma asked, as though I was forcing her to watch me pour cement.

"You sound like Millie," I said while snapping. "Yes, that's why we're here — to take pictures, *all* day."

"Well then, let's go clubbing tonight. You've earned it and I really want it."

The thought of losing myself in booming music and dancing my cares away was alluring, but the thought of going with Gemma was nerve-wracking. I had no confidence that she would care if I were attacked by unruly men, much less save me from them. I also wasn't certain she wouldn't drug me herself to get me to go home with a guy, or just allow her to do so. But Gemma would go to the club regardless of my decision, and I wouldn't let her go alone.

"Yeah okay, but Gemma—"

"I know. Call you if I leave with someone."

"No, no. Don't leave with anyone. Can't you spend just one night with me and not make me worry about you being raped by some horny Englishman?"

"But—"

"Seriously. You can shag the British army if you want, just not on a night we go out together."

"Okay, but I can dance with men, yeah?"

"Absolutely, grind away. Just keep it in the club."

"Yeah. Alrighty then, be right back."

Gemma snatched her nightclub shirt and a skirt from her purse, went into the bathroom for five minutes, and emerged a complete slut. Eager though she was, Gemma's transformation into a streetwalker was premature: it was only four o'clock. I compelled her to wait a few hours while I continued taking photos of the cathedral and its surroundings from up close and afar.

I had dinner on my own, Gemma having a strict rule against eating before clubbing. "It makes it harder to get drunk and more disgusting if you vomit," she said. I couldn't argue with such logic, but my hunger was a force stronger than her wisdom. I wolfed down two slices of pizza so greasy I could see my reflection in them from a nearby hole in the wall before we ventured to The Sugar House. The club's signage was painted on the side of a dark-colored stucco warehouse with a tin roof and no windows. I walked to the back of a long line, sad that the fates were making me wait in one, especially there. I wouldn't wait in lines to get into clubs at home; it felt too much like stalling punishment with punishment. Gemma laughed, pulled my hand, and walked me to the front. Amidst grunts and yells from the people waiting — frankly, a line of men — Gemma winked proudly at each one and said, "don't worry babe, you'll get it" or "I'll make it worth your wait."

A man so large his arms couldn't lay at his sides and whose belly obstructed his view of his feet guarded the door. Gemma whispered into his ear and he unclipped the rope and waved us in.

"What did you say to him?"

"I told him you'd shag him if he let us in," she replied.

"You what?"

"Oh lighten up, I told him I'd shag him if he let us in."

"You are a disgusting girl, Gemma. But fascinating."

The club was small and dingy, with a fetid stench of sweat wafting through the air. I didn't plan to stay long. But then… drinks were cheap. I sipped slowly, hoping to keep my inhibitions while scoping out the crowd, which consisted mostly of college-aged kids. The men were dressed in T-shirts and jeans, the girls in cheap rayon and sequins. We took limited space on a tiny, crowded dance floor and tried to move in between the stacked bodies.

"You really suck at dancing, don't you?"

"Yes, I guess I do." Though Gemma's moves were limited as well, to butt-shaking.

Before I knew it, I was truly enjoying myself. Gemma met some men she wanted to dance with and I bopped around with her leftovers. I made it a point not to let her out of my sight — except once, when, parched and light-headed, I headed to the bar.

"Stay here, Gemma. I mean it. Stay. Here."

"Yep, got it."

It took the barmaid, who was saturated with customers, at least ten minutes to hand me a bottle of water. I guzzled it in less time than it took to give the woman her tip and returned to the floor. Gemma was gone. Again.

I went to the restroom but it was blocked by a line of at least twenty women checking their makeup in their compacts and reapplying lipstick already too thick for their faces. I waited for a few minutes, my foot unable to stop tapping. It was taking too long. *What if she was snorting drugs? What if she was passed out in a stall? Good thing I know CPR!* I bravely walked to the front of the line, promising the angry ladies that I wouldn't use the loo, that I just wanted to find someone. I was called a bitch three times and shoved. *Women who have to pee are vicious.* And it wasn't worth it: Gemma wasn't there. I couldn't believe it; I had lost her again. I walked briskly back to the dance floor and searched what I thought was the whole club. No sign of Gemma.

I stood by the bar and slowly, carefully checked my phone for texts or calls. Nothing. And this time I was sure of it.

I talked with the bouncer who had let us in. He hadn't seen her, but asked me to notify him when I found her because she owed him a favor.

About an hour had gone by since I started my search. I opened the back door to get some air and possibly call Rob and Harry for help. There, in the middle of a circle of underage men was Gemma... smoking weed.

"We're going home, Gemma."

"What? Why? It's only 2 a.m."

"I couldn't find you."

"Until now."

"But you never tell me where you're going; you just leave. And I can't take it. Sorry, boys, your entertainment is leaving."

The group of men booed and called me a "boring minger" and the "buzz-killing bird"; I didn't care. I wanted Gemma to get home safely, and my fragile self couldn't handle monitoring her any longer.

But as she pleaded with me to stay, I studied her. Easygoing. Self-assured. She was a grown-up girl having a good time. She wasn't in danger, or at least she didn't think she was. Maybe I didn't need to watch her. I imagined she had been living this lifestyle for longer than I had known her; she had made it this far and appeared to be just fine. She didn't need me to be her guardian. I was doing to her what Brandon and my parents had done to me. Here I was trying to recover from their intrusive brand of parenting, but it somehow made sense when I was doing the same thing to another. But, as I knew all too well, it wasn't a fair way to treat someone.

"You know what, never mind. Stay. Call me if you need anything."

"Yep, will do."

And I left, nearly confident that Gemma would reach out to me, or the police, if necessary.

I slept more soundly than I anticipated, which helped curtail my worrying. The morning came and, though I had to sit on my hands to stop them from calling Gemma, I was rather well-behaved. Unlike Harry and Rob, I had turned into a terrible chaperone — which was just the way she wanted it. And the way it should have been. A few minutes after I went to the lobby for a black currant scone and coffee, Gemma walked through the front door.

"Brilliant evening, yeah? Where are we off to next?"

"*You're* going home. I'm going to Stonehenge today, alone, and then I am going to sleep, alone, and tomorrow I am going home to get Rob and Harry. You may leave now or you may leave tomorrow, the choice is yours."

"Did you not have fun?"

"No. Well, I did at first. But keeping an eye on you is hard work."

"Well you don't have to, do you?"

"See, that's just it. I do have to, or I feel I have to. Even though you didn't ask me to and even though you don't want me to. Look Gemm, you're fine, but I'm just too tense a person. When you're alone, I'm nervous for you. When I'm alone, I'm nervous for me. I don't want to worry about us both; it's too exhausting. It's not your fault, it's just who I am."

"You aren't giving me enough credit."

"Probably not. But I can't change that. I'll see you back at the office. Thanks so much for coming with me. Seriously. Thank you."

I didn't know how much internal change I could accomplish at age twenty-six. And though I had grown substantially over the previous few months — "old" Andrea would have run back to Rob and Harry immediately after she lost Gemma the first time — I knew, sure as Rush Limbaugh would always be an obnoxious, self-absorbed blowhard, that some things would never change, no matter what. With that knowledge, I had to orchestrate my life to put myself in situations I could manage, and wanted to manage. Watching over and worrying about Gemma did not fit into that plan. But I didn't want to be her mother either. I knew firsthand how unfair a position that was to take over someone old enough to be independent, especially someone who already had a mother she adored. The solution was easy: remove myself from the situation altogether.

I took a bus to Stonehenge. I sat by myself, staring at the countryside rolling by and listening to music through my earbuds. I met Hannah and Joe, a couple in their mid-fifties from Northern California, after they asked me to take a picture of them. It happens often: I take one picture for someone, they find out I'm a photographer, I take several more, and they try to talk with me. It's always fine; flattering, even, though talking with strangers hadn't always been among my favorite pastimes. That Hannah and Joe were newlyweds stung a little, but it was also inspiring.

Hannah and Joe launched into the story of how they had become a couple. I hadn't asked. Hannah's eyes lit up as she held Joe's hand and told a sweet tale of two people who had met at random many times, coincidentally ending up at the same dinner parties. It turned out to be not so random when they discovered that Hannah had a distant friend who knew one of Joe's distant friends. Joe finally decided their continual meeting was a sign and asked Hannah out on a date and the rest was, well, sitting in front of me on its honeymoon.

Hannah continually ran her fingers through Joe's head of thick grey hair as she told their story, and she finished even gigglier and more giddy about love than when she began — which I imagine prompted this question: "Are you seeing anyone special?" I never ask that of anyone, fearing the answer I was about to give and the awkwardness that would follow.

I had to pause for a minute to prepare myself for what I was about to say and hear. Brandon and I had in fact broken up, but it was more complicated than "I'm single" could encompass. I wouldn't lie, but I also wouldn't dole details to strangers, certainly not to ones in the midst of such matrimonial bliss. But I hadn't yet said it out loud, and I was frightened that doing so would make it even truer, if there is such a thing. I took a deep breath and attempted to smile.

"Not at the moment, no." *Ick.* The words stung my heart, as though I had received the same powerful blow the Duke of Worcester had.

And then came the awkwardness I anticipated. Hannah paused for a moment, then stammered, searching for the right words. Ultimately, she said the wrong ones, with an abundance of pity: "Aw, I'm sure he'll come along someday."

"I hope so, thanks." I allowed another smile to flash at the joyful couple and turned my face to the window to sleep.

After several hours on the lonely two-lane countryside road, the bus came to a halt at the famous pile of rocks that was Stonehenge. And that was exactly what it was: stones. Large stones, but stones all the same. I found it anticlimactic. The expectation of seeing an enormous feat of human accomplishment culminated in a pile of rocks. I didn't know how they had gotten there; most likely there was something marvelous behind the story. But to me it was a large circle of rocks in a semi-interesting pattern, some solitary and a few configured in the shape of the *pi* symbol. I took the photos I needed and managed to obtain some nice images with rays of sun shining through the empty spaces in the middle of the *pi*.

We returned to the bus. I purposely sat near the couple again so they would think the awkwardness had faded, but hoped like hell we would not converse.

Maybe it was the worry I felt at meeting a newlywed couple, or maybe I was just lonely, but after trying my hand at working alone I found I preferred Rob and Harry's company. Though they charged a fee, they were still the only people east of the Atlantic that I could call friends.

The following day I called the two and requested that they join me on the trip to Wales. Both were fired up to "get the band back together." Without much delay, we were off to the county of Gwynedd, city of Caernarfon, North Wales, to shoot Caernarfon Castle.

Chapter Thirty-Five

Caernarfon Castle was an ashen grey version of Warwick Castle. It was a colossal structure built by Edward I that appeared, from afar, to be composed of enormous sheets of stone. Up close, you could see the detail of the small stones that, like Warwick and Oxford Castles, seemed likely to crumble at any moment. With very few "windows" — *i.e.*, those slim openings in the castle walls through which warriors could fire their weapons — the castle was dismal and uninviting. However, it sat on river, with a harbor as its neighbor, which lightened the view.

We strolled through the castle grounds as I shot its different sections. It was not one of the castles we could venture inside to view an interior restored to the way it was when royalty roamed the halls, but we did walk through the expansive walkways adjoining the castle's various parts.

Harry and Rob had become an official couple. They held hands, told inside jokes, and finished each other's sentences. I guess the latter two they had done before they were "official," but now it felt different. They talked about moving in together. It seemed quick, but both were soon required to relocate from their current homes anyway, so they had decided to take the plunge. We talked a lot about areas of England they thought they might call home, and which daily habits they foresaw causing problems. Harry, a little too carefree with his clothes and dishes all over the house; Rob, too tight-arsed to allow clothes and dishes all over the house. I was definitely on Rob's team there. Brandon and I had often discussed the same issue. "No, a pile of clothes right next to the hamper isn't close enough," I would say.

Rob asked if I had talked to Brandon. I still hadn't, but felt that I might soon. Harry asked me the same of my parents. The answer was still no, maybe never, even though it was an unstable conviction. I would talk with them when the pain of their duplicity had subsided. And I learned that neither Rob nor Harry was taking extra money to chaperone me anymore.

After the castle, we walked around the harbor and through its neighboring streets. It was a surprisingly residential area; not pretty, just old. The streets were narrow and the homes appeared to be on their last legs. I noticed very few people wandering about, and the ones I did see were quite ancient, as though people came to Caenerfon to retire. It was a bleak town with little color, and it was raining. And it was cold.

Just like the "old days," we took a seat at the local pub, The Running Turtle, for a pint and a terrible dinner. I had often heard it said that the food in England is mediocre, even poor. Though I agreed, I hadn't eaten at a restaurant without something deep-frying behind the cash register in over four months — I had been saving money for the lavish restaurants I would go to during my trip with Brandon. With that change of plans, rather than get familiar with England's finer cuisine, I had ended up with a pile of extra money and an extensive knowledge of Britain's fast food scene.

Although it had been comforting to spend a day with Rob and Harry, the vibe of our relationship had shifted. Maybe it was due to their change in relationship status, maybe to my subconscious envy, but we had lost our verve. No one wanted to stay out past nine o'clock, and situations for raucous laughter were minimal. The following morning, on the return trip to London, I looked over at them as they gazed lovingly at each other, talking about their life together, and decided not to travel with them again. Not out of bitterness but out of self-preservation.

Chapter Thirty-Six

I returned to London for a breather between travels. There was still touring to do and pictures to take in London proper, including St. Paul's Cathedral, Big Ben and Parliament, and Windsor Castle. I was spending most evenings by myself, which I didn't completely mind. I bought some books on advanced photography and tried to improve my craft. I took myself to pubs a few times and chatted with the neighboring patrons, which officially changed my previously staunch conviction never to talk with a stranger — anywhere. Whether I met tourists or locals, for the first time in my life I was able to tell stories of travel and — finally — to use the phrase "you should have been there." I discovered that the exchange of ideas and stories with strangers was a horizon-broadening experience. And with this new appreciation, I decided to give a night out with Millie a try. I had been so judgmental of her, and was so intrigued by what seemed like an impossible amount of stupidity in one person, that I had written her off. Therefore, one afternoon in the office, after an inner conversation with all of my selves to ensure I was certain of what I was about to do, I popped the question.

"Millie, do you feel like going to get drinks?"

"Sure, if you feel like going."

"Yep, that's why I asked."

She seemed genuinely surprised, grateful even, and I was eager to learn her story, either in my unending desire to compare my family to others' or merely to uncover what type of family had created this seemingly blank slate.

Millie and I walked to a glossy new pub in the center of London, packed with people in suits enjoying happy hour after a day's work.

"So, how are the pictures coming out?" Millie asked before we even reached our table.

"Well, they—"

"You know, I always wanted to be a photographer."

"Really? That's great, why don't you—"

"Yeah, it seems like such fun. But I'm afraid I'm not smart enough."

"Nonsense, you can learn—"

"I do enjoy secretarial work, though."

"Oh, that's great. Where did you—"

"But I like dogs. I've thought about being a vegetarian."

"Do you mean vet—"

"Did you always know that you were going to be a photographer?"

I couldn't wrap my head around how someone could make so many comments but have a simultaneous desire not to turn them into a conversation. It was as if she adored her voice so much she couldn't stop listening to it. I wasn't given the opportunity to finish any of my own questions and, after about ten minutes of her soliloquy with no pause for her to reload her lungs, I lost my desire to try. *I really didn't appreciate Claire enough.* In between inquiries, I ordered half pints and chugged them like they were beer shooters. After several more attempts at turning *The Millie Show* into a discussion, I changed tack.

"You know, I really want to see a movie," I said. "We can eat afterwards."

"Okay, that's fine." At least she was agreeable.

Millie talked through the fifteen minutes of trailers and asked ridiculous questions about the plots of the movies in them, clearly misunderstanding the nature of a movie trailer.

"Oh, you haven't seen this one yet?"

"No, no one's seen it. It's a trailer."

"I'll ask Claire if she's seen it."

"No, see… never mind."

That said, because trailers nowadays all but give away the entire movie they are supposed to preview, I attempted to respond to some of her queries anyway. The movie finally started. Two hours of anyone's voice but Millie's was all I wanted.

In the first scene, two cars zoomed by in a one-on-one chase.

"Oh my," she said, whispering at the volume of a yell. "This is exciting!"

I leaned in and whispered, in a genuine whisper, "It is, but shush, let's let people watch."

The cars crashed. Two people jumped out and darted down the road, chased by a policeman.

"Why are they running?"

I slumped down in my chair and whispered again, "I don't know, let's watch and see."

"Who do you think will win?"

"I don't know. Let's let the movie play for a bit and then we'll see."

The chase ended and the plot began to open up. Instead of letting the movie tell the story, Millie wanted me to do it — even though she knew I hadn't seen it yet. It didn't matter. Her comments continued flowing like water from a broken hydrant.

"Do you think those two will end up together?" "Oh, he's cute. I dated a guy like him once."

People fired shushes at us from all sides.

"Oh, that girl's kind of bitchy, don't you think? I hope he doesn't end up with her." Millie was on autopilot.

"Oh, it looks like he will end up with her. I think he can do better."

Oh, sweet Moses. I felt the pent-up, seething rage I hadn't felt since I was stuck in Los Angeles traffic: anxious, trapped, and helpless against the lines of cars that boxed me in. I had no steering wheel to pound on, no windows to shield my screams. It was time to get off the freeway and take side streets.

"I'm sorry, Millie, I don't feel well."

"How will I know what happens?" Millie asked.

"I suspect if you watch the film, you'll get a clue or two. Are you okay to get home alone?"

"Shush, I'm enjoying this."

"Are you fucking kidding?" I whispered, and got up to leave.

"SSHHH!"

I left the theater feeling blue at having exhausted my final option for a friend. It wasn't a major surprise, though; after all, Millie had sent me to ruins instead of castles... twice. But then I discovered I couldn't even see a movie with her. How could watching a movie be so difficult for some people? It's one task: sitting and looking forward. Okay, two tasks. But no one has to *do* anything. That she couldn't tackle that brainteaser meant there was no friendship anywhere to be found. I walked back to my apartment feeling alone and longing for someone, anyone, that I knew to a greater extent than a few hellos and conversations about work.

I had called Ashley again, and several other friends in Los Angeles, but talking to people back home amplified my sorrow. One of my friends had gotten engaged while I was in England; I had missed the party. One of my friends had had a child while I was in England; I had missed the bris. Both of my parents had birthdays; I had missed the dinners. I found myself in the ironic situation of finally fulfilling dreams of traveling and having once-in-a-lifetime experiences, but wishing I had been somewhere else, referring to home this time. I hoped I would look upon my journey as worth it. I knew I already walked taller, less afraid. But was it enough? I was still too close to the journey to tell. But, fearful of regret, I hoped I would look back and say with certainty: yes, it was worth it.

Chapter Thirty-Seven

My next stop was in Northern England: Lancaster, in the county of Lancashire, home of Lancaster Castle and Cathedral. Millie asked if I wanted company. Although it was a polite gesture, I replied, "no, no. I'm good."

Rob and Harry asked too. "No, thanks," I said. "I'll go alone."

I was quite comfortable doing the photography part of my trip by myself; the travel and down time between shoots were more pleasant spent with people I enjoyed than alone, but better spent alone than with people I didn't enjoy. Rob and Harry were helpful during shooting and a laugh a minute in between, but the actual shot ultimately came down to my subject and me. When I take pictures, I forget everything else. In Lancaster, I forgot that I was newly single and in a foreign country with no real friends or family. It was just me — me and my connection with the focus of my picture, its environment, its landscape.

That connection began when I was ten. On the many days my parents prohibited me from playing outside, I got inventive about playing inside. One afternoon, barred from the backyard due to a red alert on the news's smog scale, I set up an obstacle course for my dog and chased her around as she jumped through it. I was thoroughly entertained. She cleared each hurdle easily and then ran to me, panting and wagging her tail for pats of approval. I wanted her to do it again and again. I couldn't get enough of how cute she looked jumping; I was so impressed with her agility. To save my poor exhausted canine, my mother handed me a camera and said, "Here,

Andy. Press this button, take a picture while she takes a leap, and then we can let the doggie rest." I snapped and snapped as she ran and jumped around the room, chasing the biscuits I had placed for her at the end of the course.

After exhausting the film in the camera, fifteen or twenty pictures later, I nagged my mother until she "braved" the heat and took me to the pharmacy to have the film developed. Too impatient to wait overnight, we took the one-hour option. I got the pictures back and, amazed b.y how a filmstrip could transform into a photo, sat in the middle of the store and looked through all of them while my mother pleaded with me to get into the car. But I didn't hear her; I saw only my dog leaping over the course, her ears flying in every direction, her tail held gracefully above her body, her tongue hanging out of the side of her mouth. "Look, mommy, I caught her in mid-air!" I said. I began to take pictures of everyone and everything, all the time. For years I poured my entire allowance into paying to develop pictures. My parents sent me to photography classes. Other than my short freelance gig as a tabloid photographer, during which I would have rather painted nails and scraped calluses off people's feet, I still get that same feeling of satisfaction when I take a picture. So I didn't mind that my camera was my only friend as I made my way through the charming town of Lancaster.

Lancaster Castle was nestled in an arboreal area of the town, atop a hill where no homes or shops were visible. It was a small, rustic castle, a pile of stones in an astonishing configuration of mushroom shades, drawbridges, and arched walkways. By this point it was nothing I hadn't already seen, but that didn't decrease its loveliness. Each castle had a unique layout and setting that film could reveal where words couldn't; I didn't envy Rob's task of having to write about each one. I circled the castle during the day, walking up and down the hill to obtain many angles and facades. I took myself to lunch at a sandwich shop and walked around the cobblestone-paved town. I shot the castle again just as the day gave way to dusk, cueing the spotlights that shone on it in the evening. I took photos of the dimly lit structure quickly, eager to be on the train before all natural light would disappear, the world would become too dark, and I would be alone in this quiet, wooded area, dining solo in another strange city.

Chapter Thirty-Eight

I fell again. I was in a department store when I slid down an aisle due to the extensive accumulation of water in the soles of my boots. I still hadn't learned to walk properly in a city where rain was the default weather pattern. From that point, if I went the remainder of my lifetime without anyone else asking if I wanted tea, I would be thrilled. If I went the remainder of my lifetime without hearing anyone else end a statement with a question, I'd be over the moon. *It's annoying, isn't it?* But what I wanted most of all was to remember England differently. I wanted the city to be cemented in my memory as I had seen it when I first looked out the cab at Trafalgar Square and pinched myself multiple times to ensure I was awake: that fresh feeling of looking at something that took my breath away and left my mouth frozen open. And that something had been real and in front of me. But I had no optimism left. I had no adventure left. And I had accomplished more than I had even wished for on my journey. It was time to leave England before the images created by bitterness and misery replaced my initial sincere and awe-inspired ones. I sat in my apartment, looked at the drooping trees outside, and turned on my computer.

Mr. Henson,

I have been going through my shots and I believe you will be satisfied. There is quite a variety and abundance — too many more and it'll be a hindrance. I think this would be a good place to stop, although I am of course pleased to continue with the itinerary or make any adjustments you would like.

Best, Andrea

[send]

Though the email was strategically worded to get my ass back to the US, I wouldn't have sent it had I not genuinely believed we could create a glorious photo display of England from the pictures I had taken. I provided Tom with a complete list of what I had shot, what I thought were the highlights, and what Rob and Harry and the writers could match with copy.

Mr. Henson's reply email was positive; he said I was relieved from my duties after one trip to the south. I was relieved, truly relieved, in every sense of the word.

Chapter Thirty-Nine

Ecstatic, elated, and motivated, I took my final trip in the UK, a day trip to the southernmost tip of the country: Tintagel, county of Cornwall, rumored to be spectacular. The destination was Tintagel Castle, in the city King Arthur had called home. The castle no longer stood, but in contrast to my trip to Manchester, I knew as much going in. Tintagel was a popular tourist spot for its dramatic setting, not for the spectacle of the castle itself. It was a four-hour train ride; the trip was not meant to be done in a day, but I would do it in a day, return to London that evening, pack up, and leave the following afternoon. I skipped and whistled all the way to Paddington Station. I didn't even know I could whistle. I was made fun of en route, the same way I had been mocked for holding a map with penis-shaped cutouts. I smiled, looked in the other direction, and continued whistling.

Coffee in hand, I hopped on the train early, just as the sun was beginning its morning appearance, and opened a book. It felt like no time had passed, but four hours later I arrived at a coastal village so spectacular my imagination was envious it couldn't have envisioned such a scene. I was overjoyed and comforted to find that I would take my final pictures of merry old England in paradise.

The ruins of Tintagel Castle sat on a lush hillside not far from the ocean, reminiscent of the scenery in *Braveheart* or *Lord of the Rings*. The crash of waves against the cliffs provided a peaceful soundtrack. The sun shone overhead without a cloud blocking its path, a slight breeze blew fresh air in my face and pulled my hair out of my eyes, and I could swear I heard bagpipes even though none were visible. It was breathtaking. I absorbed the spectacle through my camera's eye for three hours, then headed home.

Once I planted my feet on the train in the direction back to London, the realization hit me fast and furious, like I had been standing on the tracks in front of it: I was going *home* in twenty-four hours. My mind played back a highlight reel like a movie montage. The towers at the entrance of Westminster Abbey. [*Click*] The words MIND THE GAP in the subway tunnels. [*Click*] The stained-glass windows at Canterbury Cathedral. [*Click*] I love that about pictures: they freeze a moment in time without a care for the concurrent circumstances. They allow a separation of feeling and vision. I remembered the magnificence of the Canterbury Cathedral, and if I so chose I could do so without remembering my abject fear of going inside. I recalled Harry and Rob posing with John Lennon outside the Cavern. [*Click*] Robin Hood loitering in a thriving oak tree. [*Click*] Hamlet clanking swords with Laertes. [*Click*] Rob nearly planting a smooch on a beefeater at the Tower of London. [*Click*] I smiled as the pages of my mental photo album turned. Although I had a sour flavor on the back of my tongue with regard to my trip, I knew I would never see England as anything but a sweet place of splendor. In time I would forget the loneliness and my parents' and Brandon's behavior, and remember only these exquisite snapshots of Britain.

The following morning I emailed Gemma, Claire, and Millie a cordial goodbye and assured them that I would be in touch while *Adventure* continued to assemble the magazine.

Then I met Rob and Harry for a final lunch near Trafalgar Square, the place where my trip had begun. The three of us had a pleasant time, talking and laughing about all things British, the kind of conversation that half a year prior I wouldn't have understood. They used words like *loo*, *disorientated*, and *birds* (to mean ladies); I did too. And though a large part of me wished I could stay and talk with Rob and Harry for hours, it was time to leave.

"So, this is it, luv," Harry said.

I took a deep breath in. "I guess so."

"You relieved?" asked Rob.

"In some ways. I can communicate with Millie only by email now, which is nice."

"I'll bet."

"We'll miss you," they both said.

"Yeah, me too, guys," I said, my eyes filling with tears. "But we still have some work to do. You're not done with me yet."

"Yeah? Good," said Rob. He had a continual glow about him that he had never displayed while pretending, ever so poorly, to be straight.

"Guys, truly, I never could have done this without you."

"Bollocks to that, Andy. You'd have been fine," Harry said.

"Oh, I don't know—"

"Andy, you'd've been fine," Rob affirmed. "Bored, obviously. But fine."

"Remember, nothing catastrophic happened when you were alone. It was when you were with us that things burned to pieces."

"That might have been pure coincidence. But you may be right." A stream of tears was now in full force. "Keep in touch, won't you?" I said, trying to smile through the anguish.

"Oh, you've finally gotten our language down, haven't you? Of course we will."

"Absolutely, luv."

I gave them each a hug and a kiss on the cheek, moistening their faces with my tears. When I had time to process what I had accomplished, I would know that Rob and Harry were not only my chaperones: they were my guides, my teachers, and my friends. And despite the fact that my pictures might have been just as lovely whether or not they had been at my side, I actually wouldn't have completed my journey without them.

Chapter Forty

I walked through the revolving glass door of the airport, breathing somewhat heavily, my heart palpitating. I had become markedly less afraid of life over my last few months, and it was time to do something about air travel. Staring out the windows of Heathrow, I felt the warmth of the sun through the glass. I watched the planes, hoping like hell to find that they were attached to something — anything. And then I stared at *the* plane that would fly me home. I hated it for being so flipping mysterious, but loved it for being my way back. Though home was filled with more question marks than had I encountered abroad, I welcomed them. I needed familiarity and, well, family.

The announcer made the call to board and that was it. The woman who took my boarding pass gave me an enormous red smile. "Have a safe trip now, won't you?"

I smiled back. "I will."

I took one last look behind me. *Cheerio, ol' England. It's been a pleasure.*

I slept for the first five hours of the flight and then awoke, not having taken sleep medication. I watched the passengers passing the time in various ways: reading, working, playing video games, and knitting, which I thought was out of place. I decided to relax, watch one of the movies the airline so "kindly" offered for only half of what it costs to see one in the theater, and allow myself to experience the true feeling of air travel. I likened it to the earthquake scenario I had thought of in Oxford: there, in the event of an earthquake, I would have tried to run to safety and make it out alive, but at the end of the day being scared didn't make a lick of difference. On the plane, if we were to crash, whether I was awake or asleep, there would be nothing I could do. It made far more sense just to try and enjoy the time.

After four more hours, I felt the plane plummeting. It rattled my stomach and made my palms sweat, but I could handle it. We taxied to a stop at the gate at Los Angeles International. Seventy-five degrees. Sunshine.

I hopped into a cab that took me straight to the driveway in the neighborhood I had loved so dearly. I looked at the house. I knew every crevice; it was like visiting an old friend. Hopefully we'd pick up where we had left off. I hesitated for a moment, inhaled for a deep and inordinate amount of time, continuing my involuntary decision to blacken my lungs with smog, and walked up to the door. My palms clammed up again and my stomach tingled. I knocked and the door fell open slightly. Although initially amazed at why anyone would keep their door unlocked, it was midday and this was about as safe a neighborhood as Pleasantville — why not? I returned my focus to the current mission. I walked in gingerly.

"Hello?"

No one answered. I set my bags down by the door and walked through the foyer to the kitchen. Everything was where I remembered it. I loved that this house would never change; after all, home plate is always the comfortable, diamond-shaped mat the players run toward.

And there was my mom in position on her side of the table. She looked up over her glasses, which she always wore so far down on her nose that gravity should've pitched them right off. She lifted her head, steadied her glasses with one hand, and dropped her latest read, *It's OK to Crochet*, the instant she saw me.

"Andrea? You're... home!?" she squealed.

"And you're ... learning to crochet?"

"What? Oh, God," she said, stammering over her words. "Well, yeah, some girls in my knitting class wanted to try something else. Why didn't you tell me you—"

"Knitting class? When did you start knitting?" I was learning quickly that my home wasn't at all familiar.

"About two months ago. Andrea—"

"Where's dad?"

"Outside, hitting golf balls."

"On purpose? What's going on?"

Before she could provide further explanation, I saw my dad walk up to the doorway and pause. He wore a blue polo tucked into multicolored plaid shorts. I barely recognized him — that is, until he crossed his legs, folded his arms, and leaned into the doorway. Ah, there was the man I knew. I turned toward him. He said nothing. He stood, trying to stop his lower lip from quivering, but I saw it quaking through the stiffness. He walked straight up to me and threw his arms around my neck.

"I missed you."

My mother followed suit. She rose out of her chair so fast it fell behind her. She threw her tiny arms around us both. As though I was still under the English sky, my father's tears watered my shoulders and my mother's dampened my back. I had known my mother would shed tears, but the heaviest ones fell from my father's eyes. I too joined the party, sobbing for the time we had spent apart and for how we had treated each other when we were together.

"Okay, enough of this drivel, you're a grown girl."

"Oh, you know that?" I said, wiping the streams from my cheeks.

"Yes, Tom Henson told us."

"Funny."

"We saw some of your proofs at his house. He was just so pleased with the work you did," my mother said. "They're marvelous, darling."

"We're so very proud of you, Andy," my father added.

"Thank you, I'm proud too. I really can't wait to see it all come together."

"How did you get Robin falling from the tree?" my father asked.

"It's a special effect I learned. It's called the death trap."

"What?"

"Nothing," I said. "We need to talk."

We spent hours talking. I mostly confirmed what they had apparently learned after our run-in in Bath: how hurt I was that they had hired someone to watch me, and that the pain would continue. I tried to make them understand that, because I had grown up feeling like they didn't trust me and didn't think I could do things on my own, I doubted myself, my abilities, and my ability to cope with the world. And I explained that I would continue to doubt myself for as long as I felt that the two people on earth who were supposed to believe in me most didn't believe in me at all. They hadn't understood how much I had measured myself by their treatment of me. They inserted the obvious and inevitable thoughts: that they loved me, that they trusted me but no one else, that they believed in me but one could "never be too cautious" — a saying I had come to find wasn't true. The explanation made sense in a hypothetical world, but in my world, the real world, they had to let go.

"You have to love me as an adult," I said.

I talked about how selfish they had been to deceive me into breaking up with my boyfriend just so I would put off marriage and move back in with them. About how insane and hurtful it had been for them to show up in England to check up on me without calling or planning a visit. I explained that these things were contrary to how the cycle of life continues and, more importantly, that they had tremendously impeded my growth and happiness. They apologized ad nauseam for flying across the world rather than picking up the phone. And they claimed they never wanted to make me break up with Brandon, just to stave off the inevitable — they weren't ready to let me go. They thought that Harry's influence, coupled with the romance of being in England, might make me rethink my desire to be married and decide I wasn't finished dating — or, an even bigger hope, decide I wanted to be alone, left with only my parents to lean on. The biggest problem was that their scheme had worked. I had postponed my marriage to Brandon — perhaps forever. But it wasn't due to Harry's behavior; it was due to Brandon's.

"How about Brandon?" my mother asked.

"How about him?"

"Are you getting back together with him?"

"Probably not. I don't know. He took the wrong page out of your playbook."

"He loves you, darling."

"Oh, now you want me to be with him?"

"Well, I think he took the right page out of our playbook."

"I know you do."

"We didn't intend for you to break up. Just... wait a while."

"I can't be your little girl forever."

"I know, honey," my mother said.

"I'm not sure you do."

"Well, we're learning," my father added.

It was all I could expect.

"Do you want to stay with us for a while?" my mother asked, more for her benefit than mine.

My heart, heavy, fragile and without a home, fell into my shoes. "No— "

"Of course she doesn't. She wants to be in her own place."

"Dad's right. But thank you for the offer." I was apprehensive about sitting alone in my home; the last time I lived there, Brandon was constantly by my side. But it was time to continue the post-England life I created.

"I was gonna abandon her old curfew, George," my mom replied as if it added something sensible to the conversation.

"She's fine, Annie."

"Of course you would offer to abandon it when I have my own place. How timely. I'm good, though, thank you."

The one thing I couldn't yet do alone was to visit Brandon. My parents offered to pick up some things I had kept at his house, which I imagined would be an awkward trip now that Brandon knew they had hired someone for the purpose of breaking us up. I didn't take them up on that offer. Ashley offered to go with me as well, but I said no: I would take care of it myself. And when I say myself, I mean I asked Brandon to bring my belongings to my apartment when I wasn't there.

I had thought of Brandon often. I wanted so badly to see him, but I was still so angry and so utterly embarrassed. I had overreacted and screwed up and I couldn't come clean. I talked with him for a few minutes when I called to request that he bring over my things.

"Andrea, hi baby," he said, too familiar with our calling each other by our pet names to say anything else. His hello made my heart melt faster than butter in a microwave.

"Hi Brandon, good to hear your voice," I said, stuttering through the nervous swallowing and teardrops.

We talked about our friends and his work, but after fifteen minutes we paused. Was there really nothing else to say? When you want to spill your guts about your entire world but don't know where to start, or how much the other person will listen, you end up chatting like acquaintances. Like elevator conversations: you can't say nothing at all to people you know when you see them in an elevator, but there isn't time to cover anything substantial, so it ends up an uncomfortable, drawn-out meteorology report. When I remember, I wear headphones to avoid it altogether.

"My parents asked me to stay with them for a while. They're really having a hard time letting go."

"Well, they are quite overprotective," he said in a tone that acknowledged the hypocrisy.

"Yeah. They tried so hard they offered to get rid of the curfew I haven't had in over two years."

"Wow, they're really growing up."

Another awkward pause.

"How are things on the job front?" Brandon asked.

"Coming along. I couldn't get Tom to hire me on as staff, but my name is out there. I have some assignments lined up. I'm actually trying to get something else out of California or even the country."

"Wow, really?"

"Yeah, I'm eager to see what else is out there."

"That's wonderful, Andrea. I'm sure you'll do great."

"Thanks. Freelance is tough, though. You know me, always concerned that I won't get the next gig."

"Soon you'll have so many you'll forget about that concern."

"Yeah, I'm waiting on the edge of my seat for that to happen."

"You can wait on the edge of my seat, Andy. Stay with me."

"I don't think I can, Brandon."

"Things will be different, I promise," he said.

"I'm sorry, Brandon, I just don't know if I trust in us right now. I'm a different person than I was before I left."

"I know you are; and I'm so proud of you. And I'm excited to start our next chapter."

"I don't know. I need time, Brandon."

I asked for my things and then hung up, sorry that I had denied him and wholly unsure of my conviction to be without him.

Over the next several months, I became comfortable. I reconnected with friends. I got a dog from the pound, a basset hound I named Robby, after Rob and Harry. I altered my previous routines. Before my trip, I had gone running every Sunday morning, but only at 11 a.m. I wouldn't go at, say, 6 a.m. or 5 p.m. because, in my savvy thinking, evildoers lurked at six in the morning had they failed to do evil the night before, and at five in the afternoon they may have wanted to get an early start on their evening of evildoing. But at eleven o'clock, the riff-raff were most likely passed out from a drunken stupor, thrilled by the previous night's crimes but not yet ready to head out for another round. Also before my trip, I had run with pepper spray and without water, which, I feared, would tie up a hand I might need to fend off a villain who jumped out of the bushes (or an ominous shadow). After returning from my trip, I chose any time between 7 a.m. and 2 p.m. to run — and I hydrated. I found a way to strap water to myself and still have free hands to ward off criminals. I also ditched the pepper spray. I kept it in my house to defend myself in case of a break-in, and occasionally brought it out for a night on the town, but honestly, who carries pepper spray to brunch on a Saturday?

Perhaps my biggest post-trip change was the planning I immediately started for additional, numerous, trips. After experiencing people and places as diverse and extraordinary as I had in England, I would stop at nothing to discover more. I knew I would never jump out of a plane or ski down a large mountain, but I was sure I wanted a life filled with travel.

Brandon and I talked sporadically; he didn't stop checking in, though it was more to say hello than to ask what I was doing to protect myself in the event of a natural disaster. The walls I had proudly built around my heart were gradually collapsing.

The closest I came to knocking on Brandon's door was when my copy of *Adventure UK: Castles, Cathedrals and Spectacles* arrived in my mailbox. The cover: Robin Hood falling from the tree. What I had initially labeled as my greatest failure abroad had become the advertisement of my greatest accomplishment to date. I studied the magazine alone, on my couch, beaming with satisfaction. My visions of Robin Hood, The Beatles, Hamlet, Warwick, Stonehenge, Rockingham, Tintagel, Christ Church, Westminster, and more were on the pages, performing exactly the functions intended: they transported me there. Rob had written witty captions and he and other writers had woven together compelling articles describing the glorious country illustrated through pictures. The words *Photo by Andrea Lieberman* graced every page. I immediately requested and received a JPEG of the cover, and had it blown up and framed to mount on my wall. I received an influx of emails, texts, and calls from friends and family congratulating me on the issue, and a bouquet of roses from Brandon with a note: *Congratulations, Andrea! I always knew you had it in you. I love you still, Brandon xoxo.* I wished I believed in how much he claimed to believe in me.

One Saturday afternoon, returning from a jog, I saw in my mail pile a large brown metallic envelope with powder-blue script, sure to contain an invitation of sorts. Dripping sweat on the lovely packaging, I opened it up.

You are cordially invited to the commitment ceremony of Harold Eugene Randolph and Robert Alan Hays.

An enormous grin of satisfaction took over my face. The ceremony was two months away in Bath, England. I looked at the RSVP card, took out a pen, and checked off the box labeled *pleased to attend*. How could I not?

When the weekend finally arrived, my parents drove me to the airport. "Do you have your mace, your pepper spray and—"

"I have everything I need, dad."

Chapter Forty-One

I flew into Heathrow without incident and without sleep. I had work to do, so I kept myself busy that way rather than by pill-popping my way into a coma. There were a few bumps that caused me to grip my seat and look around to gauge reactions, but as the relaxed passengers went about their movie-watching or book-reading, so did I. Landing still made me a tad queasy, but it was manageable.

I arrived in London the day of the rehearsal dinner and wasted no time before taking a train to Bath. After a short day of napping and primping, I walked in to a beautiful Italian restaurant adjacent to the hotel the three of us had stayed in when we were in Bath the first time, which seemed like a lifetime ago.

I walked through the hallway to the back room where the dinner would take place and ran into Millie. Her name had made its way into a few of my travel stories, all of which I told in good humor, and most of which ended with bewilderment — "No. That didn't happen. You're embellishing." (I wasn't) and "You can't be serious, she said *that*?" (she absolutely did). I decided to say a cordial hello while mapping my escape route.

"Andrea, hi. How did you get here?"

"Hi, Millie," I said, giving her a hug. "By plane."

"Have you been here the whole time?"

"I... I don't know what you mean by 'whole time.' But I got here this morning."

"Do you live in England still?"

"What?" Although a part of me had a list of negative adjectives to throw at her, I chose politeness. She just didn't know any better.

"No, I live in LA now." I turned away quickly to avoid the waterfall of comments that would inevitably follow. I was already close to my Millie threshold. "Good to see you, Millie. I'm gonna find Gemma."

I walked further down the hall and saw Gemma in a rather conservative black strapless gown, looking lovely and talking to a handsome bloke at the entrance to the dining room.

"Sorry to interrupt. Gemma, hi. How are you?"

"Hiya! I'm good, you alright?" We exchanged hugs as well. "This is my boyfriend, Charlie."

I was floored, at a loss for words. "Wow. I… uh, well, lovely to meet you, Charlie."

Gemma and I stepped aside for a moment.

"A boyfriend? Have you been in a coma while I was away?"

"Well, he's one of two."

"Okay, you're narrowing it down; that's progress. It's good to see you. I'm going to say hello to the grooms. Let's catch up at dinner."

Dim but sparkling antique chandeliers hung overhead and five-candle candelabras graced the center of each table. Tropical vines with yellow and brown flowers lined the walls like holiday tinsel. I walked over to Harry and Rob, both dapper in jackets and ties. Rob had cleaned up nicely, and Harry, well, Harry looked like he had leapt from *Italian Vogue*, as always. Upon mutual sightings, we all screamed like sorority girls and engaged in a three-way hug.

Wiping the water from my eyes, I said, "oh, I'm just so happy for you two."

"Thank you, luv."

"Thanks, Andrea. It's so lovely to see you."

"You both look amazing."

"Yeah, I've a new exercise regime. Gotta try to stay in the same league as my man Harry here."

"Oh, you always were in the same league, Robbie Rob," I said.

"You're sweet, Andy. You look great too. Finally put together."

"Yes, well, I'm not hung over, trying to catch a train, or ducking angry football fans."

"Yes, that helps. Come have some tea," Harry said. An offer I hadn't received in months.

"I'll come and sit, but no tea, thanks."

"Oh, right. Sorry, luv."

Rob and Harry sat me at a table with the two of them and some of their fabulous, not-so-discreet friends. I learned that Harry had "dabbled with women" in the past but had always felt men understood him better. And I heard a story about how Rob had pissed on himself the first time a girl touched his penis. "It tickled," he said.

"Well then, either she did it wrong or you got your first clue that women weren't really your cup of tea," I said.

After the waiters brought the main course, but before the dessert tray came around, I walked outside to breathe in the crisp English air. I stared out at the lights beaming off the Abbey. I was just minutes from the bath where Rob and Harry's relationship had ignited. Harry sat down beside me.

"So, luv. What's going on with you?" he asked.

"Not much. Working a lot."

"No, Andy. What's going on with you?"

"I'm living with my parents."

"Oh, for shit's sake, Andy, really?"

"No, not really, just taking the piss. But frankly, they wanted me to... so badly that they offered to let me stay without a curfew."

"Well, throw a parade."

"Harry, I can't be with him."

"Why not?"

"Because what if he doesn't notice that I've changed? What if he doesn't believe I can do things on my own and then I tell him about everything that happened here? I'll never get him to believe I'm self-sufficient, and he'll do something else like he did when I was here, hiring someone to spy on me. I don't think I'll get over that twice, if in fact I'm over it this time. Or, worse than all of that, what if he *needs* me to be dependent?"

"He doesn't. And he won't do it again. Tell him. Tell him everything. Then move forward. I believe he'll understand."

"How can I tell him everything? He has no idea how scared I was here or how badly I screwed up as a result. And telling him won't change his behavior, it'll justify it."

"I don't know what you're talking about. Brandon knows you were afraid. It's okay to be afraid; what matters is how you deal with fear. And you didn't screw up. Andy, you were in England on your own for almost six months and as far as I can tell you're all in one piece. You did that."

"No, *we*, the three of us, did that."

"No, Andy. You did. Independence isn't only about doing things alone. It's about having your own thoughts and feelings and making your own decisions. It's okay to *want* to be with others, and it's okay to *need* others sometimes. It'd be weird if you didn't. It's not needy, it's natural."

"I guess. But I couldn't even ride the subway without you two. I was paralyzed."

"So you needed a little assistance riding the tube a few times; after that, you did it on your own. Sure, you got yourself into a kerfuffle or two here. You also got yourself out of them. And, you took some incredible pictures. I saw the magazine."

"It did come out pretty amazing. You guys did a fantastic job."

"We all did a fantastic job."

"Yeah, okay, we all did."

"You're bloody right. Think about what you did, what you accomplished. You have grown. You *are* independent—"

"Yes, I independently caused a fire at the Royal Shakespeare Company."

"Well, shit happens, doesn't it?"

Another rhetorical question.

"This one was a proper question. Doesn't it?"

"It does."

"We all run into good dumb luck and shitty dumb luck. It's what you do with it afterwards that matters. Andy, you made s'mores from a fire."

"What?"

"You know what I mean: lemons, lemonade, that bit," he said.

"Yeah, okay."

"You should also remember that you went for quite some time without Rob or me, just on your own, and did absolutely fine. No disasters, no calamities. Even when you took Gemma, the walking disaster herself. What I mean to say is, you have many wonderful things to tell Brandon about, apart from what you call screw-ups, that prove to him how accomplished you are. At least give him the chance to know the new you."

"I don't know. Maybe you're right."

"I am. He *really* loves you."

"You know, for someone hired by my parents, you seem to know an awful lot about Brandon."

"Yeah, well, Rob and I may have phoned him a time or two." And then the famous, irresistible Harry wink. When I winked, I looked like I had a two-by-four caught in my eye; Harry winked and the recipient bowed to the floor.

"Oh, you guys don't have to look after me anymore."

"We're not, we're looking after Brandon now. Besides, everyone needs people to look after them. Life's too hard to go it alone. Now, my beloved is waiting for me to dance, and, by God, you're going to dance with us."

We shared a dubious look. "Okay," he said. "Rob and I are going to dance and you're going to hop around like a jumping bean."

"Okay, I'm in. By the way, where are you two going on your honeymoon?"

"Greece, darling, where else?"

Damn, I thought. Another place they would get to before I did.

After the dancing, a few of Rob's and Harry's friends gave speeches. I watched them with envy. I too had something to say. I raised myself slightly out of my chair but sat back down when I saw just how many people occupied the room. But I was profoundly eager to speak. I started to rise again. But sat back down. Oh, screw it, I thought: sometimes you only get one chance, and I knew I would regret not taking this one. I stood completely up after the last of the speeches had finished and the guests had returned to their desserts.

"Um, I'd like to say a few words," I said, softly.

"Oh my god, the woman afraid of her own nose hairs is speaking in public," Rob said.

"Sod off, you wanker, I'm talking," I said loudly, prompting playful cheers from the party. I took a small sip of wine and a deep breath, and then I went for it:

"For those of you who don't know who I am, my name is Andrea. I met Harry and Rob when I was new to the Mother Country. The word fanny meant ass, a tube was just a circular box, and a queue was just a letter. But with the tutelage and friendship of these two lovely gentlemen, I now put extra syllables in words and ask a question even when I mean to make a declaration. As Harry and Rob can tell you, we had quite an adventure. I was, you see, a tad frightened of, well, living. So a castle and cathedral tour of the UK by myself might have been a disaster. Luckily, some overprotective but loving individuals brought Harry and Rob to me. Together, we rummaged through ruins to find castles, saved children from a burning building, nearly killed Robin Hood, and dodged various food items hurled by angry Manchester City fans. But I'm still here to tell about it. With the help of the dashing Harry and the adorable Rob, I am stronger and I believe in myself more now than I ever have. So as it goes, the immortal words of the iconic band that Harry and Rob both worship, and I now loathe for ruining one of my shoots, ring true: I got by with a little help from my friends."

Chapter Forty-Two

I attended a post-dinner celebration at The Choking Chicken that ended at roughly 3 a.m. Despite a long, tiring day of flying, eating, drinking, and dancing, not to mention the exertion spent coercing myself into public speaking, I couldn't sleep. True, I was caught up in the rapture of Harry and Rob's nuptials, but mostly I was caught up in Harry's words. I stayed awake for three more hours, thinking about what he said. I applied his advice to all that I had already begun thinking about: what I had done in England and how I had changed. I was proud of my accomplishments, and I was learning to be okay with saying and feeling it. It was time to measure myself by how *I* saw myself. I had learned that whenever I gave fear too much power it paralyzed me, stopped me from living. But when I moved forward, focused on a goal, fear couldn't stop me, like I was a raging bull and fear a mere ant in a matador's cape. There would be few limits to where I could go and what I could achieve. What I had said in my speech was true: it was Harry and Rob who had helped me arrive at these realizations, whether or not they knew it, whether or not they had intended to, so I had them to thank. Their words of support gave me confidence. Their mere existence made me feel safe. And I would be forever grateful to them for pushing me beyond my comfort zone and being there to support me when *I* pushed me beyond my comfort zone. And I was supremely grateful to my parents and Brandon for Harry and Rob: what I had initially thought of as a betrayal was, in reality, a tremendous gift.

I still had much to learn, but that was okay: I had time to learn it. Bravery, independence, and confidence are lessons that take a lifetime developing, and achieving perfection is impossible. Thankfully, I had people to learn these lessons with me. My American friends, my parents, my overseas pals… and Brandon. Brandon remained as close to my mind and my heart four months after my homecoming as he had been one week after I left. I had to see him. I hoped he would still love me when I wanted him more than I needed him; I was ready and yearning to find out. And I would do so soon: he would be my first stop when I landed in Los Angeles, right after I watched my good friends Harry and Rob become husbands.

After a short but peaceful slumber, I awoke to one of the ten yearly sunny days in Bath, too exhausted to move: this was the England I remembered. In the late afternoon, I walked through town, inhaling the smell of fresh bread as I passed the cafés. I walked past locals out for weekend strolls, stopping to look through the merchandise at the local shops. And I walked past numerous tourists fumbling with their cameras, trying to figure out how to get the entire length of the Abbey into a shot. I helped one of them. While behind the tourist's lens, I looked up at the splendid Abbey and was impressed that Harry and Rob were able to have their ceremony there. I shouldn't have been too surprised, though: Harry had once slept with one of the Abbey's board members and they had become good friends. Harry used his pull — British pun intended — to have his wedding there on short notice and on the cheap.

I passed the Abbey and walked up the road a bit to a park where there was a cocktail hour before the ceremony. I immediately saw Claire by the bar and began walking over to say hello, as I had not seen her the night before. I walked slowly, trying to think of questions to ask when I arrived. I was still thinking about what I would ask during the awkward silence that might follow her one-word response to "what have you been up to?" when something viewed from the corner of my eye stopped my progression. I turned to look across the lawn at the figure that caught my attention: it was a stunning vision of a tall man in a black suit, a silver tie that shimmered in the sun, and a large, welcoming smile I could see even from afar. My stomach ached, my palms began to sweat, and my knees weakened. They say weddings are the best places to meet someone. Instinctively I turned toward the figure and saw that it was walking toward me. As I got closer, I stopped and took a deep breath. *Oh. My. God.*

"It is you, right?"

And I saw the familiar, warm, chocolate brown eyes. "It is."

We walked toward each other in slow motion and stopped maybe two feet apart. We stood there silently: I kept my hands behind my back, swaying left to right, looking down but sporadically trying to catch his eyes. He kept his hands in his pockets and his legs slightly spread for a solid footing. He was cool, confident, the way I imagine Jon Hamm would stand in front of just about anyone — not intimidated by anything. Though my head followed my eyes as I looked in every direction, not a moment passed where I couldn't feel his eyes trying to achieve missile lock.

"My God, you look beautiful, Andrea."

I smiled so wide it affected my vision and I became flustered.

"What? Um, what are you doing here, Brandon?"

"Well, Harry thought you needed someone to watch you. So he hired me to attend his wedding."

We laughed. I put my hand on his cheek and he leaned into it. The world stopped; everything but Brandon's face was out of focus. I took my hand down and put my hands on my hips.

"The nerve. What, he doesn't trust me?"

"Nah. I think he just cares about you."

"Tomayto-tomahto."

We exchanged smiles.

"So, how long've you been here?" I asked.

"Just got in yesterday. Stayed with Harry."

"He's gay, you know."

"You don't say? You'd never know by looking."

"True... you didn't go to the dinner."

"No, I couldn't figure out how to make an entrance. Heard about your speech, though."

"Ah, well, I couldn't resist."

"You hate public speaking."

"I know, but I love Rob and Harry more."

"Was it awful?"

"No. You know, it really wasn't bad at all. I felt blessed for the opportunity."

"Rob did himself well with Harry. He's quite the handsome chappie."

"Chappie?" It was likely similar to how I sounded when I first arrived in England, except adorable. I had forgotten Brandon's expressions: his face contorted in the sweetest ways when he tilted his head while trying to be cute. I couldn't take the tension any longer. I finally looked straight at him, letting my eyes be caught in the crosshairs. We held each other's stare for what seemed like a day.

I continued. "Is Harry handsome? I didn't notice."

My blood pumped through my veins to my heart, which seemed to reside in my eardrums; it was pounding strong, loud, and quick.

"So... care to show me around after the wedding?" he asked.

"Sure, I'd love to."

"You can tell me all about your trip, I still don't know the details."

"I know. I will. Get ready though, cause there's some crazy shit to share... but I made it through."

"Of course you did. I'm sorry I never gave you the credit you deserved. And I'm so sorry I hurt you."

"Thank you for saying that."

Brandon took my hand and we began to walk towards the Abbey into Rob and Harry's ceremony.

"So, we'll stop at the hotel and pick up whatever you need, your pepper spray and—"

"You pansy. This is England. You don't need any pepper spray."

"You mean you didn't bring even one can?"

"I mean I don't even *own* one can."

"Really?"

"Okay, I own one, but it's for very special occasions. You're not going to chastise me for not bringing it, are you?" I asked.

"Nah, I believe you don't need it."

We reached the Abbey and looked inside the stunning room, where guests were gathering in celebration of my two amazing friends and their great love for one another. Before we crossed the threshold, Brandon stopped and turned me towards him. He stroked my hair.

"I'm so very proud of you, Andrea."

"Yeah? Me too. Thanks, Brandon."

"And I'm really excited to continue our journey together."

He smiled at me affectionately and leaned in slowly to ensure that I approved. I did. He kissed me tenderly, a kiss that had all the desire of our first and all the comfort of our last. He hugged me close and whispered in my ear.

"It's been too long, sweetie... I've missed you so much."

I reciprocated the move. "I've missed you too, Brandon... but it was worth it."

Made in the USA
San Bernardino, CA
26 June 2013